"You l...
Perhaps you should lie down."

Before Parris could proclaim that lying down could be detrimental to her well-being, Dominick had her flat on her back.

He sat next to her, his hip pressing against hers, the contact intimate and jarring. Even more jarring was the fact that he had effectively trapped her.

"Better?" he murmured. His eyes appeared to have darkened, though perhaps the room's shadows merely made it seem that way.

"I'm fine. And I'd much prefer to be sitting up, if you don't mind." She attempted to rise, but a hand at her shoulder held her down, confirming her suspicion that she would not be allowed to leave until he had succeeded in getting what he wanted.

But what, exactly, did he want?

CRITICS RAVE ABOUT MELANIE GEORGE

THE DEVIL'S DUE

"With the hand of an expert storyteller, Melanie George sends a dynamic pair of lovers on a thrilling roller coaster ride of an adventure story.... So hang on to your hearts and get set for a memorable, fast-paced tale that puts Melanie George on your must-read list!"

—*Romantic Times*

"It's a winner, with one of romance's feistiest heroines and most alluringly brooding heroes."

—*Booklist*

"Melanie George writes hot, steamy historicals with characters that leap off the page with spunk and spitfire."

—*Bridges Magazine*

HANDSOME DEVIL

"A treasure, a triumph, a treat for the heart! This second book in the Sinclair brothers' series is tender, witty, and utterly charming. You laugh, you cry, you yearn for more (much more). Ms. George just keeps getting better and better."

—*Old Book Barn Gazette*

"The romance between Nicholas and Sheridan is breathtaking, the passion is sizzling, and the story enthralling."

—*The Romance Reader Connection*

DEVIL MAY CARE

LIKE NO OTHER

Also by Melanie George

A Very Gothic Christmas
by Christine Feehan and Melanie George

MELANIE GEORGE

The Art of Seduction

POCKET **STAR** BOOKS

New York   London   Toronto   Sydney   Singapore

This book is a work of fiction. Names, characters, places and inci-
dents are products of the author's imagination or are used ficti-
tiously. Any resemblance to actual events or locales or persons,
living or dead, is entirely coincidental.

An *Original* Publication of POCKET BOOKS

A Pocket Star Book published by
POCKET BOOKS, a division of Simon & Schuster, Inc.
1230 Avenue of the Americas, New York, NY 10020

Copyright © 2002 by Melanie George

ISBN: 0-7434-4272-5

First Pocket Books printing August 2002

10   9   8   7   6   5   4   3   2   1

POCKET STAR BOOKS and colophon are
registered trademarks of Simon & Schuster, Inc.

For information regarding special discounts for bulk purchases,
please contact Simon & Schuster Special Sales at 1-800-456-6798
or business@simonandschuster.com

Front cover illustration by Kam Mak;
front cover photograph by Barry David Marcus

Printed in the U.S.A.

Prologue

She walks in beauty like the night
Of cloudless climes and starry skies;

—Lord Byron

The woman came to him under the cover of darkness, only a sliver of moonlight to guide her way. The air was sultry and warm and scented with the fragrance of night-blooming jasmine; the sounds of an orchestra's faint strains carried on the breeze.

She stood watching him, her expression unreadable, her entire aspect a mystery beneath the domino that covered most of her face, the powdered wig obscuring her hair, and the courtier's costume with its daringly low neckline, barely covering her nipples.

She walked toward him, the sensuality of her movements riveting his gaze to her hips. She spoke no words, and his tongue could not form any.

When she stopped before him, the pulse fluttering

at the base of her neck and the quick rise and fall of her breasts told him she was not as composed as she wanted him to believe. Good. Neither was he, and the realization jolted him.

Who was she?

He wanted to ask. Should have asked. But he was afraid of breaking the spell. Had he seen her inside? Had she ever attended his mother's annual costume ball before?

Did it matter? She was here now.

Dominick opened his mouth to speak, but she pressed a slim finger to his lips, silencing him. Then her fingers whispered across his jaw, slid into his hair, cupped the back of his head, and brought his mouth down to hers. The contact was explosive.

His big hands closed around her tiny waist, pulling her closer, needing her as tight against his body as he could manage. The layers of clothing between them felt confining, restrictive. Damn bothersome.

He intended to go slow, be gentle, but she changed the love play, her need insistent, inciting his senses, the heat from where their bodies touched expanding and growing beyond his control.

He eased her to the ground, pressing her down into the cool grass beside his mother's prized roses. His hands, usually so calm, fumbled against the hem of her gown.

He stroked one silk-clad thigh as his other hand tugged at her bodice. She gasped as he freed her. The moon's pale rays glimmered down on the small, perfectly formed globes. Her nipples swelled beneath his scrutiny, the sight erotic and maddening.

His gaze elevated to her eyes, whose color he could not discern, as his head lowered toward her breasts. He watched her watching him, saw her inhale as his lips closed around her nipple, drawing the taut nub into his mouth, her teeth biting down on her bottom lip to hold back the moan rising in her chest.

Her back arched, pushing that hot, wet tip farther into his mouth, her fingers digging into his hair to hold him to her. She writhed beneath him, and Dominick was lost.

Nothing—not God, not the devil, not the milling throng less than four hundred feet away in the ball-room—could have stopped the inevitable.

Perhaps if his brain had been less fogged with rampant lust, he may have recognized the signs that she was innocent—but the passion she inspired left him heedless of consequences, reckless beyond anything he had ever known.

He was enthralled by every inch of her body: the plump ripeness of her lips, the silky jut of her jaw, the long, sleek line of her neck, the delicate slope of her shoulders.

His hands slid up her firm thighs, beyond silk stockings, beyond rosebud garters, until his palms whispered over hot flesh. He cupped her buttocks, pulling her harder against his erection. She pressed upward, branding him with her heat.

Dominick groaned and curled his tongue around

her nipple, reveling in her breathy moans as his hand skimmed over her hip and then delved between her silken thighs. He slid a finger between her wet folds and stroked her swollen clitoris.

He spread her legs farther as he built the tension inside her, wanting to see her clench when he brought her to climax, a flush washing over her chest as he increased the tempo, her head tossing back and forth, the kittenish sounds she whimpered driving him wild, seeping into his bloodstream, making him feel powerful. Possessive. He didn't want to think of this angel as belonging to anyone but him.

And she would be his. Whatever it took. Whatever it cost.

When he slipped a finger into her . . . sweet Christ, she was so tight, so hot. His groan was primal, guttural, full of arrogant male pride as she began to convulse.

He had to have her.

Now.

He freed his erection, wrapped her thighs around his flanks, and entered her in one swift stroke. Her fingernails dug into his back as she tensed beneath him.

"Jesus God . . ."

She was a virgin.

Guilt and confusion swamped him. He tried to roll off her, words of apology forming on his lips, but she gripped his shoulders and tentatively, almost shyly, arched her hips against his, bringing him deeper inside.

Dominick dropped his head against her shoulder, struggling to say no, that everything had already gone too far, but the only sound he could hear was the harsh rasp of his breath.

She ran her fingertips lightly over his arms, his muscles straining from the force of his desire and self-restraint. She was soothing him. And sweet God, he let her, he needed her to assuage the recriminations pounding away in his head.

She eased her hips up again, her velvet warmth stroking him, a single, whispered word breaking from her lips.

"Please."

Please. That was all she said, and Dominick dissolved, forgot that he was a thoughtless bastard, or the second born son of a duke, or that when all was said and done he would have to offer for this girl, and he wasn't a damn bit sorry about it.

Like a man forced to the brink and beyond, he abandoned all thoughts of what he *should* do for what he *needed* to do, stroking into her as his mouth plundered hers, his thrusts escalating as he felt her start to quicken. Her lips parted, and her gaze fixed on the heavens as he brought them both to culmination.

Reality closed rank as soon as his ardor began to cool, though his senses remained ensnared by a passion so gripping it had made him forego common sense.

She rose without speaking and righted her clothes

as he grappled with the urge to tug her back down to the ground beside him, pull off her mask and demand answers.

Good Christ, she was a virgin—and he had been seduced, right and proper. Nothing in his vast sexual exploits had prepared him for this.

They heard the noise at the same time. Damn it all! Someone was coming. He cursed fluidly as he struggled to right himself while the woman who had muddled his brain drifted behind the shrubbery—a smarter idea than standing out in the open, poised like a duck about to be riddled with buckshot, like he was.

His father had probably called out the queen's dragoons to search for his delinquent son, returned only three days ago from Cambridge and already making himself scarce.

Dominick moved around to the other side of the hedge, intending to take the girl some place more secluded where they could talk, but she was gone. He swung in a circle, his gaze slashing through the darkness, but there was nothing. He was alone. She had vanished.

He caught sight of a scrap of white on the ground, partially hidden beneath a yew. He swiped up the handkerchief, the faint scent of perfume drifting upward. Her perfume.

He noted the monogram then, but was unable to make out the initials. He stepped into the moonlight and held the wispy material up for inspection.

A.S.

His hand tightened and his gut clenched. Only one woman he knew had those initials.

Annabelle Sutherland.

Dear God, what had he done?

Parris ran through the moon-dappled garden, her skirt hoisted above her ankles, her feet silent in the thick grass as tears, both happy and bittersweet, coursed down her cheeks.

She had done it.

She had made love to Dominick.

How long had she fantasized about being intimate with him? Yet had she offered herself to him, he would have turned her away as he had two years ago when she had foolishly professed her youthful feelings, thinking he would return them.

Her sister owned his heart. What man wouldn't want Annabelle? She was beautiful. She had never been a hoyden, climbing trees and sneaking around in breeches, or unearthing worms to bait her fishing rod, or riding like a wild thing through the Carlisles' estate, her hair hanging down her back in a tangled mess.

Since Dominick had returned from the university, he hadn't come to see her. Parris knew he wasn't able to face her. Ever since her declaration of love, his letters to her had become fewer and farther between.

But instead of letting go, her desperation grew, a longing building inside her to know Dominick as a woman knows a man, thinking that next time he might leave and not return, that he would marry and have children, and then she would never know his kiss, or the feel of his hands on her skin.

Alone now, Parris sank down next to the ancient oak at the edge of Archer's pond, her hand trembling as she lifted it to her lips, remembering the feel of Dominick's mouth melded to hers, those lips touching her in places no man had ever touched her.

She had thought one time would be enough. But now she knew it would never be enough.

Tomorrow she would tell him the truth.

Then face the consequences of her actions.

"That's it, sweet. Put your legs over my shoulders. Good girl."

Sweat beaded on Frederick Carlisle's brow as he pumped into the female beneath him, greedily taking what she offered, what she had been offering him ever since she had gotten breasts, those lush globes now bobbing beneath his swift thrusts, her taut nipples abrading his chest. He pinched one peak, hard, and she cried out. He smiled.

Annabelle Sutherland was a succulent morsel, but that was all she would ever be. She would spread her thighs for the Sixth Fleet if doing so would get her what she wanted. And what she wanted from Frederick was a wedding ring.

He knew she was angling for marriage, envisioning herself as the next Carlisle duchess, knowing someday his father would cock up his toes and Frederick would assume the mantle of power—which couldn't come soon enough to suit him. The old man was a bloody militant. But for the most part, he shot his poisonous barbs at Dominick.

His brother had always been the rebel of the family. Never knew how to be clandestine about a single damn thing, had fairly flaunted his friendship with the younger Sutherland chit, Parris.

Frederick knew Parris disliked him, thought he was pompous and overblown. But one day she would regret not treating him better. When he had her and her family thrown off Carlisle land, then she wouldn't be so self-righteous.

Just the thought of Parris made Freddie plow into Annabelle, taking his anger out on her, deriving some measure of satisfaction with the way she squirmed beneath his savage thrusts.

Beautiful, ignorant Annabelle. What would she think when he told her he was getting married—and that she was not the bride? She thought her beauty would eclipse her lack of a dowry, and he had let her harbor that illusion during the months he had been bedding her. But tonight she would come to understand her role in his life. Mistress. Not wife.

"Yes," he moaned, gripping her buttocks and driving into her. She played her role well, panting and whimpering and calling out his name until he climaxed.

Satiated, Frederick rolled to his side, and she sidled up next to him, the doting paramour, her fingertips lightly scoring his chest, her breasts positioned for full effect.

He toyed with one peak, squeezing hard enough to make her flinch. "You are a delight, sweet Annabelle. I don't think I've ever had a more ardent lover."

"I only want to make you happy," she purred like a true professional, her hand stroking down his belly and wrapping around his flaccid member.

If nothing else, she knew how to get him hard. She would definitely be an incentive on those nights when his future wife lay unmoving beneath him, doing her spousal duty. Lady Jane was not a passionate woman, nor would she enjoy rough play. Annabelle, and others like her, would fill the gap nicely.

Frederick gripped her hips and she mounted him, sliding down slowly onto his erection. He played with her nipples while she did the work.

A few minutes later, as his seed spewed into her for the third time that night, he said bluntly, "I'm getting married."

It wasn't the most tactful moment to make his confession, but the sex and the expression on her face were both well worth it.

She stiffened. "What?"

"I'm getting married," he repeated, removing her from her advantageous position and sitting up against the headboard. "I'm announcing my engagement at a Carlisle gala two weeks hence."

She stared at him as though he had started speaking in a foreign tongue. "Surely you jest."

He lit a cheroot and blew a billowing smoke ring. "You should know me better by now, my dear. I would never joke about something as important as my future."

"But . . . what about us?"

" 'Us'?" he laughed, choking on a puff of smoke. "There is no 'us.' We enjoy each other's bodies. That's all."

"I-I thought you—"

"Would ask you to be my wife? Really, Annabelle. I had hoped you were more realistic than that. You're a mere baron's daughter, and a rather impoverished one at that. Only my brother's foolish fondness for your sister has stayed my father from heaving you off our land." As well as the fact that the duke, licentious bastard that he was, harbored lust in his heart for the baron's wife.

It seemed all the Carlisle men had an affliction for Sutherland women. Frederick, however, used his 'affliction' to his benefit.

"As much as the old boy wants to break Dominick's will, he doesn't want to push him away entirely. Though why that is so is a mystery to me. My sibling has not a single redeeming quality."

Annabelle rose from the bed, naked and shaking with fury. "He possesses more principles than you will ever have!"

"True, and therein lies the crux of his problem. He has this bloody propensity for doing the right thing, no matter how hopeless the cause. He and your sister are rife with that annoying commodity. Good thing you and I are without conscience. We'll do just about anything to get what we want, won't we? And what I want, dear Annabelle, is a wife with a substantial purse. It makes the idea of domestic bliss much more palatable."

"Why, damn you?" she demanded. "Why didn't you tell me any of this?"

"We were always so preoccupied, there never seemed to be an appropriate moment." He reached out and stroked a finger over the curls at the apex of her thighs.

She slapped his hand away. "Don't touch me."

He rolled up on one elbow. "Now, now, sweet. It's not as bad as it seems. Marriage won't be a deterrent to our liaison. Just think of all the pleasure we can still give one another."

Her face mottled with rage, her eyes burning brightly with the full comprehension that she had been sorely used. "I'm with child, you bastard!"

Frederick took a final drag on his cheroot and then ground it out on the bedside table, knowing she lied. Her menses had come a week earlier. Did she think him stupid? "My, but that is a problem. What will you do?"

She screeched and lunged for the nearest object, hurtling it at his head. He ducked just in time, leaving the porcelain clock to crash against the wall behind him.

He clutched her wrist as she whirled away and

dragged her back onto the bed, pinioning her beneath his body, forcing her hands to curl around the iron rods of the headboard.

Pressing his mouth against her ear, he said in a silky voice, "A mistake, my girl. Now you're going to have to pay for that clock with the only thing you have of value."

Parris awoke the next morning with tears on her pillow.

She'd had the most horrible dream. She and Dominick stood in the middle of a barren field burnt by the sun, while she confessed her sins. The chilling caw of a solitary peregrine far in the distance was all that echoed in the deathly silence that ensued.

As she begged him to forgive her, his body turned to stone and he disintegrated into dust. Then a fierce wind howled out of the sky and swept him away, out of her reach.

Out of her life.

Dread settled in the pit of her stomach as she tried to banish the image, assuring herself it was only a dream even as her mind clamored that dreams could be harbingers of things to come.

The room suddenly felt stifling. She needed air. Needed time to think. She moved to the mullioned windows. The sun streaming through the small diamond-shaped panes fractured into splashes of vibrant hues, casting prisms on the floor.

She pushed open the windows, wondering if

Dominick would come to see her today. Would he recognize that the girl he had been with in the garden was she? Would he finally view her as a woman, rather than the hoyden who had clung to his every word?

Parris caught a movement on the small, shaded terrace below. Two figures stood only inches apart, deep in conversation and unaware of her presence. Dominick had his hand around Annabelle's upper arm while she rested her palm against his chest. Though Parris could not hear what they were saying, the intimacy was a blow to her heart.

Why? Why was it always Annabelle who got what Parris wanted? Hadn't God given her sister enough? She was amply endowed, blessed with lush blonde hair and had mossy green eyes like a summer meadow, while Parris was small breasted, cursed with straight black hair, and had pale blue eyes that her father had decried as haunting and unnatural. Everyone admired Annabelle, while Parris had been the child no one knew what to do with.

What was the matter with her? Why couldn't anyone love her?

But last night, in Dominick's arms, she had felt loved. He had treated her as though she was the most desirable female in the world.

Would he feel that way today?

She had to find out. No matter the consequences. Knowing she could live with. It was not knowing that was the torment.

Dressing quickly, Parris donned one of Annabelle's

old frocks that she'd had refitted to suit her smaller frame. Posing before the mirror, she scrutinized her new figure, the modest cleavage she finally had, and the nipped-in waist acquired after years of a coltish figure.

She pinched her cheeks for color and dabbed on a small dollop of the lip rouge she had filched from Annabelle's room. The color made her mouth look like ripe strawberries.

Inhaling a steadying breath, she sailed from her room. She wondered if she should wait until Annabelle and Dominick came in from the terrace, or boldly go out there.

The decision was made for her, as she found Dominick and her sister, along with her mother and father standing in the foyer at the bottom of the stairs.

Parris forced a smile to her face, though something about the assembly bothered her. A sense of tension vibrated in the air. Her legs would not stop shaking and her stomach twisted into a knot.

Please Lord, she silently beseeched, *let nothing ruin this moment.*

But the Lord was not listening to her that day, for as she descended the stairs, she heard Dominick say to her father, "I wish to marry your daughter, sir. I would like Annabelle to be my wife."

For as long as he lived, Dominick would remember the look on Parris's face that morning two weeks ago.

Her gasp had brought his gaze swinging up to

where she stood poised in the middle of the staircase, those riveting pale eyes huge in an equally pale face, her gaze centered on him with despair.

Two years, he had stayed away. Two years of feeling like a lecher and the worst sort of human being for finding himself falling for a girl barely out of the schoolroom.

He remembered every detail of that day by the pond when she had professed her love for him. She had been only sixteen but already beautiful, a girl on the verge of being a woman.

She hadn't known what she was saying. She had spoken with the emotions of a child who worshipped him, not as a woman who understood the nuance of love. She was too young. Too inexperienced.

Too everything. Parris had always been larger than life.

But Dominick had understood the danger, how easily she could make him forget himself, succumb to his growing desire for her. And so he had stayed away. Anything to place distance between them.

He needed time to acclimate himself, to come to terms with whatever emotion it was that burned inside him when he thought of her.

When he had come to confront Annabelle the day after the ball, he had prayed the incident in the garden would not be as it seemed, that the handkerchief had simply been lost.

But as soon as he saw Annabelle crying out on the terrace, genuine tears that he had never seen in all the years he had known her, he could no longer deny the truth. He had taken her virginity, and no matter her role, he had to pay the price.

How ironic that both he and his brother would be announcing their engagements tonight. Neither of them had made a love match, but love had never been a requirement for Freddie. Unlike Dominick, who had vowed that when he finally took a wife, she would be a woman he could cherish for life. He'd seen too many of his peers wed out of duty, their lives thereafter a continuum of discreet affairs. He hadn't wanted that for himself.

Yet, here he stood on the cusp of his engagement to a woman for whom he did not feel even the remotest amount of affection—until a deplorable act of lust had driven him to make an irrevocable mistake.

Once more he stood alone in the garden, bathed beneath the same moonlit sky, thinking about a woman he wasn't sure had ever existed except in his mind. It was hard for him to envision Annabelle, so coolly beautiful and composed, as the woman who had writhed passionately beneath him, who had whispered a sweet plea for surcease against his lips.

Dominick tried to block out the image, quaffing another swig of brandy from the bottle he clutched like a lifeline. The liquor created a warm path down his throat, numbing him another degree.

The orchestra began to play. He looked toward the house, where the windows glimmered like jewels in the overly warm night, pressing heat into every crease of his body, weighing him down like another burden on his soul.

His blurry vision focused on a movement. A darkly cloaked figure exited the French doors leading from the library. The person glanced about furtively before hurrying across the lawn toward the summer cottage. A flash of skirt told him his target was female.

Dominick's gaze tracked the woman as she made her way toward the cottage, slipping quickly inside. A sliver of light spilled from the open doorway, conveying that someone else waited inside.

Was his father meeting one of his paramours? The place had always been his favorite spot for illicit rendezvous. Even tonight, Dominick would not put it past the old man to disgrace his wife right under her nose.

Grimly, Dominick waited, his gaze fastened on the little house, the liquor an accelerant to his mounting frustration and disgust.

Finishing off the remaining brandy, he tossed the bottle against a tree, feeling a savage satisfaction at the sound of splintering glass as he stalked toward the cottage.

Soundlessly, he opened the front door. The tiny parlor, with its heavy exposed ceiling beams and rustic furnishings, was dim with a solitary candle burning on the mantle. He could hear the muted sound of voices, then a female moaning.

Christ, this would be sweet, watching the expression of shock and humiliation on his father's face as he was caught in the act of adultery.

A strong sense of vengeance took Dominick to the open doorway of the bedroom, where two figures grunted and groaned amid the twisted bedsheets.

His fiancée on her hands and knees.

His brother entering her from behind.

Frederick spotted him first, a satyr's grin curling one corner of his lips as he thrust in and out of Annabelle, who was oblivious to Dominick's presence, her head angled down, her mass of blonde hair veiling her face, her pointed nipples pushing against Frederick's eager fingers.

His brother slid his hands down and gripped her waist, guiding her movements, enjoying a few more seconds of torturing Dominick before finally deigning to say, "Look who's come to watch, sweet. Your darling bridegroom."

Annabelle's body jerked as though she had been lashed with a whip. Her head snapped up, her eyes wide with shock. "Dominick!"

He didn't allow her the time to formulate any excuse. "Either you cry off on our engagment or I will." Then he turned on his heel and departed.

One

∞

*Half our mistakes in life arise from
feeling when we ought to think, and
thinking when we ought to feel.*

—John Collins

LONDON, 1850

"That's the spot, love. A little harder. Right ... there ...
ah, yes."

Dominick's fingers tightened around the waist of
the barmaid who was straddling his lap, her hands,
deft and incredibly masterful, working their magic on
his heated flesh.

Blessed Jesus, she was good. He had never been
massaged in quite this way, amid a crowded taproom
with a mountain of cleavage staring him in the face,
only the barest wisp of material covering the girl's
enormous breasts.

He hooked his finger over the top of her gypsy
blouse, lightly caressing her dewy skin, watching as her
nipples peaked and strained against the flimsy cotton.

She gazed at him with heated eyes, her look amply conveying that he could do whatever he liked, that she did not care about the onlookers gathered around them, drool practically dribbling from their mouths.

Perhaps this time he would take her up on her offer. "My lord?"

"Ssh," he murmured, sweeping the very tip of his finger over one hardened nub, hearing her quick intake of breath and smiling. She squirmed against him, wanting more. He obliged.

He dipped a hand inside her blouse, boldly cupping her while keeping his prize hidden from the leering eyes hoping for a glimpse at Sally's elusive bounty.

"Please, sir."

How could he deny her when she begged so sweetly? "All right, my girl. You've won."

Dominick leaned forward, very slowly tugging the material down, his tongue running over his lips as he anticipated the unveiling of that dusky pink tip.

"Sir?"

He scowled as the voice beckoning him changed from soft and infinitely feminine to grating and annoyingly male.

The barmaid's image began to waver, as though he looked at her through a water-filled glass globe. Then, like a vapor trail, she disappeared.

Damn.

"Sir?" croaked that same bloody voice, ruining a perfectly lascivious dream. "Are you awake?"

Dominick growled and rolled onto his back, grabbing the pillow under his head and throwing it at the speaker. "Bugger off, damn you!" he barked as reality pummeled him, along with a throbbing in his skull that told him he had imbibed far too much at his club the previous evening.

"Are you all right, sir?"

No, he bloody well wasn't all right. Since his homecoming a week earlier, everyone felt inclined to ply him with drinks as though he were some conquering hero, instead of a retired army colonel who had returned only because he had been forced to.

With a great deal of reluctance, Dominick lifted his forearm off his face and was immediately assaulted by a brilliant burst of golden light.

He closed his eyes against the unwanted intrusion. "Sweet Jesus," he rasped, "what is that?"

"The sun, my lord," replied that now familiar voice, creaky as an unused gate and just as irritating. Hastings, his bloody butler. Soon to be his *ex*-butler for waking him.

"Good Christ, is it always that . . . bright?"

"For as long as I can remember, sir. Yes."

Dominick groaned. "What time is it?" His throat felt like someone had poured sand down it.

"Two in the afternoon."

"On what day?"

"Friday, sir."

"Friday?" Dominick frowned. He remembered Monday fairly well. Tuesday was a bit hazy. Wednesday was somewhat of a crapshoot, and Thursday . . . well, what could one say about Thursday? Nothing, apparently.

Emitting another painful groan, he levered himself up onto his elbows. Once settled in his new position, he fixed his irritated gaze on his rigidly erect, gray-haired butler, who had been with his family since Dominick was in short coats, and who took it upon himself to peck at Dominick like a mother hen whenever Dominick got out of line—which had been quite often as a youth, and almost as often as an adult.

It didn't seem to matter to Hastings that Dominick was now the ninth duke of Wakefield, albeit ushered into the position reluctantly because of his older brother's untimely demise in a hunting accident.

It was still damned hard to believe; Freddie had been only forty years old. But Dominick felt little loss. He and his brother had not spoken since the night he had found Freddie in bed with Annabelle Sutherland.

But Annabelle's perfidy had not caused the rift. He and Freddie had always been rivals rather than brothers, and the way the bastard gloated as he fucked Annabelle had irrevocably severed any remaining familial bond.

Dominick figured he deserved what he got for being such a gullible sod and falling for Annabelle's ploy. She had had one Carlisle; why not another? Being a duke's wife was certainly more appealing than being the wife of a lowly second son. But when Frederick had tossed her aside she had come crawling back to Dominick, begging his forgiveness.

Seeing him unmoved by her tears, she changed from contrition to indignation, her acting skills laudable. Later, in front of the assembled guests, she had even produced a single fat tear as she told them she could not marry him, allowing her tortured expression to imply that he was the dishonorable party.

Dominick had nearly applauded, but then he caught sight of Parris's stricken face in the crowd, those eyes branding him with all the heartless traits that Annabelle's silent censure had heaped upon him.

Her look of betrayal and anguish still haunted Dominick. He had hurt her, destroyed something special and rare. Somewhere in the mess that had become his life, he had lost the only thing that had truly meant anything to him. Parris.

He forced down the regret that churned in his gut whenever he thought of her, and concentrated his efforts on glaring at his butler. "Hastings, a bit of advice?"

"Yes, Your Grace?"

"It would behoove you to keep in mind that I've killed men for lesser offenses than rousing me from sleep." Let the fastidious old prune digest that. Dominick had to set the tone for his reign as reluctant liege, and thus far, either he hadn't made himself clear or Hastings was dense.

"My most heartfelt apologies, sir," Hastings intoned, not looking the least bit worried. "I would not have disturbed you had I not been led to believe the matter was of some importance."

"And what matter is that?"

"Lord Stratford is here to see you. I told him you were abed, but he said it was imperative that he speak to you. He looked rather agitated."

Good Christ. Stratford thought telling the world he had a hangnail was imperative. Why Dominick had remained friends with the annoying blighter all these years was another of life's little mysteries. Perhaps it was merely ghoulish curiosity about what might befall the man next. Trouble seemed to always be just around the bend wherever Jason was concerned.

"He awaits you in the library," Hastings added.

"Bloody hell." By now, Jason would have worked his way through half of Dominick's finest liquor and pocketed several of his expensive cigars.

"Might Your Grace like a spot of tea to refresh himself before rising?" Hastings inquired, clearly assuming that Dominick would not tell him to pitch Stratford headlong into the street.

"No," Dominick grumbled, concluding that the only thing more annoying than Hastings's infernal presence—besides Stratford's infernal presence—was Hastings speaking in the third person. "His Grace does not want any damn tea."

Reluctantly, Dominick swung his legs over the side of his bed. "Guess I might as well rise, since the best part of the day has been shot to hell."

"Shall I call Smithson to assist you in dressing, sir?"

Dominick slid a sidelong glance at Hastings. "I've

been dressing myself my whole life; why the hell do I need someone to help now?"

"If I may be so bold as to remind you of your station in life. You are a duke now and no longer serving in Her Majesty's Royal Army. There are certain things expected of you."

Dominick gritted his teeth. He did not need another reminder of his responsibilities. Every day, they were there, ready to irritate him, like a bucket of cold water to the groin. Glorious freedom had become an elusive commodity.

For eight years he had been a soldier, living hard, playing hard, and all this damn mollycoddling was grating on his last bloody nerve.

"I don't need Smithson," he bit out, stalking nude past Hastings and throwing open his armoire. "I can put on my own blasted clothes. Get rid of him." Dominick could almost feel the stiffness creeping into his butler's limbs at his last remark.

"I would be remiss in my duties were I to do such a thing, Your Grace. No person in your position can be without a gentleman's gentleman."

It was on the tip of Dominick's tongue to inform Hastings that he first had to have a gentleman to work with, but he refrained. Between his throbbing skull and his throbbing leg—compliments of a gunshot wound to the thigh while on maneuvers in the Peninsula—he wasn't quite up to having holes bored into the back of his head as his butler glared at him in silent umbrage.

Stoked by renewed disgust at the unexpected turn his life had taken, Dominick grabbed the drawers Hastings held out to him and shoved his legs into them. Then he yanked on a pair of black trousers, threw his arms into his shirt, and fumbled with the buttons.

Grimacing, he stared at his reflection in the mirror, catching only a shadowy outline of the tattoo on the left side of his chest: a hissing serpent that coiled in an S-pattern, the tail curling around his nipple.

He had gotten the tattoo shortly after he had joined the army. The snake seemed appropriate, considering his experience with gardens and forbidden fruit. It served to remind him of his folly.

His day now thoroughly soured, Dominick rolled up his shirtsleeves and brushed past Hastings, who stood like a wax effigy holding out his waistcoat. Dominick grabbed it and headed resolutely toward the door.

Hastings beat him to it. "Your jacket, sir." He held up the garment and Dominick's brows drew together, warning the meddling little philistine not to push. The warning went unheeded. "Here, let me help you."

The next thing Dominick knew, his sleeves were rolled down, his cuffs fastened with gold links bearing the ducal emblem, and the jacket was sliding up his arms. Then his cravat was looped around his neck like the hangman's noose it resembled and properly tied in the requisite number of knots.

"There. That's better." Hastings smoothed the

jacket's lapels. Dominick growled, but his butler merely glanced at Dominick's earlobe, holding out his hand. "The stud, please, Your Grace."

Dominick leaned down close to Hastings's face and said through gritted teeth, "Over your dead body." Then he nudged the irritating specimen aside and practically sprinted from the room.

Hastings got the stud before Dominick had reached the landing.

Muttering curses all the way down the stairs, Dominick entered the library to find his assumption had been correct. Stratford was helping himself to a fresh glass of port, most likely his third or fourth by now, and had one of Dominick's finest cigars clamped between his teeth.

Jason was the fifteenth earl of Stratford, and the youngest at thirty-one years of age. He was also a prime example of vice if ever there was one, well on his way to becoming a complete degenerate.

Dominick had met the heir apparent to the Stratford fortune at boarding school. Both their fathers had claimed they were in need of discipline or else they would grow up to be complete wastrels, a possibility they both courted with a near religious fervor.

Together, they rebelled, bucking the restrictive ties of being born into the aristocracy, with all the minutiae it entailed. Expulsion loomed on the horizon during their entire academic careers.

Stratford, however, had drawn the line at army life

and shivered at the prospect of such a regimented existence, unwilling to go that far to stay free of the tentacles of his title.

Some females—who were blind to Jason's numerous faults—might call him handsome with his dark, unconventionally long hair, his swarthy features, cobalt blue eyes, and his height of six-two.

His body, like Dominick's, had been honed in the boxing ring, where Jason delighted in pummeling unwitting dupes who were ignorant of his skill.

Stratford needed to remain fit, so he could fend off the irate husbands looking to end his life in the most painful way possible—an idea that held a great deal of merit at that moment as Dominick observed the rotter pocketing his antique sterling snuffbox.

Stratford caught sight of him then, grinned like the unrepentant roué he was, and raised his glass in salute. "Ah, the prodigal son has arrived! Let us all hail this miracle."

Dominick growled in response. His head still pulsated from the previous night's overindulgence, and he was not in a particularly benevolent frame of mind.

Not that Stratford deserved any form of benevolence; the man was irritating at his best and a rousing pain in the ass at his worst. It defied logic why Dominick liked him.

Jason quirked a brow. "Someone's in a foul temper today. That glower is practically blinding." He gave Dominick a quick once-over and remarked, "Let me guess? Hastings?"

Dominick scowled and held out his hand for his snuffbox.

Jason chuckled, clearly amused by Dominick's black mood as he offered up his pilfered booty. "I cannot begin to fathom why you let the frail old boy irritate you so. He's just doing his job. You can't fault the man for that." He eyed Dominick's attire, adding in a tone that proclaimed his jaw was asking for a punch, "Besides, I think you're looking exceptionally handsome today. All the other dukes will be green with envy."

"Unless you're hoping to leave here with fewer body parts than when you arrived, I would advise you to refrain from further comment."

Jason held up his hands in supplication, but his mocking grin only broadened.

Dominick shoved past the idiot and strode to the sideboard to pour himself a drink. Normally he waited until the evening hours to indulge—a growing habit of late, considering the company he had been keeping—but something told him he was going to need the mellowing aspects of alcohol this afternoon.

He downed a half glass of Madeira, felt it warm his gut and begin to spread before he turned to face his friend. "So what's on your mind? If you'll forgive the overstatement."

Jason flopped down in one of the chairs scattered about the library and hooked a booted leg over the arm. "I received a letter."

That revelation straightened Dominick up. "From her?"

"The lady herself. Lord, the termagant has got brass; I'll give her that. She left her little love note inside my coach. The witch is like a bloody phantom. Nobody has ever caught a whiff of her."

So the infamous Lady Scruples had struck again, and very close to home this time. She was a menacing enigma, keeping London's entire male population on their toes, wondering who would be her next victim.

She had been dubbed Lady Scruples because of her moral do-gooding on behalf of women everywhere, and damn if she didn't intrigue Dominick as nothing else had in a long while.

The uproar she had been causing in town for the past few months was all people could talk about. Men everywhere were nervous. Though Stratford tried to hide his concern behind his insouciant manner, Dominick knew better: The man was a wreck.

"What is she threatening?" The revenges the lady came up with to put the targeted male in his place were not only inventive, but sometimes vastly entertaining.

Stratford scowled. "The shrew told me that if I do not stop seeing the Earl of Markham's daughter an unpleasantness would befall me. More specifically, she said I would be afflicted by a flaming attack of conscience in the one place I cherish most."

Dominick let out a bark of laughter.

"Not funny, you miserable sod."

Dominick imagined that whatever punishment the lady had in mind for Stratford, she wouldn't disappoint. He couldn't help being reluctantly intrigued by the puzzle she presented. He seemed to have cultivated a certain unhealthy fascination for women who were shrouded in mystery.

He suspected that in real life Lady Scruples was a dour-faced spinster who was taking out her unhappiness on the male population of London, whom she blamed for overlooking her.

"I wonder if she's ever been bedded," he mused.

Jason shot him a look over the rim of his glass. "What difference does it make?"

"It could make quite a big difference. Unlike you, most people generally do things for a reason. Perhaps you could offer up your services? Put yourself out there for stud purposes, so to speak. I realize you're spread rather thin at the moment, with all your incoming and outgoing conquests, but consider this a humanitarian effort."

"I know my prowess is legendary, but jealousy does not become you, old boy. And let me point out that as a member of the male populace, you are not immune to becoming an object of female vengeance."

"I haven't been home long enough to corrupt anyone. And I suspect it would take me twelve lifetimes to catch up to you."

"I do a rather brisk business, don't I?" Jason reflected, radiating cockiness. Then he sighed and regarded the shine on his Hessians. "But now we must consider our innocent brothers-in-arms who are being tormented by this virago."

"Innocent? We know most of these men, and everything they have been accused of has been true. Even your crimes, Stratford. You have been making a habit out of tupping chits barely out of the schoolroom recently."

"So?" Jason said petulantly. "Perhaps I've grown bored with married women. There's simply no sport in the pursuit these days. It's like having nothing but brisket for six months, and then seeing a succulent braised duck and knowing you simply must have it or you'll go mad."

"What an interesting analogy," Dominick murmured dryly, trying his damnedest not to be amused.

"Besides"—Jason shrugged—"it's not as if I'm going after these women. They are coming after me—rather ardently, in fact. And as you well know, I'm an obliging sort of fellow. I did endeavor to protect my virtue for as long as I could, but I am a man, not a saint—so please refrain from going pious on me."

There was no arguing with Stratford on this particular issue. When it came to women, he could be so narrow-minded that should he fall on a pin, he would be blinded in both eyes.

Dominick leaned against the sideboard. "Well, it seems your newly acquired love for braised duck has earned you a formidable rival."

Jason brushed a speck of dust from his trousers. "I'm not worried."

Dominick raised an eyebrow. "No? Then why are you here? If I recall correctly, you had Hastings wake me from a dead sleep, claiming it was imperative that you speak to me."

Stratford rendered such a perfect expression of affrontery, his ancestors would have been proud. "The man exaggerated."

Dominick highly doubted that. Hastings prided himself on being utterly precise when relaying a message, to the point that Dominick often considered killing the man justifiable homicide.

"If that's the case, then what did you want to talk to me about that couldn't wait until later?"

"Later I will be attending the Beechams' rout, where I hope to make an assignation to meet a special friend at a dark, little tavern on the outskirts of Spitalfields tomorrow night."

"I see. And would that 'friend' happen to be the rebellious Lady Claire Markham, belle of this year's crop of hopefuls, who apparently doesn't realize she's playing with fire?"

"And if it is?" Jason returned defensively.

"Then I guess I'm just curious as to why you felt it necessary to tell me of your plans—as if you thought I might care."

Jason avoided looking at him and instead concentrated on the dwindling alcohol in his glass. "I thought you might like to join me?" His attempt to sound offhanded fell short of the mark.

The unspoken request was that Dominick stand vigil and make sure Stratford didn't suddenly vanish from the face of the earth or develop a painful case of hanging testicles, due to defying the avenging angel of women everywhere.

"I'm not into threesomes, thank you."

Jason pushed himself from the chair and stalked to the sideboard, glaring at Dominick. "You're being a rotter, you know."

"I know."

"Just come tonight, will you? By now, everyone must know of your return. This evening's event will solidify your homecoming and get all those tedious greetings and insincere well-wishes out of the way."

That much was true. Dominick had been acquiring invitations since the moment of his return, and steadfastly avoiding all of them. Every mama with an available daughter would parade her in front of him now that his status had sufficiently elevated.

But perhaps tonight he could finally put to rest the speculation about his hasty departure eight years ago. It was well past time to bring everything full circle. But that didn't mean he couldn't enjoy another moment of making Stratford sweat.

"Look," Jason said, his tone bordering on desperate, "it'll be worth your while. There's a new batch of beauties just waiting to be plucked. They'll be fawning all over you, salivating at the prospect of catching your eye and becoming the next duchess, to which you can dash all their hopes with that surly expression."

Dominick held out a moment longer, then sighed like a martyr. "Fine. I'll go." Let the man believe he was interested in immersing himself in a gaggle of tittering misses, who would probably faint dead away should he tell them about his time in India, of the rebellions, the poverty—and what fate would befall any man who found himself inside the maharajah's harem.

"Good." The glint returned to Jason's eyes as he swigged down the last of his drink and plunked the empty glass on the sideboard. "I'll see you tonight." He turned to go. "Oh"—he paused, pivoting halfway around—"and keep tomorrow evening open."

"Why?" Something told Dominick he wasn't going to like whatever scheme Stratford was hatching.

"We're off to the Wrack and Ruin for a bit of fun."

Dominick cocked an eyebrow. "We?"

"You, me—and Lady Claire, should I succeed in my mission. For a bit of blunt, you can get a tumble from one of the serving wenches. They're a voluptuous bunch. The proprietor only hires ones with big—"

Dominick held up his hand. "Pray, do not elaborate."

Jason gave him a cocky half-grin, then turned on his heel, calling over his shoulder, "See you tonight."

Dominick watched his friend depart, wondering what he was getting himself into by agreeing to go slumming in the East End with Stratford.

The Wrack and Ruin. How apropos. Something told Dominick that tomorrow night would be more than just another drop of water in the ocean of pointless frivolity that was Stratford's life.

And his own, if he wasn't careful.

Two

Virtue that transgresses is but
patched with sin; and sin that
amends is but patched with virtue.

—Shakespeare

"Lady Gwendolyn Fairchild and the Honorable Miss
Parris Sutherland!"

The footman's bellow jolted Parris, who had been
unprepared for such resonating volume coming from
such a wisp of a man.

As she stood on the precipice of the unknown, she
hoped she didn't appear as if she might bolt at any
moment—which was a definite possibility as she
stared down into the Beechams' crowded ballroom.

"Relax," her cousin whispered as they descended
the massive marble staircase. "Take a deep breath and
keep smiling. Don't let them think you have a care in
the world."

Easier said the done, Parris thought. Her cheeks felt
as though they might crack from the bright smile she
forced to her face as she nodded her head at one per-

son, then the next, pretending she didn't notice the women gossiping behind their fans.

"Lord," Gwen muttered in an exasperated tone through her smile. "You'd think we were cattle about to be bartered at the market, the way everyone is staring at us."

And people were definitely staring. Every eye in the room was focused on them as they circled the outer edge of the dance floor where gaily dressed couples whirled. Champagne sparkled in fluted crystal glasses atop silver salvers, carried by liveried servants attired in the Beecham colors of blue and gold.

The twinkling lights from the magnificent chandelier glittered off the jewelry draped around the women's necks and dangling from their earlobes, and the flickering sconces scattered about the room lent a fairy-tale atmosphere. Parris wished she could have appreciated it more. As it was, she'd be happy just to make it through the night.

She knew the crush of preening women and foppish men were not gawking at Gwen, even though her cousin looked enchanting in the pale pink creation Madame Savina had delivered just that morning.

No, they were staring at Parris; shocked, she imagined, that she had finally appeared out in public after nearly four months of forced seclusion.

She had not been seen since the "Scandal," as society had labeled her crushing humiliation at being deserted by her bridegroom on her wedding day.

Little did they know that she had been saddened,

more than anything else, for she had hurt James with her confession—and that was something she had never wanted to do.

She'd first seen James at the Duvalls' cotillion, nearly two years earlier. His back had been to her, but the breadth of him, the way he stood with unrestrained grace, his dark hair as sleek as a sable pelt, had captured her full attention. He had reminded her of someone else. Someone Parris had never forgotten.

Then he had turned, caught her staring, and smiled, and that smile had been warm. Parris had instinctively returned it, even though her heart faltered at the realization that he was not the man she had hoped.

She had not given James any reason to believe there would ever be more between them than friendship, and yet, after only six months of being acquainted, he proposed.

Parris had been shocked, never expecting anyone would want to marry her. At twenty-six, most people considered her on the shelf.

"Oh, look," Gwen remarked. "There's Lady Claire. My, but she is glowing tonight. Makes one wonder if she is not as averse to Lord Stratford's attempts to seduce her as one would think."

Parris glanced over at Lady Claire Markham, who was holding court on the opposite side of the ballroom. She looked radiant, dressed in a peach silk gown, slightly off the shoulder, a skirt with an empire waist falling away from a snug bodice trimmed with Valenciennes lace. Her blonde hair was a halo around her piquant face, making her appear angelic and serene.

Lady Claire reminded Parris of her sister, Annabelle. Both women had the power to capture men's attention, and both used their beauty to their advantage. Men flocked to Annabelle like bees to a honey pot, until she'd finally landed the one she wanted. The man Parris had once loved so desperately.

Parris still felt a burn of pain in her heart whenever she thought about her childish declaration of love to Dominick Carlisle, and the way he had taken his love and given it to Annabelle.

She and Annabelle had never been sisterly, but in the years since Dominick's defection, their relationship had completely disintegrated. Annabelle had grown colder, more vindictive, destroying whatever small bond there might have been between them.

Parris wanted to feel sorry for her. Annabelle had been crushed when she found Dominick with another woman on the eve of their engagement.

But Parris could summon only despair for herself and an odd sense of relief knowing that Dominick would not be marrying her sister. How could she have ever lived with that?

"Lord, it is a crush in here," Gwen said, pulling Parris from images that still had the power to defeat her. "Oh, look at your mother. She is radiant tonight!"

The baronness was smiling up at Lord Randolph as he guided her elegantly about the floor, her deep rose-colored gown accentuating her lithe figure. Her face was flushed with pleasure and her eyes twinkled more magnificently than the chandelier above their heads.

Parris was glad her mother had finally found some measure of happiness. Her husband had certainly not given her much. Though he had preached propriety to his wife and daughters, the sermon never extended to himself. He had maintained a mistress for years. Many a night, Parris had listened to her mother's weeping, the sound heart-wrenching in the darkness.

Parris had vowed that she would never give a man the power to hurt her like that.

She suspected it was during those long, painful nights that the persona of Lady Scruples had begun to take shape, her anger at the way most women were treated making her want to do something about it. That was part of the reason she had agreed to attend the Beechams' rout: to keep an eye on Jason Fielding, Earl of Stratford—her current target.

The earl had a propensity for seducing girls who were not worldly enough to recognize a master libertine at work. Instead, they were flattered by the attentions of such a handsome lord. Lady Scruples had already issued one warning. Tonight she would discover if sterner measures would be in order.

As though Parris's thoughts had conjured the man up, she heard Gwen say, "There's the earl now. Good Lord, look at him circling his quarry like a vulture ready to swoop."

Parris watched the earl as he ranged the perimeter of the pack of men fawning over Lady Claire, looking like a gloriously sinister archangel in search of his next soul.

His rugged physique was trimmed in a perfectly tailored black suit, and his white cravat emphasized his bronzed skin. The half-grin he sported was utterly wolfish as he cut a swath through the throng to boldly take possession of Lady Claire's hand, bringing it to his lips and lingering a trifle too long for propriety.

"The man's a barbarian," Gwen huffed, a flush staining her cheeks, which Parris suspected was not entirely due to indignation on Lady Claire's behalf.

Two weeks earlier, Lord Stratford had passed them on the street and had bestowed a look on Gwen that could only be described as devouring. Gwen had shot him her most quelling glare, but he had merely smiled the devil's own smile and inclined his head to her. She had been seething ever since.

"There's the dowager now," Gwen pointed out. "Situated discreetly to the right of Lady Claire."

Parris spotted the dowager, Honoria Prescott, widow of the late earl of Linton. The dowager gestured with her fan, a signal that she wished to be closer to hear the exchange between the earl and Lady Claire.

When the dowager moved, Parris caught sight of a man standing in the shadows near the open balcony doors. A man whose gaze locked with hers, causing her chest to constrict painfully and her heart to thump in an erratic rhythm.

She blinked to clear her gaze, sure she was seeing things, but the image did not dissipate. And when the man raised the glass in his hand in a silent salute, Parris knew her mind was not playing tricks on her.

He was real. He was alive.

And he was here.

Heaven help her . . . Dominick Carlisle had come home.

Dominick's hand wasn't quite steady as he put his drink to his lips. His gaze did not waver from Parris, who stood directly across the ballroom from him, the light from the sconces behind her making her upswept ebony hair shimmer with golden streaks.

Parris. Sweet little Parris.

No, not little anymore. A woman now. A beautiful woman, who had taken his breath away when he'd seen her descending the grand staircase after the footman had announced her.

The very sound of her name had sent a sizzle down Dominick's spine, and he had completely ignored the woman at his side. Not exactly a difficult task, considering the woman—Annabelle.

God, the witch was unbelievable. Upon spotting him, she had sailed to his side as though pulled by some atmospheric force, putting on a great show of letting bygones be bygones. How had he ever thought she was worth the effort?

Dominick studied Parris. She had amply fulfilled her potential. The sculptured features he always knew existed had asserted themselves, showing off high cheekbones, a stubborn jaw, and a delicate nose. Her complexion was kissed with color, telling Dominick that she still turned her face up to the sun.

And her mouth, what could he say about that mouth? He remembered the first time he had taken notice of those lush lips. His thoughts hadn't been particularly neighborly. He had been disgusted with himself over his fantasies about all the wicked things she could do with that sweet mouth.

This was Parris, after all. Parris, who had always looked up to him, and who had, for a time, believed the world rose and set at his feet. He had loved her adoration, knowing a deep sense of satisfaction at being needed.

That last summer they were together, before life had turned upside down, she had unwittingly driven him mad in slow, torturous degrees. Her body had lost the gawky lines of youth and filled out in the all the right places.

He remembered the day he had discovered her out by the stables wearing a dress meant for a younger girl and far too small for her new figure.

But instead of the girlish attire reminding Dominick of how young she still was, it had only enhanced each new curve and hollow.

Her breasts were small, but they had rounded just enough to fit nicely in the palm of a man's hands, and that mental image had had Dominick continually making fists to keep from touching her.

Something inside him had changed toward her that summer. He'd tried, but he could no longer see her as the dirt-streaked imp who used to follow him around, or the one whose haunting blue eyes had glimmered with unshed tears at the callous way her father treated her.

He had never acted on the growing attraction he felt toward her, yet neither had he been able to shake it. Even now, all these years later, she aroused a fierce longing in him. God, how he had missed her.

Dominick didn't realize he had pushed away from his safe haven in the corner and started moving across the room toward Parris until a hand gripped his upper arm, stopping him.

He shot a glare over his shoulder and found Stratford standing there, one eyebrow quirked in an amused question mark.

"Must you always wear that unwelcoming look?" his friend asked. "It grows wearisome."

"What do you want?"

"To remain free of marriage, eternally youthful, and stinking rich. For the moment, however, another glass of champagne will suffice." Jason swiped the requisite flute of bubbly from a passing tray and tipped the glass to Dominick in salute before downing its contents.

Then he said, "Dare I ask what has caused your current black mood? You have been most popular with the ladies this evening, and I don't believe it is entirely due to the fact that your pockets have recently acquired significant blunt. One or two of these females might actually like you—well, for you. Some women find the tortured, brooding male irresistible. Clearly there is no accounting for taste."

Jason deposited his empty glass on a passing servant's tray and hoisted another from a salver coming in the other direction. "All right, old boy, spit it out. Or am I to guess all night?"

Dominick debated the wisdom of confiding in Stratford. "I see a friend."

"A friend, you say? Well, this 'friend' must be quite extraordinary, as I don't believe I've seen that glint in your eyes since I took you to Madame Lacey's whorehouse when we were fifteen, and that lovely Asian girl gave you your first hair massage—among other carnal delights."

Dominick could only marvel at the things that had molded Stratford, the childhood that had inspired his single-minded point of view.

"So, where is this friend?" Jason prompted.

"If you can restrain yourself from being overly blatant, then she's over there. Second pillar to the right. Crème-colored gown."

With an exaggerated amount of sangfroid, Stratford turned to look. As Dominick should have expected, Jason's lazy regard sketched slowly down Parris's body and then up again.

"She is a morsel, isn't she?"

"Be careful what you say."

Jason's amused gaze slid to Dominick. "Marking our territory, are we?"

"She's a friend. I won't have you maligning her."

"All I said was that she was pretty. How is that maligning?"

Dominick silently cursed himself, realzing he had spoken too quickly. But he had felt more than a little irritated seeing Jason looking over Parris as though she was another potential conquest.

"She won't have any interest in you, so leave off."

"I don't believe I expressed an interest in pursuing her, though now I cannot help being intrigued. And how is it that you know she won't like me? I can be quite charming when the mood strikes."

Dominick had to remind himself that Stratford was merely being his prodding best. "Let's just say she has scruples, which we both know you don't possess, and leave it at that."

Jason grimaced. "Please, do not use the word 'scruples' around me."

"Ah, yes. That's right." Dominick had forgotten about the note from the mysterious lady, which had been the impetus behind his attending this function. "Any trouble so far?"

"No, thank Christ. But I must admit to feeling as though I'm being watched."

"Self-aggrandizing, perhaps?"

"I won't discount it." Then Jason shrugged. "But back to your lady friend." He ran a hand over his jaw. "Something seems familiar about her."

His brow puckered in a rare bout of thought, and Dominick felt a bead of worry over what might issue from his friend's mouth, something to the effect that he had once attempted to seduce Parris. Knowing Stratford, that was not outside the realm of possibility.

"Ah, yes. Now I remember." Dominick steeled himself. "She's the chit whose fiancé left her on their wedding day. Haven't seen hide nor hair of her since then. Not surprising, though, as the ton can be a bunch of barracudas with such juicy gossip."

Dominick stood in stunned silence. Christ, she must have been devastated. In the past she would have come to talk to him about her hurt, but he hadn't been there for her.

"How long ago was this wedding to have taken place?"

"About four or five months ago, I believe. It was all anyone could talk about for the longest time. I felt rather sorry for the girl. Being the brunt of so much speculation couldn't have been easy."

"What was the speculation?"

Jason shrugged. "The usual. Did the bridegroom have a lover? Did the bride? That sort of thing."

Did she have a lover? More than one, perhaps? Parris had always been on the wild side as a girl, headstrong and stubborn as a mule when she set her mind on a plan. The very things that had exasperated Dominick were the same things that made him admire her, as well.

He felt a desperate need to speak to her, to see if anything about her had changed, and find out how she felt about his return. Yet he also feared discovering the answers to those questions.

"I'll assume the lovelorn expression on your face is directed toward Miss Sutherland and not the girl next to her," Stratford remarked. "Seeing that I'm tipping the inebriation scale at the moment and my vision is blurry, I cannot be entirely sure whom you ogle."

"What are you babbling about?"

"The goddess next to Miss Sutherland. Have my eye on her, old boy. Take that as fair warning."

Dominick's gaze flicked briefly to the young woman next to Parris. She was pretty in a provincial sort of way, but she could not hold a candle to Parris.

He was surprised that Jason had an interest in the brunette. She seemed too innocent looking, by half. Then again, Jason was in his braised duck period and ruining women at a steady clip.

A well-dressed, older fellow sauntered up to the ladies, smiling at the brunette before extending a gloved hand to Parris, clearly looking for a dance partner.

With a brief glance in Dominick's direction, she nodded to the man and he swept her out onto the dance floor—and Dominick felt his face turn to granite.

After downing another glass of champagne, he had resolved to cut in, but the music came to a stop and her partner returned her to her previous spot, bowing gallantly and pressing a kiss to the back of her hand, spending a moment too long doing so.

"Good Lord, man," Jason chuckled. "Go and speak to her. You're scaring off all the women with that black glower."

Before Stratford had finished his sentence, Dominick

was striding across the room, cutting a path directly through the dancing couples.

He caught the look of alarm on Parris's face as he advanced, and watched in consternation as she hiked up her skirts and practically fled the room, exiting through the French doors that led to the garden.

Three

*. . . the sky grows darker yet
And the sea rises higher.*

—G. K. Chesterton

Parris didn't even know where she was going as she pushed her way through the crowd. She knew only that Dominick was heading toward her and she didn't want to speak to him.

Seeing him so unexpectedly had left her unprepared. She needed time to steel herself, to hide her heart, to cover up any remnants of the young girl who had once loved him so desperately.

He had joined the army within a week of Annabelle's crying off their engagement, creating a major scandal. His father had been furious with him, but not because Dominick hadn't married Annabelle: The duke hadn't wanted to be related in any form to the Sutherlands in the first place. No, his anger had stemmed from the fact that Dominick had embarrassed him in front of his peers.

Dominick had left Carlisle Manor that night, left behind his family, his friends—her—and disappeared into another world where she knew nothing of him, besides the occasional newspaper clipping touting him as a war hero.

Two years after the furor, the duke had died, and Dominick had not even returned for the funeral. It was whispered that the rift between father and son had done in the old duke. Once more, Dominick's behavior had been fodder for the gossip mill, dredging everything up just when Parris thought she might be able to forget him.

It was hard to believe he had shown up tonight. People had long memories, and loved to rehash any sin. Parris knew that all too well. She had heard the talk, comparing her to Annabelle, that there must be something wrong with the Sutherland women that did not inspire love and fidelity in men.

Out of breath, Parris finally stopped running. Looking around, she discovered she was out in the middle of the garden. It seemed a cruel joke to find herself in a similar place to where her life had completely and irrevocably changed, eight years ago.

She wondered what Gwen would think about what she had done back then. Parris rarely talked about the life she had known before London.

When her uncle, Gwen's father, had requested that Parris come to town to be a companion to his only daughter, Parris hadn't hesitated. She would have done just about anything to get away from the memories that plagued her in Kent.

In Gwen she had found a friend she sorely needed, who had come to mean so much to her that Parris had not wanted to risk telling her the truth, for fear her cousin would look at her differently.

Now, with Dominick's sudden appearance, the orderly world she had so carefully cultivated had been thrown into upheaval.

Parris pressed a hand to her stomach; it felt as though it was twisted in a hundred knots. She spotted the gazebo, secluded and lit by only the sprinkle of stars overhead, and hurried toward it.

She moved up the few stairs and sat down, leaning back against the post and closing her eyes, taking deep breaths to calm her nerves.

She was just beginning to relax when a deep voice said, "Hello, Parris."

Parris's eyes flew open and she went rigid. She did not move, *could* not move. There had been so many times over the years when she had heard that voice in her head, imagined what Dominick's homecoming would be like. But nothing could have prepared her for it.

Her heart thumping wildly, she slowly rose to her feet, praying for the strength to get through the next few minutes. Taking a steadying breath, she turned to face him, and very nearly staggered back under the force of the six-plus feet of sinfully handsome reality standing just beyond arms' reach.

He blended perfectly with the night in a formal black frock coat and trousers, his silky dark hair pulled back in a queue, emphasizing a face that had sharpened and grown more arresting with the passing of time.

Only his pristine white shirt, with its starched points and cravat, stood out against the landscape of his body, his attire delineating the shoulders and chest that had broadened, the muscular arms that the jacket could barely contain, the lean hips and long legs that conveyed masculine grace.

He was too beautiful for words, and it was so viciously unfair. He didn't deserve to be so perfect, so divinely flawless. His sins should have ravaged him, instead of making him look like a fallen angel as he stared at her with eyes that had plagued her dreams.

Parris wanted to go back in time to the days when life had been simpler, and their friendship had been a certainty. But the mature woman who needed to salvage her pride maintained her distance and her poise.

"Welcome home, Your Grace," she murmured stiffly, executing a light curtsy, a feat it had taken her graceless body years to perform with any adeptness.

She thought she saw Dominick's eyes narrow and his jaw tense, but the expression was so fleeting that perhaps it was a trick of the moonlight.

Then he said, "So it's to be like that, is it?"

Parris's fingers tightened in the folds of her skirt, and she realized she was still holding it up. Abruptly, she released the wrinkled material.

"Like what?" she replied, feigning an innocence that was transparent to both of them.

"We are to act as if we don't know each other." He leaned against the railing leading up the stairs and regarded her with unfathomable eyes, eyes that appeared as black as the night, but which she well recalled were the lightest shade of brown she had ever encountered, like warm honey.

"I'm not sure I understand what you're suggesting, Your Grace."

"We are going to act formal and highly proper and follow protocol for old friends long separated, as though I didn't once tend your scraped knees and you didn't make me laugh when you would mimic Frederick at his most pompous. In other words . . . like strangers. But we're not strangers, are we, Parris?"

That he could ask such a question after all the years of separation revived Parris's anger. She would not allow him to walk back into her life as though the last eight years had never happened, as though he had not once intended to marry her sister, and think all was forgiven and forgotten.

"Yes, Your Grace. We are strangers."

"I see." He continued staring at her, his gaze watchful, unflinching. Unnerving.

"If you'll excuse me, I must be returning to the party. I merely came out here for a breath of air."

"You came out here to run away from me."

That he had so accurately seen through her rubbed a raw nerve. Had she some forewarning of his return, her composure would have been intact. She fought to regain that balance.

"You've overestimated your appeal, Your Grace."

"Perhaps. But that doesn't change the fact that you were hiding."

Parris's hands clenched. How she wanted to slap his handsome, arrogant face. "Think what you will."

He shook his head. "Still a handful, I see. And wanting to blacken my eyes, no less. Now, is that a nice way to treat an old friend? I thought a kiss was standard practice."

"Go to blazes—Your Grace."

A hint of a smile lifted the corner of his lips. "Been there already. I don't recommend it." Then he shrugged. "Some things never change, do they? You still have a hair-trigger temper—stunningly packaged, though it may be." His gaze slowly sketched down her body, and it was all Parris could do not to fidget under his scrutiny.

"And is that your reason for following me? To make me angry?"

The ebony backdrop of the sky was a perfect foil for his dark and disturbing presence, the diamond-shaped stars no match for the glint in his eyes. "Perhaps I was hoping you would welcome me home."

"With open arms?"

"All the better." Sobering, he confessed, "I've missed you, Parris."

Parris didn't want him to affect her, didn't want his presence to lull her, or his sweet, empty words to disrupt her sense of balance. And yet he managed to do all of that with ease. She had to harden her heart, or this man who had once been her very world could ruin her.

"What is it you want, Your Grace?"

He stared up at the stars before returning his gaze to her. "Absolution, perhaps?"

"Then speak to a vicar, for that is something I cannot give."

"Isn't it?"

Parris forced herself to say nothing, to stand firm under the barrage of those beautiful eyes that seemed to silently vow that he would batter down her defenses.

"I never expected that the hoyden I once knew would become the hardened woman I see today."

Parris met his gaze squarely. "Not hardened, Your Grace. Self-assured. Less likely to repeat the follies of my youth. Perhaps that is what you didn't expect."

He regarded her for a long moment before murmuring, "Is there nothing left, Parris? Of us?"

"There never was an 'us.' There was you. There was me." A well of emotion suddenly rose up inside her, threatening to overwhelm her as she said, "And there was Annabelle."

He came up one of the steps and Parris took an involuntary step back. He stopped, and a sliver of moonlight slanted across his chiseled features.

"Would it make a difference if I told you that I never loved Annabelle?"

In another lifetime, Parris would have given anything to hear those words. But it didn't matter now. He had walked away and not looked back. He had made his choice, and Annabelle's specter would always loom between them.

"You really have developed tremendous conceit. Why would I care if you ever loved my sister?"

"Maybe because you still love me. Do you remember when you told me you did? I do; I've never forgotten."

Parris held herself steady by a sheer dint of will. What had made her think she could ever have prepared herself for this? For him? She wanted to get away, but his big frame blocked the stairs, as if knowing she would bolt.

"I . . . I was just a girl."

"A beautiful, sincere girl." He came up the next step. "One who I always knew would grow into an enchanting woman." He took the third step. "Who would give a man the chase of a lifetime before allowing him to capture his prize." He took the final step and stood before her, the space inside the gazebo shrinking with his presence. He tilted up her chin, his breath a sweet whisper across her cheek. "Who would well be worth the effort."

Parris trembled beneath his touch and the heated look in his eyes. How many years had she longed to see that very expression directed at her?

She jerked away from his fingers. "I don't have to listen to this." She tried to brush past him, but he reached out and took hold of her wrist.

"Do you remember when I fished you out of Archer's Pond?"

Parris felt as though she were a ship being tossed from one swell to the next, the way he kept her constantly unbalanced, her feet unable to find solid ground.

"Release me," she demanded, trying to free herself from his unrelenting grip.

"You climbed up that old oak and shimmied out onto the limb," he continued.

"I don't remember any such thing." He had begged her to come down, warned her that she could hurt herself. But she had not heeded his plea.

Instead, she had balanced herself on that branch, easing farther out until it wobbled under her weight. Then suddenly the limb had snapped and she had fallen hard into the water, the wind knocked out of her.

Dominick was beside her in an instant, scooping her up, holding her close to his chest, his shirt plastered to his body, showing her that all the whipcord strength that had once belonged to a boy had turned into the thick, hard muscles of a man. And when she'd looked up into his eyes, for a heartbeat she had seen something there, something her body had responded to.

"I've never met anyone as brave as you, minx," he had whispered in her ear. "Don't ever change."

But she had changed. The world had transformed her, as had her love of a man who had not returned her feelings, a man who had wanted someone like Annabelle.

"God, how I want that girl back," he said, sounding almost anguished.

Parris very nearly reached up and brushed her fingers along his jaw, wanting to ease his tension. Instead, she remained unmoving, the night closing in around them in a hush of silence and memories.

"Did you understand why I had to go, Parris?" His

voice was a low, sensuous thrum in the dark, and Parris was struck by each word as though they were arrows flung against her.

Did she understand? Yes. And no. He had deserted her, cast aside their friendship. But what had been left for him, after all? A girl whom he had never seen as anything more than an amusing nuisance, and Annabelle, whom he must have had *some* feeling for, if he had wanted to marry her.

Perhaps that was what had truly destroyed all that remained in Parris's heart: Dominick had felt something for Annabelle that he had never felt for her. In time she might have recognized that he had been uncomfortable with a young girl's adoration.

If only he hadn't chosen her sister over her.

Parris gazed up at the night sky, burdened by the sadness that washed over her, thinking about all she had lost: a friend, a confidant. A hero.

Those days were long past, those memories locked away. Now she had to focus on the present, on the life she had mapped out for herself, and on doing whatever it took to get by.

"I have to go." The words sounded like a plea.

He didn't release her.

Instead he turned her toward him, most of his face shrouded in shadows except for his eyes, where moonlight sliced through the lattice that rimmed the roof of the gazebo.

Suddenly there were so many things she wanted to say, so many questions she wanted to ask about his life since he had left, about the army; what it was like, if he had ever been scared, lonely, homesick, if some of the tales she had heard about the battles he'd engaged in were true. There was a time when they could have spoken about anything. Now the words would no longer come.

"Parris . . ." Dominick's eyes captured hers as his head slowly descended, his gaze lowering to her lips, her breath locking in her throat even as her mind clamored that she should protest.

"Parris?"

Parris was jolted at the sound of a voice calling from the house, where a shimmer of golden light outlined the figure of a woman. Gwen.

Parris's gaze locked with Dominick's, something intangible moving between them. Reluctantly, he released her. Her wrist tingled and her body trembled.

"Run away, Parris." The mockery in his tone was an unexpected cut. "Go on, little girl. Fly home, where you'll be safe."

Parris hated him in that moment. Hated him, but wanted him. Longed to strike him, but ached to kiss him. He angered her as no man ever had, had hurt her in a way that nearly broke her, and yet he ran through her veins like a drug she could not shake.

Without another word, she lifted her skirts and hurried down the steps.

"Parris," he called out, stopping her even as she told herself to keep going, her heart pounding wildly as she forced herself to face him.

He stood at the edge of the steps, his eyes obsidian

disks in the darkened overhang. "I'll be coming by your house tomorrow morning. I hope you'll be there."

"No." She shook her head. "I don't want you to come."

The hiss of a flame and the small glow of light illuminated his face as he lit his cheroot, showing her the steely determination in his expression.

"Be waiting."

"You're not invited."

"I beg to differ. I have an engraved invitation."

"From whom?"

"Whom do you think?"

The answer came to Parris in an instant. Annabelle. Of course. Parris had seen her sister standing with Dominick in the ballroom, flirting with him, and in that brief flash of time, it was as if all the years had washed away and she was once more the anguished young girl watching Annabelle take away the only thing she had ever wanted.

With old insecurities welling up inside her, Parris picked up her skirt and fled from the garden.

Dominick watched her until the darkness had swallowed her, cursing himself roundly for his stupidity.

Damn it. What the hell had happened to his common sense? Or even self-preservation? The last thing he should be thinking about was paying a visit to the Sutherland household. Such a maneuver only invited speculation and rumors.

As it was, a good portion of society thought he had hired someone to do away with Frederick so that he could get at the dukedom.

Well, talk was bound to happen, slander and caustic gossip bound to wind their way through drawing rooms and clubs alike. No one was immune to it.

Parris had been brave enough to face it tonight. Many women would have gone abroad for a spell and waited for the furor to die down before returning. But not Parris. She wasn't like other women. She wasn't like him. She didn't run away.

Yet hadn't she run from him tonight? From the moment he'd come upon her—her eyes closed and her skin shimmering like pearlescent silk in the moonlight—she had been angry and bitter and hating him. Which Dominick deserved, though that didn't make it any easier to accept.

He wanted the exuberant, always-happy-to-see-him Parris, the one who had looked upon him as though he was her knight in shining armor whenever he chased off Freddie, or when he told her that she could do anything she put her mind to ... or when he assured her that someday she would be more lovelier than her sister.

And she was. God, how she was.

Her beauty had rounded on him like a sharp, unexpected jab to the gut. The slim frame and boyish lines of her youth had changed into lush curves and supple hollows.

The bodice of her gown shaped her breasts, the soft

mounds pushing above the material and quivering with indignation as he crowded her, pressed her, forced her into some kind of reaction, inciting every sense he possessed. He had wanted to kiss her, and had been about to do so when fate, in the form of her cousin, had intervened.

Bloody fate. When had it ever served him well where Parris was concerned?

The Parris of his youth was gone, and in her place was a formidable woman armored in a fashionable gown and perfectly coifed hair, with skin that looked as though it had not seen a smudge of dirt in years.

Dominick raked a hand through his hair and took a long drag from his cheroot, trying unsuccessfully to block out the images of what had transpired in a garden very much like this one in another lifetime, memories of a seduction that nagged at him still.

And memories of a life he wanted back.

The carriage ride home was interminable.

Parris longed to escape, to fly to her bedroom and close the door. She needed time to think, to plan, to contemplate the merits of visiting distant relatives in America. Perhaps then she would be safe from Dominick.

Safe from Dominick.

The thought seemed so foreign. There had been a time when the only person who had made her feel safe *was* Dominick. How easily his presence tonight had thrown her entire world into chaos.

And tomorrow he would be coming to visit.

Annabelle had invited him, so surely he would show up. Parris thought to make herself scarce. Just because he had ordered her to be there when he arrived did not mean she would yield to his demand. Now was the time to set him straight. Let him see that she was no little girl that he could imperiously tell what to do.

The coach rattled to a stop outside the town house, and with great relief, Parris put the steps down before the driver had alighted from the box. He hurried down in time to offer his hand to her mother, Gwen, and Annabelle, whose expression throughout the trip home was nothing short of gloating.

Parris wanted to be alone and hoped to make it upstairs before anyone asked her any questions, but Gwen whispered in her ear, "I wish to speak to you. Come to my room before you retire."

Her cousin afforded her no time to protest as Gwen hastened up the front steps and into the brightly lit foyer, where the butler divested them of their cloaks.

Parris had seen that light in her cousin's eyes before. Gwen intended to pry. She had been fair to bursting since Parris's return to the ballroom, where every eye had scrutinized her, perhaps expecting to see her disheveled and breathless.

She must have countless lovers, had been the whispers trailing her since her wedding day. *Why else would a decent man like James have left her?* Parris could imagine the matriarchs gossiping as she crossed the ballroom. *There goes one of those Sutherland girls, on the verge of another scandal.*

Parris sighed. She had dealt with much over the past few months, but she wasn't sure how well she would weather this latest crisis. Dominick had returned at a vulnerable time in her life, and she had every reason to believe he would exploit that weakness. Best not to give him any opportunity.

At the landing, Parris started as a hand gently gripped her shoulder. She turned to find her mother standing beside her, a worried expression on her face.

"Is everything all right, darling?"

"Fine." Parris essayed a light smile, but could tell she had not convinced her mother.

The baronness paused, as though weighing her words, and then said, "So, the Duke of Wakefield was in attendance this evening."

"He was." Parris endeavored to keep her voice neutral.

"You were out in the garden together." There was no accusation in her mother's voice, only concern.

"Yes."

"Did anything happen?"

More than Parris cared to admit. "No."

Her mother's gaze searched her face. "I realize you're a grown woman, but I still worry about you."

"There is no need to worry, Mother."

The baronness nodded, and then asked hesitantly, "Is he home for good?"

That question had lain heavily on Parris's mind, as

well. It was one thing to put Dominick from her mind when he wasn't there. But what would she do if she were forced to live in close proximity to him? To pass him on the street? To catch sight of him at a ball?

To see him with a woman?

"I don't know. I suppose so. He's the duke now and cannot ignore his responsibilities."

"You two were very close once."

Closer than Parris had ever been with anyone. To this day, she had not found anyone to replace him.

"You were crushed when he left," her mother added. "I thought you would never come out of your despair."

"I wasn't . . ." The look in her mother's eyes halted Parris's words of denial.

"I felt so helpless then. There seemed to be nothing I could do to help you. Do you know, I always thought you and Dominick would eventually marry."

Instead of denying that such a thing could have ever happened, that she had never thought what it would be like to be Dominick's wife, Parris said, "He loved Annabelle."

Her mother shook her head. "If he ever felt anything for your sister, it was the superficial emotions of a boy. The deeper emotions were never there. I love your sister dearly, but she could never have given Dominick what he needed. I'm glad they didn't marry. It would have been a disaster."

"You never told me this."

"I'm not sure you would have heard me back then, and I suppose I didn't think any of this would soothe

the pain you were feeling. I continued to hope that in time you would move on, find someone else. Then James came along . . ." A sad smile crossed her face. "But your heart was not in it." She took hold of Parris's hand and gave a gentle squeeze. "I just don't want to see you hurt again, now that Dominick's come home."

Parris did not want that, either. The first time had been too painful. She had believed she'd found a safe place to store the memories of what she had once shared with him. But the moment she'd looked into his eyes, she realized how strongly he could still affect her.

Parris placed her hand over her mother's. "I'll be fine. Dominick and I were friends a long time ago. He chose his life and I chose mine. And regardless of what happened between James and myself, I'm very happy."

"Are you?"

"Yes," she lied.

"That's all I want, you know. For you to be happy."

Parris smiled lightly. "Then put your mind at ease."

After a moment's hesitation, her mother gave her hand a final squeeze. "Well, I guess we should get some sleep. It's been a long night." Her mother leaned forward and kissed her cheek. "Good night, darling."

"Good night." Parris watched her mother until she disappeared from sight, knowing only one of them would find any rest.

four

*Two roads diverged in a wood,
and I took the one less traveled.*

—Robert Frost

"You didn't come to see me last night."

Startled, Parris glanced up from the roses she was trimming to find Gwen standing on the threshold that led from the breakfast salon to the small terrace. She looked lovely, as always, in a demure dress of sprigged muslin, entirely opposite from Parris's boyish attire of an old, favorite pair of breeches and a shirt with a dirt stain on it.

But Parris had no intention of entertaining any company today, regardless of what a certain autocrat had commanded. Let Annabelle fawn all over His Grace. Parris would remain back here in the garden.

"I'm sorry. I fell asleep." Parris hid the lie by concentrating on retrimming the same thorny branch.

As much as she had tried to block Dominick from her mind, visions of his hard, unyielding body, and the way his eyes had drilled right through her, and the touch of his hand on her wrist, conspired to keep her tossing and turning all night. One more grievance against him to add to all the others.

Parris had thought to travel into town at first light to avoid her unwanted visitor, but then decided hiding in plain sight was the better option.

Dominick had tracking abilities that rivaled a bloodhound's. Should he want to find her, he would, and then he would accuse her of running away again—which would just make him cling to that ridiculous notion that she still cared for him. She felt nothing for him but irritation at his persistence.

"You're mangling those poor roses, cousin."

Parris glanced at the rosebushes. She had nearly denuded every stem, the heads lying in a sad pile on the ground, petals broken off and scattered beneath her feet.

Lord, she was a horticulturist's nightmare. She sighed and wiped away tendrils of hair from her forehead with the back of her hand, inadvertently smudging dirt over her cheek.

Her hair was slipping from its tight coil and curling riotously around her face, and a light sheen of perspiration clung to her throat and upper chest.

It felt wonderful.

Ever since she had arrived in London, she had been trussed up in dresses and coifed to within an inch of her life, with maids fussing and clucking over her.

Sometimes two or three at a time would study her

thick, unruly hair as though the fate of the country depended on finding just the right style.

"If I didn't know better," Gwen remarked in a measured tone, plucking the last remaining rosebud from the bush and holding it up to her nose, "I might think you were purposely trying to avoid me, cousin."

The truth was, she was avoiding everyone. The fewer people who knew her whereabouts, the better. Besides, Gwen was just looking to wrench details out of her about Dominick, the one topic she did not wish to discuss.

Parris put down her shears and removed her gloves. "I wasn't avoiding you. I was simply exhausted and couldn't keep my eyes open another moment."

"Hmm." Gwen came to stand before her, studying Parris as though she could read the truth on her face. "We're to have a visitor, today, I recall."

"Yes." Annabelle had chirped the news to all and sundry the night before. This morning her sister had risen almost as early as Parris, a feat of biblical proportions, as Annabelle generally disdained any hour before noon.

Hoping to deflect her cousin, Parris said, "We're to meet Honoria Prescott and some of the other ladies this afternoon to discuss the future exploits of Lady Scruples."

Gwen's nose wrinkled. She and the gruff Lady Prescott did not always see eye to eye on matters of men, most recently coming to loggerheads over Jason Fielding and whether he needed to be dealt with in so urgent a fashion.

Gwen tucked the rosebud behind her ear and regarded Parris, not waylaid from her chosen path. "The duke is very handsome, isn't he?"

Too handsome.

When he had come to stand before her in the gazebo, his tall, broad form draped in shadows, making him look dangerous and forbidding, Parris had found it difficult to breathe. He epitomized masculinity and authority. Both traits he was born with, making him a perfect candidate for the army. And now for his role as duke.

"I imagine some women would think so," Parris said with a shrug, forcing her attention back to the mauled roses.

"You imagine? I don't believe I've ever seen a more beautiful-looking man. Such piercing eyes and wide shoulders. I doubt his tailor uses an ounce of padding in his jackets. And he is so very tall and dark. Quite mysterious and exciting."

"To some, I suppose." Since Parris was studying the headless stems as though they were the most fascinating thing in the world, she missed the piqued expression on Gwen's face.

"I hear he's an army man."

"Was. He retired to resume the duties left him when his brother died."

"Ah, yes. Frederick Carlisle. What a little toad." Polite lying had never been Gwen's strong suit.

"It's not nice to speak ill of the dead." Though Parris had thought the same thing about Frederick growing up.

He *was* a toad, and lorded the fact that he would someday be the duke over everyone—even his own brother.

"Well, I guess everything happens for a reason," Gwen observed philosophically. "But you know what this means, don't you?"

Parris cast a sideways glance at her cousin. "Means?"

"This turn of events. His Grace is now no longer just a lovely specimen of manhood, but an incredibly wealthy and titled specimen of manhood. Every eligible female is going to try to land him. The man won't be safe until he slips a wedding ring on some lucky girl's finger."

Gwen was right, of course. Dominick would be considered eminently suitable for any young woman looking to snare herself a husband.

A tiny gnawing ache tightened Parris's stomach. If she wasn't positive the problem stemmed from having missed breakfast, she may have thought she was bothered by the thought of Dominick getting married. But she was no longer the sixteen-year-old who had been madly in love with him. And Dominick no longer held any control over her emotions.

Yet, why hadn't he gotten married all these years? Was it simply because he was in the army and unwilling to burden a wife with his frequent absences and the possibility that he might never return? Or had he just not met the right woman for him?

What type of female *would* be the right woman for him?

Eight years ago, Parris had believed she had known the answer to that question. Now, so much time had passed. He had changed. She had changed. How could she begin to comprehend what he wanted anymore?

The gnawing in her stomach increased. "And what about you, cousin? Will you be making a bid for the duke's hand?"

A whimsical smile curled Gwen's lips. "It is a lovely thought, I will admit. He is so splendid, after all. I suspect many women would want him even without his money and title." She leaned forward and added in a conspiratorial tone, "I hear he is an excellent lover."

"Gwen!" The outrage in Parris's voice was far more than the situation warranted, but for Gwen to discuss such a thing . . . and for Parris to feel her body go up in flames, knowing firsthand how wonderful a lover Dominick was.

But clearly other women knew as well. He had carved quite a swath, it seemed. Where had he found the time? Between destroying Parris's hopes and ruining her sister, he must have been very busy, indeed.

"Why, cousin," Gwen said in a laughing tone, "I didn't know you were such a prig about such matters."

"I'm not . . ." Parris stopped, catching the teasing light in Gwen's eyes. Her cousin was purposely prodding her, figuring if she didn't get answers one way, she would get them another.

Parris returned her attention to the sickly roseless bush. "Your plan won't work," she said, wondering if her mother would believe an animal had destroyed her prized blooms.

"Whatever do you mean?"

"You know exactly what I mean. You're trying to get me to confess my feelings for the duke, to tell you all the sordid details of our youth, perhaps to confide that I was once madly in love with him." Why had she said that? "Well, your endeavors are in vain. My lips are sealed."

"Now, that is truly a shame," a new voice drawled. "As they are such beautiful lips."

Parris froze. Dominick. How had he found her? Guests generally arrived by the front door, not by creeping around the side of the house and coming through the walled-in terrace. Blast him!

She pivoted to face him. He stood at the edge of the terrace, resplendent in a suit of navy superfine with a waistcoat of crème brocade over a crisp, white shirt with perfectly starched points. A dazzling sapphire winked from the folds of his cravat. His jacket outlined the generous shoulders Gwen had spoken of with admiration, and his trousers delineated the muscular power of his legs.

Heat rose to Parris's cheeks as she realized where her gaze was going, and when she glanced up and met his eyes, his smile was wicked—as was the way his gaze made a leisurely perusal down her body, as if telling her fair was fair. And yet, the way he did it was so much more . . . intimate.

Every place his gaze touched brought heat. She tried

to remain poised, hoping the chill in her eyes conveyed what she thought of his unscrupulous behavior, when his gaze finally returned to hers. Instead it only amused him, his lips lifting in a taunting half grin.

In return, Parris dropped into a deep curtsy rife with mockery and murmured, "Good morning, Your Grace."

He had caught her looking her worst, soiled with dirt and garbed in breeches. *Not* that she wanted to look good for him; of course not. But she knew he was thinking he had gotten the upper hand.

Straightening, Parris glared at him. "We weren't expecting you back here."

"Hiding again?"

Flushing, Parris flicked her gaze to Gwen, who was grinning unrepentantly. Clearly, her cousin was not only enjoying Parris's predicament, but she could have warned her of the duke's arrival, and had purposely chosen not to. Her cousin was developing a terrible propensity for mischief.

Parris gave Dominick a cool look. "Hiding? Why ever would I do that?" To change the subject, she gestured to Gwen. "Have you met my cousin, Lady Gwendolyn Fairchild?"

He turned that sumptuous smile on Gwen. "No, we have not been formally introduced. But I certainly could not forget such a winsome smile. You were at the Beechams' gala last night, I believe?"

"I was. A lovely affair."

"Indeed," he murmured.

An unexpected spurt of jealousy sprang up inside Parris as she watched her cousin and Dominick, who made a stunning pair. Gwen's lithe figure complemented Dominick's muscular build. And here *she* looked like something dredged up from the bottom of a swamp.

She knew she should be proud of the fact that she had shown Dominick how little his coming today had affected her, that she had no intention of making herself pretty for him.

Yet she yearned to make a hasty exit and storm about in her room, cursing Dominick with every breath.

Dominick leaned over and said something to Gwen that made her blush, causing Parris's pruning shears to drop from her hands with a loud clang, bringing the couple's gaze to her.

Dominick cocked an arrogant, inquiring eyebrow, the insufferable beast, while Gwen hid a grin behind her hand. Parris wished a hole would open up beneath her feet and suck her in.

"Gwen, would you be so kind as to show His Grace to the morning salon, while I inform Annabelle and my mother of his arrival?"

The devilish look in Gwen's eyes told Parris that her cousin had no intention of helping her out of this situation. "Oh, cousin, I would love to, but I'm running late for a fitting with my modiste. I simply must dash off."

Gwen turned to Dominick, dropped a quick curtsy

and said, "Charmed, Your Grace. I hope you will pay a call on us again, so I may have the chance to hear about your many heroic deeds to protect our beloved England."

"Not very heroic, I assure you." Dominick lifted Gwen's hand and placed a light kiss on the back. "But I would be delighted to visit again, my lady."

"Until then." In the next instant, Gwen disappeared around a tall topiary . . . leaving Parris very much alone with Dominick, a fact he clearly meant to take full advantage of.

"It seems it is just you and I now, Miss Sutherland. Shall I call you Miss Sutherland? Or"—he began to close the gap between them until he stood a scant foot away—"will you grant me permission to be more . . . personal?"

The fact that his nearness somehow intimidated her, and his words chased goose bumps over her skin, angered Parris. "I believe I asked you not to come here today, Your Grace."

"And I believe I told you I was coming whether you liked it or not." He stared down at her with intent in those golden-flecked eyes. "Your sister invited me. Remember?"

How would she ever forget? "Then I'll go get her for you. I'm sure you two have lots of catching up to do." And she hoped they both choked on it.

Furious, Parris marched toward the French doors leading into the house, but Dominick blocked her path.

"Move," she demanded.

"Make me."

Parris's hands fisted at her sides against the urge to do exactly that as his taunting words vibrated through her body. "Leave. Me. Alone."

He swept a single finger along her jaw. "I can't. Riling you is far too enjoyable. There's just something about you when you're angry that can blindside a man. Besides, I don't like being ignored."

So *that* was what this was about: His pride was pricked. "Well, Your Grace, you had best get used to it."

"Dominick."

"What?"

"You know my name, Parris. Stop trying to anger me with your formality." He crowded up close to her, endeavoring to overwhelm her. And succeeding. "Now, let me hear you say my name."

"I won't."

He took hold of a lock of her hair, fanning the strands between his fingers as his gaze held her captive. "Do you know how many times I've heard your voice in my head over the past eight years? Your laugh? How you sound when you're trying not to cry? Or the way you make that breathy little gasp when something surprises you? Do you know how many nights the memory of you sustained me? When I was stuck out in the middle of nowhere, waiting for a faceless enemy? Don't you care at all, Parris?" He took another step closer, the lapels of his jacket brushing her breasts. "You used to care."

It was all she could do to remain standing, her legs were so shaky. "Yes—*used* to, Your Grace. Used to."

A muscle worked in his jaw. "You do know how to cut a man down to size, sweet. Is this how you treated your fiancé? If so, it leaves much to be desired."

"James is none of your business." She turned to go. Let him stand out here all day and rot, for all she cared!

He grabbed hold of her arm, bringing her to an abrupt halt. "So what happened? Did he really leave you at the altar? He was a jackass, if he did."

Parris heard the warmth in Dominick's voice, saw that warmth reflected in his eyes, along with an apology, and hated herself for responding to it. "I don't want to talk about it."

Parris thought he would push. He was fond of doing so, after all. Instead he loosened his hold, but did not release her. His hand slid down her arm, his long, lean fingers lacing between her cold, stiff ones.

She looked at their clasped hands and wondered why she did not pull away, and why the feel of Dominick's skin against hers was so comforting, when that was the last thing she wanted from this man.

Parris jerked back when he rubbed his other thumb over her cheek. "What are you—"

"Smudge," he replied.

"Oh." For some reason, she didn't tell him to stop. The gentle motion of his finger was hypnotizing, even as her mind told her that the dirt streak had to be gone by now.

The rest of him was just as distracting, the breadth

of his chest and the way the muscles in his arm strained the seams of his jacket as he held his hand to her face.

Lord, but his arms were enormous. What had he been doing in the army to build such muscle? No gentleman of her acquaintance had a body like Dominick's.

"Do you remember when you saved my life?" he said, shaking Parris from her contemplation of his physique, a dangerous place for her mind to be.

"What?"

"On the old post road. We came across that merchant beating his horse, and you grabbed the whip from his hand before he even knew what was happening. Then you hit the little slug and asked him if he liked the feel of the whip. You didn't hesitate; not a second. I think you were only fourteen or so at the time, but damn if you weren't the bravest girl I ever knew, even then."

They had been walking together on the dirt road that rimmed the back edge of Carlisle land when they had come upon a grubby cart vendor beating his horse. The animal was trying to shy away from the bite of the whip, but the man held the reins tightly.

Even from a distance, Parris could see the welts on the horse's hide, and she had been furious. She flew at the man and ripped the whip from his hands, fear and rage giving her the strength to shove him into the dirt and bring the whip down on his thigh hard enough to draw blood.

Unfortunately, she made the mistake of then turning her back on him to soothe the frightened animal. The man grabbed hold of her hair, swinging her around to face him, prepared to strike when Dominick plowed into him, his head ramming into the man's stomach, knocking the air out of the merchant in a loud *whoosh*, and sending them both headlong into the ground.

The man turned out to be more wiry than Parris imagined and managed to get out from beneath Dominick, his hand reaching for the gun tucked in his boot.

When the man leveled the gun at Dominick, Parris had simply reacted, grabbing up a large rock and hurling it at the man's head as he cocked the trigger to fire.

She could still remember the thud as the rock connected with the merchant's head, blood dribbling down his brow as he stared at her in stunned disbelief before toppling facedown into the dirt.

At first she thought she had killed him, but Dominick had checked his pulse, and told her he was only unconscious. Parris had never known such relief—besides that of Dominick being unharmed.

Dominick had tossed some money onto the ground next to the peddler to compensate him for his loss, and they had taken the horse and quickly gotten away.

"My recollection on the situation is a bit different," Parris said, trying to ignore the heat radiating from Dominick's body. "You saved me. Not the other way around."

"A matter of opinion, certainly. Had you not thrown that rock, you might now be putting flowers on my grave." He canted his head slightly. "Would you do that, Parris? Put flowers on my grave, perhaps even shed a few tears over my untimely passing?"

"Don't talk that way."

"It bothers you, does it? To think of me dead."

"It bothers me to think of anyone dead."

"Am I just anyone, Parris?"

No, he wasn't. She only wished he was. "Annabelle has been waiting anxiously to see you." As Parris slipped her hand from his, he stroked the tips of his fingers over her palm.

She shivered. And he noticed.

"Anxiously, you say? One would think she wouldn't want to see me again."

"Perhaps my sister is a forgiving soul."

"What about you, Parris?"

"What about me?"

"Are you a forgiving soul?"

"I don't wish you ill, if that's what you mean."

"No," he said. "That's not what I mean." He was so close she could see the tawny flecks in his eyes, and how perfectly his valet had shaved his face, and the way his pulse pounded a steady tattoo in his neck.

God help her, it was still there—that heat, the racing of her blood that had become her constant companion since the year before Dominick departed for the army. The sensation had not lessened. If anything, it had only increased.

*   *   *

Ardor slammed into Dominick with the force of a lead pipe to his gut as he stared down into her turbulent blue eyes, eyes that had once looked at him with youthful adoration.

He had been enticed by some of the most beautiful women in the world: harem girls in Turkey, a sheik's daughters in Arabia, a voluptuous princess in Spain. But never had he experienced the hunger that now sluiced through him.

He wanted to touch her, to smooth back the riot of curls seeking to break free from the loose chignon at the back of her head, to hear her whisper his name with passion in her voice.

Eight years, he had been gone. An eight year gap between them, built in the hopes of overcoming the incessant need that had plagued him when she'd changed from a girl to a young woman, tying him into knots of desire and confusion.

There had been several occasions when he had almost taken a chance, almost risked their friendship to quell the lust raging through him.

For years, he had told himself that he had joined the army to get away from Annabelle and Frederick and his father's constant disapproval.

But Dominick realized now that the real reason was standing before him, angry, indignant, and so bloody glorious, he ached from restraint.

He had been given another chance, and he didn't intend to ruin it. As much as he wanted to beat the bastard who had hurt Parris by crying off on their wedding day, he couldn't help being glad the man was gone.

He hadn't meant to be such a swine by throwing the incident in her face, but damn it, no woman had the capacity to make him as angry as Parris.

He needed to talk to her about what had happened, but this was not the place or the time. He had to find his way back into her good graces, and though he hadn't acknowledged it last night, that was what had motivated him to come here today.

"There's a chasm between us," he murmured, loving the way her eyes seemed to absorb him. She still cared; he knew it. "And I intend to repair that breach."

"And what if I don't want you to?"

He leaned down to say, "Then I guess I'll have to work harder, to make you want it as much as I do."

"Don't." Emotions Dominick thought never to hear from her rang in that solitary word. "Just . . . leave it in the past."

"I can't." He wanted to kiss her. Badly. To savor those soft, lush lips against his own, to slake just an ounce of the hunger she so effortlessly aroused in him.

Desire overcame common sense, and his head lowered toward hers. He watched her eyes widen, her mouth parting, a kittenish sound whispering from her lips, stirring his blood and enflaming every male instinct inside him that yearned to possess her . . .

five

Still nursing the unconquerable hope,
still clutching the inviolable shade.

—Matthew Arnold

"Parris!"

Annabelle's high-pitched voice snapped Parris from her daze, making her fully cognizant of just how close she stood to Dominick, her breasts lightly brushing his chest, her hands clasped intimately in his.

She had almost kissed him, wanted to kiss him, had inched forward without even knowing it, certain she had seen the same need in his eyes.

What was the matter with her? This was the man who had betrayed her heart, who had wanted her sister and left his friendship with Parris behind. Had Annabelle not come along, Parris might very well have lost the only thing she had managed to retain during the long years without him.

Her pride.

She tried to ease her hands from his and encountered resistance. Her gaze snapped to his, noting the hint of wickedness in the curve of his lips, and the challenging light in his eyes.

Disconcerted, Parris yanked her hands away. She could practically hear Annabelle gnashing her teeth.

Dominick chuckled low in his throat and murmured softly, "Still every bit the hellion."

Parris shot him a quelling look before turning to her sister, who stood on the threshold in the exact spot Gwen had occupied a short while earlier. But unlike Gwen, there was not a shred of fondness in Annabelle's eyes, just her usual dislike and accusation.

"Good morning, Annabelle."

Her sister swept regally out onto the terrace, and said, "Lord, Parris, must you always look like a rag picker?"

Eyes gleaming, her sister dismissed her and turned a practiced smile on Dominick, looking beautiful, as always, and exuding a grace Parris had yet to master.

Would the feelings Dominick once had for Annabelle resurface now that they were together again? She wondered. Or had he been too hurt when her sister had cried off on their engagement?

He'd tried to talk to Parris the night before he left, coming to her bedroom window under the cover of darkness and tossing pebbles at the glass, the way he used to when they were younger and he wanted her to sneak out so they could sit on the porch steps and talk about what they wanted out of life.

Parris had wanted only one thing. Him. Though

she'd held that secret inside her until her heart could not bear the burden any longer, changing everything.

She had not spoken to Dominick that night. Instead she had hid in the shadows on her window seat, tears coursing down her cheeks as she watched him, wanting to go to him but wishing desperately that he would go away.

He did.

And he had not come back.

What might he have said, had she pushed open her window and spoken to him? Would he have asked her to come down? Would he have explained what had happened between him and Annabelle? Or had he simply hoped Parris would intervene on his behalf with her sister? She had been too afraid, too hurt, to take the chance.

With a heavy heart, Parris watched Annabelle float across the terrace with the grace and elegance she had always possessed in such abundance.

Stopping closer to Dominick than Parris thought necessary, her sister dropped into a curtsy, the bodice of her square-cut gown revealing a good portion of her ample bosom.

Parris darted a glance at Dominick to see if he was appreciating the view afforded him. He only looked upon Annabelle with mild inquiry; then his gaze cut to Parris and caught her staring. He treated her to a conspiratorial half-grin, which infuriated her almost as much as it warmed her.

"Your Grace," Annabelle murmured in a breathy

voice she only used when she had spotted a new conquest, making every muscle in Parris's body stiffen in revolt. Certainly her sister wouldn't try to seduce Dominick? Not after all that had happened between them?

Dominick briefly inclined his head. "Annabelle."

"It is a pleasure to see you again." Annabelle straightened slowly.

"Really?" Mockery flashed in his eyes.

"Why, of course." A slight flush tinged Annabelle's cheeks. "I was forever worrying about your safety while you were gone."

"How kind of you," Dominick drawled.

Parris couldn't remember a single time that Annabelle had spoken of Dominick in anything but a disparaging tone. But now that he was a duke, her sister clearly intended to sweep the past under the carpet and take up where they had left off. Annabelle had always been persuasive; would Dominick succumb again? And why did Parris care even the smallest bit if he did?

"I hope you haven't been waiting long?" Annabelle inquired.

"My time has been well spent." His amber eyes slid Parris's way, making her acutely uncomfortable. She could feel her sister's furious regard.

"I see," Annabelle said with a forced smile. "Parris, as you may recall, is too often caught up in her own little world to be burdened with such trivial matters as the social graces."

Dominick came to her defense. "I remember everything about Parris, and my memories are somewhat different than yours, Annabelle. Your sister was always putting others' needs before her own."

How did Dominick manage so effortlessly to keep her feeling continually off balance and conflicted? She didn't want him defending her, yet she felt grateful that he had. It reminded her of how it used to be the two of them against the world. Dominick had been her barrier, her solace, and it was as if all the years of separation had floated away and nothing else existed but them.

"You always were a protector of the less fortunate," Dominick murmured as he looked at Parris, feeling drawn to the softness in those pale blue eyes. "There was always someone you were trying to save."

He remembered the day they had come across an injured puppy lying by the side of the road. The little dog had been tossed from a passing conveyance as though he were so much fodder, discarded and unwanted.

His leg had been broken and the whimpering had cut through Dominick's heart like a hot knife blade. But even after all the puppy had been through, it looked up at Parris with trusting dark eyes, too weary to raise its head.

The tenderness Parris had shown the injured animal had touched Dominick. How gently she had crooned to him, how carefully she had picked him up and cradled him in her arms, taking the utmost care with his injured leg. The sky could have fallen from the heavens before Parris would have let anything happen to that puppy.

Dominick had known as well as she that Sir Oliver would never allow any animals in the house, but Parris had been determined to take care of the animal, no matter the backlash. His heart had twisted painfully when she had looked up at him, tears streaming down her face as she uttered only one word.

Why?

She had not comprehended such cruelty, such callous disregard for suffering, and Dominick had hated the world at that moment for showing her that cruelty, the underbelly of the worst people had to offer. He had protected her as best he could. Even now, he felt that protectiveness thrum through his veins as he looked at her.

"Your absence had been sorely felt, Your Grace." Annebelle's voice had risen a degree and was edged with irritation as she extended her hand for an obligatory kiss.

Dominick hesitated only a moment, then took hold of the offering, placing a light peck on the back of her hand. "You're looking lovely as ever."

Annabelle flushed with pleasure and shot Parris a brief, triumphant look before briefly lowering her eyes in a show of demureness that would have rivaled any thespian's best acting.

Then Dominick said, "Marriage has only enhanced your . . . voluptuousness."

Annabelle's eyes widened, the meaning behind his cleverly chosen words clear. She had gained weight since she had had her children, and though her figure was still lovely, there was much more of it.

Every morning Parris heard squeals and shrieks issuing from her sister's bedroom as her maids struggled to get her waist down to its pre-birthing size of twenty-two inches, which never happened, but the corset managed to redistribute the extra flesh upward. Hence her overflowing bosom, which she flaunted at every opportunity.

Parris wasn't sure what to think about Dominick's knowledge of her sister's life since they had parted ways. Had he been interested in finding out what had become of Annabelle? Or had the news managed to reach him where he was? Her marriage had certainly not been a secret.

Annabelle had wed a man she barely knew shortly after her engagement with Dominick ended, causing a stream of nearly unending speculation.

Looking flustered, Annabelle struggled for composure. "My beloved Harry is deceased now. A stagecoach robbery gone horribly wrong, I'm afraid. May God rest his soul."

Parris gaped at her sister. May God rest his soul? Annabelle had cursed her "beloved" Harry to the rafters when he had hied off to America to get away from her constant barrage of demands and nagging, leaving her with "two squalling brats," as she had referred to her children more than once.

Parris felt sorry for her niece and nephew. Philip was almost eight and Mary only five. They were good children, and didn't deserve the hand they had been dealt.

"I'm sorry to hear of your loss," Dominick said.

As if on cue, Annabelle tugged a lace handkerchief from her sleeve, dabbing at her eyes as she dangled the wispy scrap of material above her cleavage.

"We all suffer losses," she said in a martyred tone. "One must carry on in the face of adversity."

Dominick's expression sobered. "A friend of mine once told me that he expected me to get roaring drunk on each anniversary of his passing, to honor his memory."

"Did your friend die in the war?" Parris heard herself ask.

"Yes." His voice was somber, and his hand drifted to his thigh in a subconscious gesture.

Watching him brought to mind the news Parris had read in the newspaper five years earlier. "You were injured."

He nodded, the movement stilted, as though the subject was an uncomfortable one. "I took a bullet in the thigh."

"Does it still hurt?"

He shrugged. "Mostly when the weather grows cold or it's about to rain." A wry smile twisted his lips. "My friends use the throbbing of my thigh as a weather barometer. They haven't been caught in an unexpected rain since."

Parris knew he was trying to lighten the mood, but such an injury had to be painful. She had read that he had nearly died from an infection. She remembered how scared she had been at the possibility.

If he had only written her, asked her to come, told her that he needed her, she would have faced any obstacle to be by his side. But the weeks came and went with nothing from him. And when next she heard of him, it was again from the newspapers, saying he had recovered and had received a commendation from the queen for bravery above the call of duty, for saving four of his men from certain death.

"Oh, how horrible!" Annabelle exclaimed, regarding him with wide eyes that appeared sufficiently awed. "And here my sister has left you standing about when you are obviously in pain."

"Actually," he said, "movement is better for the wound than sitting. It cramps up."

Her concern rebuffed, Annabelle flashed a brief, venomous glance at Parris as though she were at fault for her faux pas. Just as quickly the light, practiced smile returned to her sister's face as she looked at Dominick.

"Are you home for good, Your Grace?"

He hesitated, turning his gaze to Parris before replying, "Yes . . . I'm home for good."

Parris hadn't realized how much she had wanted to know the answer to that question, until that moment.

"Wonderful!" Annabelle chirped. "Then we must have a dinner in your honor, to welcome you back."

"That's not necessary."

"Don't be silly. I'll arrange everything with the staff. Would next Friday evening be convenient?"

Parris could see that Dominick didn't want a fuss made over him. But she knew her sister would keep after him until he relented. Obviously, he recognized that fact as well, because he nodded. "That'll be fine."

"Shall we head inside, then? I'm sure my mother is eager to visit with you." Annabelle remained poised before him, apparently waiting for Dominick to take her arm and lead her into the house.

He properly looped his arm through Annabelle's, but when she made to move forward, he held her at bay and glanced over his shoulder at Parris. His eyes held a distinctly challenging glint as he offered his other arm to her.

Parris didn't want to touch him, didn't want to feel those muscles flexing beneath her fingertips. He was a danger to her peace of mind. But mostly, she didn't want Annabelle on his arm, too, feeling those same muscles.

Parris had not wanted to share Dominick as a child. And God help her, nothing had changed.

She swept past him regally in her dirty breeches, feeling his gaze searing into her back as he and Annabelle followed closely behind.

They were halfway across the morning salon when a high-pitched shriek reached their ears, then another voice vowing, "I'm going to get you!"

In the next moment, two small bodies came careening through the door, running full-tilt, skidding to a halt a second too late and crashing against Dominick's midsection.

Absolute silence reigned for the space of three heartbeats as two youthful faces stared unblinking up at the adults gazing down at them.

Then Annabelle, looking mortified by the all-too-natural actions of her children, berated in a strangled voice, "What is the matter with you two? Can you not see we have a guest? Is it not possible for you to *ever* behave yourselves?"

Any joy that lingered on their impish faces immediately dissolved at their mother's reprimand. "We're sorry, Mama," they uttered in unison.

By the rigid set of Annabelle's jaw and the way she darted anxious glances at Dominick, Parris knew her sister was far from mollified. "And what do you say to His Grace for your horrendous behavior?"

"It's all right," Dominick said. "They're simply being children. No harm done." His good-natured remark and the broad smile he bestowed upon Philip and Mary immediately won them over.

He bent down and fixed curly-headed Mary with the full impact of that smile, which clearly melted the little girl's heart. Mary was a female, after all, and Dominick had always possessed an abundant supply of charm.

"And what is your name, my girl?"

Mary executed a curtsy, but her feet tangled together and she almost toppled over.

Dominick gently righted her and brushed back an errant ringlet from her forehead. Mary beamed at him in a way that made Parris's heart catch.

"My name's Mary Elizabeth Marbury, sir, but my brother calls me mop-head 'cause of my hair. That's why he was chasing me, 'cause I told him he was a big dummy."

"I see." A hint of amusement tinged Dominick's voice, though his look conveyed all that was serious. "Older brothers are like that. I had one who called me names, too."

"You did?"

"I did."

Mary cocked her head to the side as though trying to discern if he was telling her the truth. Then, in the way only a child could manage with any aplomb, she said, "Do you think I'm a mop-head?"

"Absolutely not. Do you want to know what else I think?"

"What?" she asked in a near whisper.

"I think that you'll be the belle of the ball when you're all grown-up. And I hope when that time comes, you'll honor me with a dance or two."

Mary's face brightened immeasurably. "Oh, I will!" Then she peeked over her shoulder at her brother and prodded, "See, Philip? I'm going to be the . . ." She glanced back at Dominick. "What am I going to be again?"

Dominick ruffled her curls. "The belle of the ball."

"Oh, yes." She returned to taunting her sibling. "I'm going to be the belle of the ball, just like Auntie Parris said, and now this nice man, too." To bring her point home, she stuck her tongue out at her brother, who promptly rolled his eyes.

Dominick laughed, patting Philip on the shoulder as he stood up.

Mary turned back around and craned her neck to look up at him, commenting bold as brass, "You're pretty."

"Mary Elizabeth!" her mother gasped.

Parris laughed, silently agreeing with her niece. Dominick was very pretty, in the most masculine way a man could possibly be.

"Where is Matilda?" Annabelle demanded of her children, speaking of their nursemaid, who always looked beleaguered. Matilda was a sweet, good-hearted person, but she was getting too old to handle her rambunctious young charges.

The children exchanged a glance, and then Philip replied sheepishly, "We sorta tied her to one of the chairs in the nursery."

"You *what?*"

"We didn't mean any harm. We were playing pirates. I was Blackbeard and Mary was my captive—though she kept trying to steal my sword, which is against the rules." He gave his sister a pointed glare, to which she responded by scrunching up her face in her best imitation of a wilted prune.

Annabelle's expression became thunderous. "Why have I been cursed with you little heathens? Can you not stay out of trouble for even a moment?"

The cutting remarks struck right at the children's heart, bringing tears to Mary's eyes.

Parris was prepared to give Annabelle a scorching piece of her mind, but Dominick spoke first. "Go find the nursemaid," he told Annabelle in a tone Parris suspected he'd used with the men under his command.

Looking more than a bit cowed, Annabelle nodded docilely and hastened from the room. But even with her departure, nothing could fix the moment, as evidenced by the two forlorn little faces staring at the floor.

Parris knelt down and kissed the children's foreheads, wishing she could do more for them. Whenever she tried, though, Annabelle would get angry and accuse her of trying to steal her children's love away, threatening to take Philip and Mary someplace where Parris couldn't interfere.

Heartsore at the thought of losing her niece and nephew, Parris often had to restrain much of her natural inclination to rush to their aid. The only people who would suffer Annabelle's wrath were Philip and Mary, and Parris couldn't bear that to happen.

Mary, sounding almost shy now due to her mother's scolding, leaned toward Parris and whispered, "What's the pretty man's name?"

Parris smiled and tucked a lock of her niece's silky curls behind her ear. "This is the Duke of Wakefield, sweetie."

Mary hazarded a glance up at Dominick. "Do I call you duke?"

Dominick hunkered down beside Parris, his grin infectious as he patted his knee in invitation. Mary hesitated only a moment and then scrambled over to him.

"How about we make a deal?" he said. "I'll call you Mary and your brother Philip, if you call me Dominick. All right?"

Mary glanced at Parris for confirmation, and when Parris nodded, the little girl whispered, "All right."

Parris looked over at Philip, who stood a little away from them, a flush on his cheeks, having taken his mother's scolding harder than his sister. Parris held her arm out to him. He scuffed his shoe on the floor and then ambled over to her side.

"Did your Aunt Parris ever tell you that she and I used to play pirates?" Dominick asked Mary, who looked adorable huddled in his lap, fascinated by the diamond stud in his ear, which Parris hadn't noticed until that moment, and which gave his face a hint of the pirate he had once imitated to such perfection.

"You and Auntie Parris played pirates?" Mary asked in awe, turning to stare at Parris as though seeing her in a new light.

"We certainly did. Though your aunt refused to be my captive. She was very stubborn. And she always was taking the sword, too—and we know only the men should have the sword, don't we, Philip?"

Philip, who had inched closer, gave Dominick a tentative nod. "Only men should have swords. Girls'll just get hurt and cry."

"Nah-uh!" Mary hotly contested. "Girls are just as good as boys. Right, Auntie Parris?"

"Right, Mary." She looked from her niece to Dominick, who regarded her with a raised eyebrow.

"I think we're being challenged, Philip," Dominick said without removing his gaze from hers.

"I think so, too, sir."

"What shall we do about this stain upon our illustrious persons?"

"Stain, sir?" Philip frowned, appearing perplexed as he eyed his clothing and Dominick's. "I don't see any stains."

Valiantly, Dominick remained straight-faced. "Our good names are being sullied, Master Philip. This calls for action. How shall we salvage our honor?"

Philip, seeing that Dominick was asking his advice, puffed out his chest. "I say we lock 'em in a closet until they beg for mercy."

"Hmm." Dominick did his best to appear as though he was pondering Philip's suggestion.

Then Mary chanted, "Duel! Duel!"

"Yeah!" Philip piped in. "A duel—between you, sir, and Aunt Parris."

Parris blinked at this unexpected turn of events. "Now, Philip, His Grace does not . . ."

"A perfect idea!" Dominick interjected, speaking over her. "A duel it shall be."

"I'll get the swords!" Mary scampered off Dominick's lap and ran from the room before Parris could protest.

Dominick rose to his feet, his expression wicked as he held out his hand to her. Parris hesitated, and then accepted his assistance, once more finding herself within inches of that hard, heated frame. She was all too cognizant of the hand he still held.

"It seems we are to be opponents," he murmured. "I'll try not to trounce you too soundly."

"And I'll try not to make *you* beg for mercy—at least not for too long."

"Philip?"

"Yes, sir!" The little boy dashed to his side, as though summoned by his captain, his square little frame erect.

"Will you be my second?"

Philip blinked, and then his serious expression changed, his lips spreading into a grin. "Yes, sir!"

"Good. Now, I think we will need medical supplies, so we can aid our rivals once we've bested them."

"I'll get them!" And like a flash, Philip, too, was gone . . . leaving Parris very much alone with, and very much aware of, the man whose gaze had yet to waver from her face.

The whole event seemed orchestrated, as though Dominick had known from the onset exactly what he was doing.

She extracted her hand from his. Once more, his fingers brushed her palm, the slow, sensual curve of his lips telling her that he was enjoying her discomfit.

She took a half step back, which he matched. "You are overly confident in your prowess, sir."

His gaze dipped to her lips. "To which prowess do you refer, Miss Sutherland? I'd like to think I possess more than one."

Parris fought down a flash of unexpected heat. "That of your swordsmanship, of course. If I remember correctly, I beat you more than once when we were children."

"That's because I allowed you too much leeway back then. Things are greatly different now. I'm a man. And you . . ." His gaze drifted over her body. "You are most definitely a woman. The rules have changed. I can only hope you're up for the challenge, for I know I am."

Parris tipped up her chin and returned his gaze squarely. "I have never shied away from a challenge, Your Grace. And I can assure you, there will be no doing so now."

"It does my heart good to see that you still have more than your fair share of spirit, misplaced though it may be." He closed the small bit of space between them, bringing them so close that his thighs brushed against hers.

Parris started when one large hand cupped her face, his thumb stroking gently, almost tenderly, over her cheek. "Ssh," he murmured, his warm breath stirring the loose tendrils at her temple. "More dirt."

Parris licked her suddenly dry lips and his eyes lowered to her mouth, watching intently. Had he moved closer? Or had she leaned farther into him? Either way, they were very, very close. Were she to rise up on tiptoe just then, she could touch her mouth to his.

"Parris," he whispered in an almost tortured voice. The next moment, however, he stiffened. "Damn."

Before Parris had completely surfaced from that gauzy world into which she had disappeared, an excited voice exclaimed, "Dominick Carlisle! Oh, dear boy, is it really you?"

Reality jolted Parris to awareness. Guiltily, she pushed away from Dominick as her mother entered the room. Sweet heaven, that had been close. Too close. Thinking about what could have happened, had someone not interrupted, was a disaster too monumental to contemplate.

Parris prayed her face gave nothing away as she turned to her mother. "Good morning, Mother. I was just about to come and inform you of His Grace's arrival."

Her mother greeted her with a smile of genuine warmth, but something in her eyes made Parris feel as if her mother knew she wasn't being entirely truthful.

The baronness glided into the room, dressed impeccably in a dark blue tea gown that brought out the vibrant color of her eyes and accentuated her still slim figure. She was as lovely today as she had been when Parris was growing up, with only a sprinkling of silver streaking her thick, auburn hair to indicate the passage of time.

She stopped in front of Dominick, the expression on her face one of joy as she took hold of his hands and said with quiet feeling, "Welcome home, my boy. It is so good to have you back, safe and sound."

Her mother had never held Dominick accountable for what had happened between him and Annabelle. She had always been the most forgiving person Parris knew.

"Thank you, ma'am. It's good to be home."

"You've made quite an impression on my grandchildren. They have been singing your name up and down the hallways, and rattling on about some sort of duel."

Heat rose to Parris's cheeks at the reminder. "Not a duel, really . . ."

Dominick chuckled at her chagrin. "What your daughter is trying to say is that I have challenged her to a mock duel."

Her mother's eyes twinkled with delight. "So you're still challenging my daughter, you scoundrel?"

"That I am, ma'am." Dominick's grin was unrepentant.

"It seems you will never learn." She laughed lightly. "So what spoils go to the victor?"

"As to that," Dominick said, sparing Parris an appraising glance, "we have yet to discuss the terms. I was thinking that if I win, your daughter might accompany me to Saint Bartholomew's Fair."

"She was always clamoring about going to that fair when she was a child."

"I remember."

Parris couldn't believe Dominick would remember something so trivial as her wanting to attend the fair. She had tried to hide her disappointment when her father would refuse her year after year until, finally, she had stopped asking.

"What does my daughter get if she wins?" her mother asked.

"Anything she wants," he murmured, the seductive timbre of his voice vibrating through Parris's body.

The children's excited voices and running feet heralded their arrival a good thirty seconds before their bodies actually barreled through the door, breaking the spell Dominick's intense regard had cast over her.

Mary held up two wooden swords, and Philip presented the requested medical supplies, which appeared to consist of every ointment and bandage in the house.

"Grandma!" Mary exclaimed in a voice made breathless from having run full out to accomplish her mission before her brother. "Auntie Parris is going to pummel Mister Dominick 'cause he said Philip had a stain and that girls shouldn't have swords."

"I heard, darling." She bent down and smiled lovingly at her granddaughter. "It is all very exciting. But I think the opponents will need a bit of sustenance before the battle." At Mary's confused look, her grandmother explained. "They need to eat, sweetling."

"Aw, Grandma," Mary and Philip said in unison, looking deflated.

"You will join us, won't you?" her mother asked Dominick, her expression clearly communicating she would not take no for an answer.

"I would love to." Then he chucked the children under their chins. "Cheer up, you two. First we eat, then we battle. And if your aunt loses, which we know she will, because I'm the superior swordsman, we will all go to Saint Bartholomew's Fair to celebrate. But if by some chance she wins, well . . ." He left the sentence purposely unfinished.

Parris narrowed her gaze on his devious face. He was setting her up to lose by implying that if she won, it would be all her fault that none of them went to the fair.

Her mother hid a smile, clearly enjoying the underhanded tactics of her guest. "Well, come on, children. Let's eat." Her comment appeared to be directed at Parris and Dominick, laughter dancing in her eyes as she led Mary and Philip from the room.

Dominick waved Parris ahead of him. "Losers before winners."

"That would be you, then," she returned.

"I guess that leaves us to depart together." He smiled down at her, linking his arm with hers and steering them toward the door. "Fair warning, Miss Sutherland: I play to win."

"Fair warning, Your Grace: so do I."

Six

The fierce wretchedness
that glory brings us.
—Shakespeare

Dominick won their duel.

But he had arrived at his victory unfairly. His underhanded tactics with the children kept diverting Parris's attention.

Poor Mary looked so conflicted. While she wanted her Aunt Parris to win, and thereby prove that girls were as good as boys, she wanted to go to the fair even more, and had begun cheering Dominick on when he got the advantage.

Between Parris's distraction with the children and Dominick's unsettling presence—his muscles flexing beneath his shirt, his trousers molding rock-hewn thighs with each mock feint and parry—she had been doomed from the start.

Though she was still greatly put out about the whole affair, she had more pressing matters on which to concentrate at this moment—such as maintaining her disguise as a barmaid. No easy feat, considering the tavern she and Gwen found themselves in that evening was smoky, and her blonde wig was hot and beginning to itch her scalp.

Parris was a stickler for having accurate information and making sure that whatever scoundrel she chose to pursue as Lady Scruples was indisputably guilty of the crime with which he was being charged.

The dowager, Honoria Prescott, had tracked the Earl of Stratford's movements the entire evening of the Beechams' soiree, and had overheard him coaxing Lady Claire Markham into a private assignation at the Wrack and Ruin, an appropriately named tavern on the outskirts of town where Parris now found herself, with Gwen.

She glanced around the crowded, smoke-filled taproom searching for her cousin, who had gone off in pursuit of the earl and had not yet returned.

"Hey, sweet piece, stop standin' there an' get t' work."

Parris turned to glare at her employer, though she doubted he caught her expression as the demi-mask she and all the barmaids were forced to wear hid most, if not all, of her disgust.

Fish, as the proprietor was aptly called, had taken one look at Gwen's ample bosom when Parris and her cousin had shown up a few hours earlier, claiming they needed work, and muttered something about business picking up once the patrons got a gander at her. Little did he know, they wouldn't be around long enough for that to happen.

Parris loaded mugs of ale onto a dirty tray and began to make her way through the boisterous crowd, endeavoring to ignore the catcalls and barely managing to refrain from clobbering a few heads.

Through a break in the smoky air, she spotted Gwen, and for a moment, Parris could only stare. Who would believe that beneath the flared peasant skirt and ruffled petticoats that showed an inordinate amount of calf, the flimsy white gypsy blouse, and the tightly laced red corset worn over it, which very nearly caused her cousin's breasts to spill over the top, was Lady Gwendolyn Fairchild, cream of this year's debutantes?

Though thoroughly schooled in the proper manners of a young lady of means, Gwen fit in surprisingly well with her surroundings, appearing far more comfortable in her temporary role than Parris did.

At last, Parris caught her cousin's eye and Gwen nodded, signaling she had spotted the earl. Then she glanced toward the stairs leading to the tavern's upper level, where a man could get a room to sleep off his overindulgence—or take part in other pursuits, should he feel inclined.

Parris watched her cousin steathily disappear up the stairs, and sent a silent prayer heavenward that they would both get through the night without incident.

Then she took a deep breath, mentally arming herself as she stopped in front of the table of men who had been waiting for their drinks.

While most of the patrons had kept their hands to themselves, these men had not, and Parris did not relish having to come within their sphere of drunkenness again. Unfortunately, there was no avoiding it.

Over the rim of his glass, Dominick's gaze followed the petite blond barmaid as she headed toward a group of rowdy patrons. He had seen her steps slow, the closer she got to them, and knew she really didn't want to go near the swines again. He didn't blame her.

His senses were on full alert—trouble was brewing. He hadn't spent his nights crawling into enemy camps on his belly, keen to each sound carried on the wind, to not recognize when tensions were escalating. His men had called his intuition uncanny. Dominick simply considered it a strong will to survive.

But he had not come to the tavern that night to watch this girl, compelling as she was with her tiny waist and sensuously swaying backside.

He was here as a favor to Jason, who had, before disappearing abovestairs to rendezvous with his current paramour, returned with a drink for Dominick, a lovestruck expression on his face.

"I just spotted my next mistress," he had said, grinning like the unpenitent roué he was. "A blonde serving wench with breasts that could make a man drool. If I were not otherwise engaged this evening, I would have to sample her many delights. Ah, well, another time."

Stratford then took himself off, leaving Dominick

to wonder if the serving wench in question was the same one *he* couldn't seem to take his eyes off of. From what he could tell, she did have lovely breasts. Small, but definitely a nice handful.

Christ, where was his head? He was acting no better than bloody Stratford, who seemed to drift through life with his brain in his trousers.

However, the stirring in his loins reminded Dominick that it had been a long time since he had lost himself in perfumed skin, or felt a woman's body quicken with desire, heard her moans, her pleas for surcease, and then felt that sweet, gloved warmth tightening around him when she found her release.

His palms began to sweat and he tossed down another slug of his drink, his thoughts drifting to Parris, as had been happening with annoying frequency since seeing her at the Beechams' ball. She had been a vision, standing there in the moonlit garden, all grown-up and more beautiful than any woman had a right to be.

God, what a jolt it had been when he'd seen her that morning garbed in breeches that clung to her every curve, a powerful reinforcement that she was very much a woman.

Her body had filled out, ripened, and Dominick had been in awe, and yes, in lust. Seeing those nicely rounded buttocks molded by her breeches had nearly been his undoing, his reaction immediate and bordering on painful. Luckily she had been facing away from him when he arrived, which alloted him a moment to regain his equilibrium.

Her cousin, on the other hand, hadn't missed the appreciative gleam in his eyes. Lady Gwen might be young, but she was not naïve.

Jason would have his hands full if he attempted to pursue that particular lady. She would lead him on quite a chase, which was exactly what the jackanapes deserved.

Dominick was jarred back to the present at the sound of raised voices. He knew what was coming before it even happened, his body moving toward the barmaid before she had uttered a shriek of outrage as the biggest of the four men squeezed her buttocks.

"Come on, sweet thing. Give it up for ol' Jake," the dirty bastard slurred, his eyes gleaming with too much drink and escalating lust.

"Don't touch me!" she fumed, trying to fend off the hands coming at her from all directions.

The men guffawed, then Jake's counterpart said, "That's it, darlin'. Fight us. We like it."

"Leave me alone or I swear y'll regret it!"

Jake whooped, an idiotic grin splitting his ugly face. "Make me regret it, girlie. Make me regret it *real* bad."

"All right. Y' asked for it." She slammed the heel of her hand into Jake's nose, causing it to gush blood.

Stunned, the man wiped the back of his hand beneath his nose and stared down at the red smear left behind. When he looked up, his eyes glinted with fury. "Y'll be sorry for that."

The chair scraped back and clattered to the floor as he loomed over her. He swept his arm back to strike her, but the blow never fell. A large hand clamped around Jake's wrist, holding him immobile.

"Touch the lady," came a voice full of dark menace, "and I just might have to kill you." With a force that rattled the table, Jake was shoved back into the chair.

Parris froze.

She knew that voice, but it couldn't be. Not here.

Her gaze slowly rose from Jake's bloody face to the man holding him captive in the chair, locking with eyes that appeared almost black in the muted, smoky light.

Oh, God, he *was* here, big and solid and furious. Did he recognize her under the wig and mask? If so, would he give her away? Demand that she tell him why she was in disguise in a tavern on the disreputable side of town?

Then a realization dawned on her. He must have come with the earl. She had seen Dominick talking to the man at the ball, but she had not taken this possibility into account.

"Are you all right?"

It took a moment for Parris to realize he was speaking to her. She nodded, afraid to utter a single syllable. Even though she had perfected her cockney accent, having heard it often enough from several of the maids her uncle employed, it might not fool Dominick.

Never had she seen him look so dangerous, his gaze briefly scanning the onlookers and warning everyone away. Not a single man made a move to interfere.

Then his gaze returned to her and skimmed a measuring glance down the length of her body and back up again. When his eyes met hers once more, Parris sucked in a breath at the hot look reflected back at her. Never had she seen such a look directed at her, desire and restraint clashing in his eyes.

He wanted her.

The discovery made her heart slow to an erratic thump. How many years had she waited to see Dominick look at her that way? She might have taken some pleasure in the fact, had she thought he was actually seeing *her* rather than a scantily clad barmaid.

The man called Jake glared up at Dominick. "Who the hell are you?" he demanded, trying to rise again but unable to move an inch, even though Dominick had only one hand on him.

"Don't worry about who I am," Dominick rumbled with menace. "Worry about how you're going to chew your food without teeth."

The man across the table from Jake challenged in a slurred voice, "Y' don't scare us." He began to stagger to his feet. "We'll wipe the floor with—"

Dominick's right fist shot out and cracked against the man's jaw with the resounding impact of bone against bone. Parris flinched as the man went spinning to the floor. From his ignoble position, he stared up at his attacker with a dazed expression, rubbing his injured face.

"Whaddya do that for?" his cohort asked. "He ain't done nothin' to y', mister."

"Take that as a warning," Dominick told them. "Touch the lady again and I won't be so nice. Do we understand one another?"

The men, who looked as if they would stick a knife in his back the minute it was turned, reluctantly nodded and grumbled amongst themselves. Without another word, Dominick came around the table, startling Parris as he took her by the hand and led her away.

For some reason, she followed him rather meekly. Perhaps it was not meekness, though, as much as an inordinate amount of curiosity, and unease, about what he would do next.

Would he denounce her now? Demand to know what she was doing? Rail at her for being so foolish as to come to such a dangerous place?

Or did he intend to follow through on that heated glance? Would he kiss her? Touch her? Would she let him, even if he thought she was someone else?

Parris knew she was playing with fire, that he very well might ruin all her plans, but she simply could not, for the life of her, pull away. The large, warm hand holding hers so firmly felt too warm . . . too right.

Before she knew what he was about, Parris found herself in a dark corner of the tavern with Dominick looming in front of her, looking like some wild, beautiful pagan, with his silky black hair, defiantly long, brushing the shoulders of his jacket collar.

But what was worse was his heat, his closeness, the

way he radiated every ounce of his nearly over-whelming virility in her direction without a single effort.

He said nothing. Just stared down at her with those unfathomable eyes, and the first threads of panic rose inside Parris.

What was he waiting for? Had he recognized her or not? Did he expect her to break down and confess under his intense scrutiny?

She had to do something, or else she would scream. She averted her gaze, pretending interest in a stain on her skirt. The gentle touch of warm fingers beneath her jaw, tilting her head up, startled her, and uncon-sciously she took a step back. The wall pressed against her spine, conveying she was trapped.

But it was what she saw in Dominick's eyes that was nearly her undoing. The desire she had glimpsed ear-lier had not abated, but had intensified instead.

Parris didn't realize she had her bottom lip tucked between her teeth until his gaze dipped to her mouth . . . and his head descended.

No words crossed his lips. No words of protest crossed hers. She wanted this, had wanted it since she was old enough to understand that she desired Dominick, and through all the long, lonely nights when she had dreamed of him.

Warm, sweet lips nudged gently against hers, entic-ing her, savoring her, coaxing her to open her mouth so that his tongue could slip inside and mate with hers.

A soft moan rose up her throat, which made him

groan in return and press flush against her as his kiss became hotter, more demanding.

Parris's hands fisted at her side, when they really wanted to fist in his hair—but some small shred of sanity yet remained, reminding her that she was not who he thought, and that he would probably hate himself, and her, if he learned of her deception.

But for one insane moment, Parris wanted to continue in her role as the barmaid if it meant that Dominick would continue kissing her.

But it was wrong and she reluctantly pulled away, placing her hands against his chest, though not pushing him away. That she could not do.

Instead, she reveled in the heavy thump of his heart beneath her palm, so strong and fierce, she could feel it even through his jacket and see it pounding in a vein in his neck.

A silky lock of hair tumbled across his forehead. Impulsively, she rose on tiptoe and gently blew it back. Stunned by what she had just done, her gaze locked with his, and the hands he had placed at her waist gave a gentle squeeze. He looked conflicted, and heartbreakingly handsome.

How she wished she could pull off her mask and reveal herself, say the things she had wanted to say for as long as she could remember. It seemed as if a mask of one kind or another had always been standing in their way.

Even after all this time, nothing had changed: not her heart, not her mind. She cared for him still, but revealing herself was out of the question. Once more, she had chosen a road from which there was no turning back.

"Forgive me," he murmured, seeming reluctant as he released her and took a step back. "I guess I had more to drink than I thought. My sincerest apologies."

Too much to drink. Not desire. Parris's chest felt tight and she wanted to rage against the unfairness of it all, to be forever doomed to care for a man who had never returned her feelings. If Dominick had ever felt anything for her, he would not have left her, not have chosen her sister over her.

Tears threatening, Parris ducked beneath his arm and fled into the crowd.

Dominick reached for her, then lowered his arm, tracking her as she hastened across the room and disappeared behind a set of double doors.

It was for the better. He didn't need any complications in his life, and something told him the little barmaid would be a definite complication.

His mood darkened, and he hoisted a mug of ale from a passing tray and indulged in a healthy swig, in the hopes it would return him to his senses.

God, he had kissed her, hadn't asked for permission, hadn't warned her, hadn't said anything. He had seen what he wanted and taken it, obeying a piercing need in his gut to feel those soft lips on his, when all he had intended was to make sure she was all right. But a single glance at those lush lips, and all his good intentions had been shot to almighty hell.

Disgusted with himself, Dominick finished off the remaining ale. A good bender might be exactly what he needed. The alcohol would numb his ability to care about what he was doing and why, or who he was pursuing, and Lord knows, he couldn't kick the idea of pursuing the barmaid.

Where had she learned the move she had used on that piece of garbage who had groped her? Never had he encountered a woman so fearless, so capable of defending herself.

The only other woman who might have been able to pull off such a maneuver was Parris. He had taught her a similar move shortly after a stable boy had cornered her and tried to steal a kiss when she was thirteen.

She had vowed she would never again feel so defenseless—not that the lad had gotten off easy, not by a long shot. Parris had grabbed the rake that was used to muck out the stalls and bashed the cretin over the head. Little did she know that Dominick had added his own right jab to the boy's jaw later that day.

So, he wondered, was it the clever move the barmaid had made that had been the catalyst of that kiss? Or was it the mask? Something about her had caused him to lose his control.

Or was there more here than he was actually seeing? Something gnawed at him, and his instincts were rarely wrong. They had seen him safely through war, political intrigues, and one maharajah's daughter.

At the very least, he owed it to Stratford to dig a little deeper, to hang around until his instincts were thoroughly appeased.

And if he just so happened to get shed of that grating nobility along the way . . .

So be it.

Seven

The depth and dream of my desire,
The bitter paths wherein I stray.

—Rudyard Kipling

Her heart rapping out a wild tattoo, Parris ducked into the back room of the tavern. Hanging in the shadows, she surreptitiously watched Dominick.

He still stood in the corner where she had left him, but now he had acquired a drink and seemed to be downing it at a rapid clip.

Could their kiss have affected him as much as it had her? Or was he simply berating himself for his impulsive actions, wishing he had never touched her? He claimed to have drunk too much. That had stung, though his words had been meant to explain his conduct, not wound.

Parris wished she could produce a similar excuse for her behavior, could rationalize a good reason why she had allowed the kiss. But there wasn't one.

Those few moments in Dominick's arms and the

taste of his lips had been like a potent drug, muddling her senses, quelling common sense.

Yet, she couldn't help wondering what he might have done if she hadn't fled like some tremulous virgin. And what might he do at the moment if she were to return to his side, take the mug from his hand, and lead him to one of the rooms above the tavern? Would he come with her?

It was best not to know. She'd had the nerve to seduce him once before, and it had ended with a shattered heart.

Knowing he was still out there kept Parris from resuming her duties, worried that he might approach her again. The next time, he might recognize her.

The next time, she might not pull away.

She would have to hope Gwen had succeeded in finding out what Lord Stratford was up to so they could depart without delay.

Now, where to find Gwen?

Parris's gaze lit on the stairs at the back of the room, next to a door that led to the alley behind the tavern. That would be the way she and Gwen could leave undetected.

Parris took one last glance at Dominick, her fingers itching to brush back that silky lock of hair that had once more fallen across his brow. Before the urge overcame her, she hastened to the stairs. She had just topped the rise leading to the upper level when she spotted Gwen.

Though her cousin's face was partially hidden by

her mask, Parris could immediately tell something was wrong. "What's the matter?"

Gwen took her by the arm and turned her back toward the stairs. Tension vibrated through her cousin's fingertips. The moment they reached the bottom of the steps, Parris faced her.

"Something's happened. Tell me. Did the earl catch you? Does he know he's being watched?" Then her thoughts progressed further. "Oh, Lord . . . he didn't hurt you, did he? I promise, if he did, I'll—"

"No. It's nothing like that." Gwen averted her gaze. "Well . . . not really."

"What do you mean?"

Gwen's cheeks grew flushed and her eyes didn't quite meet Parris's, which alarmed her even more, since very little ruffled her cousin. "I made a mistake."

"What kind of mistake?

"He saw me."

"Saw you? As in . . . ?"

"No." She shook her head vehemently. "My disguise remained intact. But he . . . he cornered me outside his room." Then she rushed out, "I didn't think he would suddenly open the door!" Her already rosy cheeks flamed with color. "I was trying to listen and then I glanced up . . . and there he was."

"What did he do?"

"Nothing, at first. But he . . . he wasn't wearing a shirt, only his trousers—and the top button was undone! Showing all this . . . this . . ."

"Skin?"

"Yes! An obscene amount of broadly muscled skin."
Gwen inhaled a deep breath.

If Parris didn't know better, she might think her
cousin was thoroughly infatuated with Jason Fielding,
but Gwen was a level-headed girl and wouldn't possibly fall for a rake.

"And his stomach!" her cousin went on. "It was like
he had swallowed a washboard. A little soap and water,
and I could have cleaned my blouse and hung it up to
dry on the arm he had braced across the doorjamb."
She fanned her face with her hand, appearing a bit
dazed. "Worse, he didn't even care about his state of
undress. Instead, he stood there looking all pleased
with himself—you know, like an tomcat who had just
raided the creamery."

Parris knew that look well, as Dominick had
sported such an expression that afternoon when he
had beaten her in their mock duel.

"Then what happened?" Parris prompted.

"Well, he came out into the hallway, like he was
stalking me. I couldn't look away, couldn't run. It was
as though he had put a spell on me. Those blue
eyes . . ." She blinked, as if still under the strange
enchantment. "Then I felt the wall against my back. I
was trapped . . ."

"And?"

"And . . ." Gwen's voice dropped, an expression of
mortification on her face, and something else Parris
couldn't quite define, as she finished, "He kissed me."

"He *what?*"

"Kissed me." Then she blurted out, "I slapped him, of course."

"What did he do?"

Her cousin frowned. "He laughed."

"Laughed?" Now Parris frowned.

"The brute thought it was all very amusing. He grinned like a satyr as he pressed me back against the wall, and I was afraid . . . but then . . . well, it wasn't at all like I had thought it would be. His lips were warm and he tasted of brandy." She glanced down at her hands. "Then he disappeared back into his room . . . to the fancy woman waiting for him."

"A lady of the evening, you mean?"

Gwen's shrug had a sulky quality to it. "That's what she looked like to me, with her bosom practically spilling out of her bodice. It was scandalous!"

Though both she and Gwen had confronted unexpected complications—six-plus feet and two hundred pounds' worth of it—they had managed to obtain the information they had been seeking: the earl had not rendezvoused with Lady Claire.

"I think it's best if we leave," Parris urged. "The less time we spend here, the better." Especially with Dominick and the earl too close for comfort. "Travers has parked the coach around the block, and will be waiting for us at the corner."

Gwen nodded, her thoughts clearly elsewhere as Parris led her to the back door, and together they stepped out into the alleyway.

*   *   *

Dominick was glaring at the bedchamber door when it opened and out sauntered a very satiated and self-satisfied-looking Stratford.

Dominick had been waiting in the seedy hallway for almost ten minutes, his head beginning to throb from imbibing one too many mugs of ale in rapid succession.

He could imagine bloody Hastings now, speaking in that creaky voice that grated on Dominick even when sober. "A duke never loses control of his senses. He must maintain the utmost decorum at all times." He would then drone on about how a duke never consorted with riffraff, or those people who did not bathe as a matter of course.

In return, Dominick would inform the interfering little martinet that if he knew so damnably much about what a duke should or shouldn't do, that he could bloody well take over for Dominick and stop being such a rousing pain in the backside. It was a vicious cycle, and somehow, Dominick never won.

"Waiting long, old man?" Stratford inquired in a droll voice as he stepped out into the hallway, the top button of his trousers undone and his wrinkled shirt hanging off one shoulder.

"Hurry back, lover," a voice crooned from inside the room.

Dominick glanced over Stratford's shoulder and glimpsed a young tart propped against the pillows on the bed, a sheet draped over her nude body, her gaze following Jason's every move.

"Keep yourself warmed up, my sweet," Jason said with a leer. "I'll be back for the encore momentarily." He closed the door and leaned against it, grinning wolfishly.

"I see that's not Lady Claire. Came to her senses, did she? Or could it be you fear the potential backlash of one Lady Scruples?"

"First of all, I'm afraid of no woman. Secondly, Lady Claire would have come had she not had a previous engagement."

"And what engagement would that be? Avoiding you?"

Jason smirked. "You'd like to think that, wouldn't you? Always did envy my way with the women."

"It's a wonder your big head doesn't snap your neck."

"Mock me if you will, old man. But you know you'd like to be the arrogant ne'er-do-well you used to be back in the hallowed days of Eton and Cambridge. The devil himself, you were. There were times I truly admired the way you could juggle the women. They should have commissioned marble busts of the two of us and proudly displayed them in the square. Then you had to go off and ruin it by becoming responsible." Jason shook his head in disgust. "The downfall of another good man."

Dominick didn't know how much he liked the idea that he had become responsible, considering it was a fate he had avoided at all cost when he was younger, and the cause of many of the problems between himself and his father.

"So when do *you* plan to do the Elder proud and become a scion of virtue instead of vice, Stratford?"

"Banish the thought, old boy! I'm in my prime. Don't intend to waste that precious commodity locked behind office doors."

Dominick shook his head and returned to the point. "I'm departing now, so keep an eye about you for women wielding threatening letters."

"You *are* feeling droll tonight, aren't you? Well, that's fine. You go home and let Hastings tuck you in. Perhaps he'll sing you a lullaby. I, on the other hand, intend to find the blonde I spotted when we arrived, once I'm through here."

That last part rounded on Dominick like an unexpected right hook. "The blonde?" Surely Stratford was not referring to *his* blonde?

His friend nodded. "Caught her up here a short while ago, listening at the door."

"Why would she be listening at the door?"

"Curiosity about my sexual prowess, I suppose. It was like a blast of hellfire to the groin, finding her there. Then she gave me these doe-eyes. You know, trying to look innocent. Couldn't help myself. I kissed her."

Dominick straightened away from the wall that had been propping him up. "You what?"

"Kissed her. Rather enjoyable, too. If I hadn't been otherwise occupied, I would have pressed my good fortune. But with one lady waiting . . . Well, you know. Had to be a gentleman, and all."

Christ, Dominick couldn't believe it. He just couldn't. The girl had kissed Jason? No, Jason had kissed *her*, he said. But had she wanted Stratford's attention? Had that been why she had fled from Dominick?

The thought was like an iron fist to the gut. He didn't know why he couldn't get the girl off his mind. Something about the feel of her, the taste of her lips ... like a potent elixir holding him in thrall.

"Well, good night, old man," Jason taunted in a cheery tone that made Dominick want to bury his fist in his friend's face. "Try not to hurt yourself going down the stairs. You may want to think about investing in a cane."

Dominick gritted his teeth, but decided to let the blighter think his taunts had changed Dominick's plans.

"Actually, *old man*, I think you're right. It's too early to go home. How about we head over to my club and break out a few bottles of cognac? See who can drink whom under the table. If memory serves, you never could hold your liquor worth a damn."

Stratford's eyes took on a new gleam, and he grabbed the bait. "From your private stock?"

"Would I give my friend anything less?"

"Well, if you feel up to it ..."

"Oh, I feel up to it, all right." Anything to keep Stratford from pursuing the barmaid.

For Dominick fully intended to pursue her himself.

*   *   *

Parris covered her nose as she and Gwen stepped out of the tavern and into the dark alleyway. The rank smell of rotting garbage and damp earth wafted around them, making Parris glad she had not eaten anything recently.

Empty bottles rattled at their feet. She pushed them out of the way with the tip of her lace-up boots, the tough leather pinching her toes. She longed to remove them and soak her poor feet.

"A rat's paradise," Gwen declared, wearing the same expression of distaste as she glanced about.

The queasiness in Parris's stomach redoubled at her cousin's remark. She had managed not to think about the bewhiskered creatures until Gwen had brought them up.

Her gaze skirted the area, sure now that every bottle harbored a beady-eyed rodent just waiting to pounce on an unsuspecting passerby.

"I cannot wait to get home," Gwen said, articulating Parris's thought. "Between the smoke and ale inside, and the stench out here, it will take hours of bathing before I feel clean again."

Parris nearly groaned out loud. Her tired body ached with the desire to sink down into hot, steamy water, the smell of rose oil perfuming the air while she closed her eyes, breathed deeply, and melted away into blissful oblivion. So enraptured was she by the image that Gwen had to lightly shake her to bring her back to the present.

They started down the alleyway, but had barely

gone twenty feet when a noise behind them raised the fine hairs on the back of Parris's neck.

"Well, well . . . lookie what we got here. If it ain't that troublemakin' bitch who done busted m' nose."

Parris halted and exchanged a quick glance with Gwen before they slowly turned to face the man. But it was not just Jake behind her, his nose swollen and canted at an unnatural angle, but the three other men who had been with him inside. The man Dominick had punched now sported a huge black-and-blue mark on his right cheek and jaw.

"What do you want?" Parris demanded with far more bravado then she actually felt. She knew that showing these men any fear would give them exactly what they wanted.

"Actin' all high-falutin' now, are we? Too good for me and the lads?" He jerked his thumb over his shoulders at the men leering at her and Gwen, one slimy toad licking his lips as his lecherous gaze raked her cousin's body. "Don't think I like that much. No, don't like it much a'tall."

"Leave us alone," Parris told him, backing away as Jake advanced, her hand clasped in Gwen's.

She glanced over her shoulder and estimated the distance to the street. Not far; they could make it. They were in much better condition than Jake and his druken cohorts.

But then what? Would Travers be waiting on the corner to help?

"Don't even think about it," Jake warned, catching on

to what she was planning and increasing his stride, now just a few feet from them. "You and me got unfinished business, girlie. Y' got away from me earlier 'cause of that gentry-mort. It ain't gonna happen again. No one in this bunch is gonna help y', so you best treat me real nice . . . real nice, indeed."

Before Parris had a moment to react to the smile that slithered across his greasy face, Jake raised his hand and slapped her, hard, sending her reeling to her knees, the material of her skirt rending. She could taste blood on her tongue.

"*Parris!*" Gwen cried in alarm, dropping down beside her and trying to help her to her feet.

"That's what y' get for sassin' me," Jake growled. Then he snapped his fingers and the man with the swollen jaw grabbed Gwen in a bear hug and yanked her away, lifting her feet clear off the ground.

Gwen squirmed and kicked out at him. "Let go of me, you filthy cur!"

"Y're a feisty one," the man said with a grunt. "I like that." He tried to lick Gwen's cheek, but her cousin wrenched her head away. The man chuckled. "Let's you and me get better acquainted, sweet piece."

Gwen let loose a scream that reverberated off the moldy brick walls and certainly had to have been heard for blocks.

"Shut her up!" Jake barked.

The man clamped a hand over Gwen's mouth and growled something in her ear that Parris could not hear, but which made her cousin's eyes grow wide with fear.

"Now get her outta here," Jake ordered, sending the brute who held Gwen tromping down the alley.

Parris sprang to her feet to go after her cousin, but Jake seized her roughly around the waist. "Where d'ya think y're goin', eh? We got things to do, you and me."

"Don't touch me!" Parris struggled to wrench her arm free, but her actions only served to make Jake's grip grow more punishing.

"Don't make me any angrier than I am. I ain't a nice man when I'm mad." He began dragging her in the opposite direction from where his chum had taken Gwen.

Parris looked back and saw her cousin still wrapped up in the man's brawny arms, struggling wildly . . . and then disappearing from view behind a stack of crates.

Panic sluiced through Parris's veins and roared through her blood like wildfire. *Scream!* her mind hammered. And she did, as though her very life depended on it.

Dominick descended the tavern stairs with Jason in moody silence, the idea of Stratford minus teeth looking more appealing with each passing second.

But hitting Jason would only be a temporary, albeit enjoyable, measure. If for some unfathomable reason the girl preferred Stratford, what could he do about it?

Kill Stratford? his inner voice prompted.

As loath as Dominick was to admit it, the clod had his good points, even if not a single one came to mind at that moment.

All right, so killing Stratford was not an option. That meant Dominick would have to be at his most charming and persuasive when next he saw the serving girl.

To avoid her now, he led Jason down to the back door instead of out through the taproom. He'd return tomorrow night and discover the lay of the land.

He was engrossed in his plotting when a putrid smell assaulted his senses as he stepped out into the alleyway, his boots crunching on glass. Then a piercing scream rang through the air, ramming a spike of dread into his gut.

His gaze swung toward the sound and he saw a woman struggling wildly with a man who had her pinned up against a wall, his hand raising to strike her.

Dominick took off toward her at a dead run; Jason a few steps behind him.

"Bitch!" Jake hissed, spittle dribbling down the corner of his chin as he clamped a hand over Parris's mouth. "Y' just don't learn your lesson, do y'? Well, you'll understand the meaning of obedience before this night is through."

He raised his arm, and Parris flinched in anticipation of the blow. But in the next moment, Jake was spun about and a fist flew out of nowhere, impacting violently with Jake's face, sending him flying back onto the ground, his head lolling to the side, his nose gushing blood again as he lay there unconscious.

"Bastard," a furious male voice spat, bringing

Parris's gaze swinging around, her heart nearly stopping when she saw the towering, enraged figure of the man who had been her protector as a child coming to her rescue once more.

Fury simmered in Dominick's eyes as his gaze turned her way. "Are you all right?"

Parris nodded, her throat closing up on her. She yearned to toss off her disguise and throw herself into his arms, like she used to do when she was younger, so he would soothe her and swear that he would make everything all right.

Her lapse of weakness went as quickly as it came, thankfully. Her attention was diverted when she spotted the man standing beside Dominick, wearing the same expression of disgust as he stared down at Jake—a man almost as tall and broad shouldered as Dominick, with hair the same unconventional length, but whose eyes, when they lifted to her, were the most glittering shade of blue Parris had ever encountered.

Lord Stratford. The man for whom she and Gwen had risked their necks to spy on.

Oh God, Gwen!

Parris spun on her heel, needing to find her cousin, to save her before that hideous slug hurt her. A viselike hand wrapped around her wrist, hauling her to a stop.

"Where are you going?"

Parris had sense enough to disguise her voice and not say Gwen's name. "My friend! She's been taken away by some men. Please, y' must help her!"

"Where'd they take her?" Lord Stratford demanded, his features hardening.

"Back behind the alley." Parris pointed to the spot where Gwen had disappeared.

"I'll go," the earl told Dominick. "Stay here with her. There's about to be bloodshed." A grim smile crossed his face and he took off at a dead run.

Parris shuddered, knowing the thug who had gone off with Gwen would greatly regret his actions when Jason Fielding was through with him. The man may be a philanderer, but he was also a prized pugilist.

Unfortunately, his departure had left her completely alone with Dominick, who was staring at her in a way that made her heart falter.

Eight

*My soul, like a ship in a black
storm, is driven, I know not wither.*

—John Webster

Reality struck Dominick like a poison dart to the neck,
swift and jarring.

Parris. Good sweet God. The woman beneath the
wig and mask and phony accent that had given her
away the moment words had tumbled from those
rouged lips—lips that had nearly driven him to madness when he had succumbed to temptation and
tasted their sweetness—was Parris.

Blessed Jesus . . . that kiss.

Never had there been a man so twisted into knots
as he was at that moment. Thoughts avalanched
through his mind, and yet the brief contact he had
shared with Parris in the tavern was the sticking point
in his mind.

After all these years of tormenting himself, wondering how she would feel in his arms, how she would

taste, of what their first kiss would be like, and he had missed everything.

Except the fact that she had kissed him back.

And she had known his identity.

That realization jarred something inside him violently, but with an equal amount of pleasure.

For a long time, he had contented himself with being her protector and friend, glad just to be a part of her life. But lying dormant was a need to be her protector and friend *and* lover, to feel her beneath him, her body arching up to meet his, her soft moans driving him over the edge as he slid into her silky heat . . .

What in the name of Jesus had the girl done to him? With a single kiss she had shattered all his good intentions, laid waste his plans of a gentlemanly pursuit, and kept him from staying the course of renewing their friendship first.

One kiss. One deep, erotic, inferno-building kiss.

Though he hadn't left her much choice in the matter, she could have slapped him, tried to push him away, shouted her outrage—and yet she had done none of those things.

His amazement quickly turned speculative as yet another thought struck him. Had she been shocked and scared of him rather than aroused? Trapped in a situation from which she did not know how to extricate herself? Too afraid that he would recognize her to do anything but submit to the onslaught of his demand?

Christ, was she thinking about his aggressive behavior right now, worrying what he would do next? She was regarding him warily, which told him that either she wanted to bolt or she was concerned he would unmask her, literally and figuratively.

The thought made Dominick wonder about the very thing that should have concerned him from the start, had he not been so wrapped up in that kiss.

What was she doing here at this run-down hole-in-the-ground tavern, dressed in a disguise that she desperately didn't want him to see through?

The little fool! She could have gotten badly hurt, both inside the tavern and out. Had he not come along . . . The mental image of what could have happened to her made his gut clench.

Fury rose inside him like a living entity, his gaze slashing to her fallen attacker, his fists clenching with the need to beat the bastard's face to pulp.

A light touch on his forearm stayed him. "Are you all right?" she asked, concern in her voice.

Hell, no. He wanted to demand some answers, rattle them loose, if need be. His jaw ached from how tightly he clamped it, to keep from saying anything until he had himself under control.

Where had she picked up the hackneyed speech? And why, even when she was speaking words that butchered the English language, did she still sound as lilting as an angel?

"I'm fine," he said tightly, staring at the delicate hand on his arm, all his muscles bunching in tension from that simple touch.

Noting the direction of his gaze, she quickly dropped her hand. "Thank you for y'r help." The words were a near whisper and she wouldn't meet his gaze directly. "I must go find my friend now. So I'll bid y' good night."

Dominick moved in front of her as she attempted to walk by him. She would not get away that easily. Since his return home, she had been trying to outmaneuver him at every step. Well, no more.

"She'll be fine. Stratford will see to her." Dominick wondered who the mysterious friend was that had come with her.

On the heels of that thought came a rather startling revelation.

Lady Scruples.

That was why Parris was at the tavern tonight. She was following Jason. That could be the only reason, for certainly she was not following him, no matter how much he would like to believe otherwise.

He remembered how startled she had been when he had suddenly appeared at Jake's table, and the way she had run away from him.

She had not been expecting him. In fact, Dominick suspected he had put a chink in her plans—and that was why she had been sneaking out through the alley.

Damn her for an obstinate brat!

For as long as he had known her, she had been embroiled in one form of trouble or the other. That trait, combined with the fact that she had always fought for those who couldn't fight for themselves, would make the role of Lady Scruples irresistible to her.

How could he not have connected the pieces sooner? No female of his acquaintance was as bold and undaunted by potential harm as Parris.

Well, this was where the game ended. She'd had her fun tormenting the male population, and now it was time to retire Lady Scruples. He'd just have find a way to occupy her evenings so she wouldn't feel inclined to go stirring up trouble.

Since she clearly had a knack for slipping from her house undetected, the thought of protecting her for her own good was a daunting prospect. But he was ex-military. Daunting prospects were his specialty.

Dominick's concentration on her was so complete that Parris held her breath in anticipation, of what, exactly, she wasn't sure.

If he had found her out, he'd undoubtedly be upbraiding her for her foolhardy behavior. Still, her nerves would not settle down.

Here he was, in front of her, and they were alone . . . and he had kissed her earlier. Was he thinking of that kiss? Perhaps wanting to kiss her again? And would she encourage him? Would it be right?

Each moment she kept the truth about her identity from him only widened the chasm between them. She didn't want to put another lie in their path; then she'd be back where she'd started, and the only way she could be with him was if she were cloaked in pretense.

His gaze was fierce and yet oddly tender as he stared at her, his eyes dropping suddenly to her mouth. Parris touched the cut there with the tip of her tongue, knowing only one thing would soothe the pain: Dominick's lips on hers.

The touch of a warm, slightly callused finger against her chin caused Parris to flinch. "Ssh," he murmured, his voice a husky growl as he tipped her head up. "I'm not going to hurt you. I just want to see how badly you're injured."

Parris shivered from his touch. She wanted to ask him why he didn't see her, recognize her, and why he had been willing to kiss the barmaid but not her. To pull the barmaid close, but not touch Parris in more than a brotherly fashion.

Her body thrummed with the thought that now, in her disguise, she could do what she wanted to him, as she had done one night in a garden.

She could smooth her hands over his broad shoulders, unbutton his shirt and feel the contours of his chest, press her lips to the pulse that beat, strong and steady, at the base of his neck.

"That lip needs to be looked at," he murmured. "It might need a stitch or two."

He withdrew a pristine white handkerchief from a pocket inside his jacket, the initials *D.C.* monogrammed in gold thread in one corner. Carefully, he dabbed at the small cut on her lip.

Parris would never have believed so big a man could be so infinitely gentle. The sweetness of his gesture almost undid her, almost had her confessing her sins, which seemed to multiply with each passing second. But, heaven help her, she didn't want this to stop.

Somehow they had moved closer to one another, his thighs brushing against her skirt, her breath arresting in her throat at the way he stared at her lips.

In the next moment, he released her and took a step back, muttering a curse. Then he grabbed her hand and led her out of the alleyway. A hackney sat beneath a flickering gas lamp. The driver appeared to have nodded off.

She thought Dominick meant to put her into the waiting conveyance. Instead, he steered her toward a black coach that suddenly materialized, as though conjured up magically by the night.

"Good evening, Your Grace," said the liveried driver on the box, tipping his hat at Parris. "And where might I take you and the lovely lady, sir?"

"Home, Benson," was Dominick's brisk reply, holding up his hand to stop his driver from alighting to open the door. If the man thought there was anything strange about his employer taking a tavern maid home, his expression gave nothing away.

Parris panicked, grinding to a halt as Dominick put his hand at her elbow to assist her into the coach. "Thank you for y'r help, y'r lordship, but I'll be fine now."

"Nonsense, my girl. I wouldn't dream of leaving you here unattended."

"But—"

"I consider it my duty." Though his tone was all that was polite, the steely determination in his eyes told Parris he intended to get his way. He had always been the only person who could get her to do what he wanted.

Parris made one last attempt. "My friend . . ."

"Is in capable hands. Have no fear."

The brief, wry twist of his lips reminded Parris quite jarringly of who had gone after Gwen. The earl!

The man was done for now. If there was one thing Lady Gwendolyn Fairchild could not tolerate above all else, it was a philanderer; the very trait Jason Fielding epitomized. Her cousin might be in capable hands, but Lord Stratford could not even begin to fathom the handful he would find in Gwen.

Dominick must have thought her hesitation stemmed from concern, because he said gently, "I promise you that no harm will come to your friend."

Parris was forced to look into his eyes once more, and what she saw there told her how important it was to him that she trust him. "All right," she murmured. "If you promise."

The half grin he bestowed upon her was devastating. "I do. Now climb in."

Parris turned toward the coach, telling herself that if she had come this far, she could see herself through the next ordeal.

She would let Dominick tend her cut if it would make him feel better, then she would go on her way. If she was brave enough to take on the patrons of the

Wrack and Ruin, she was certainly capable of handling one misguided, well-intentioned, but far too distracting duke.

She caught a movement out of the corner of her eye then, and her heart lurched as she spotted her driver, Travers, hustling in her direction. She had completely forgotten about him!

Well, there was only one thing that would save her now. Whirling around, she flung her arms wide, and launched herself against Dominick's chest, making him stumble back a few steps.

Wrapping her arms around his neck, she thanked him profusely for the kindness he was showing her, all the while waving away Travers.

"Your gratitude is admirable, my girl," Dominick murmured close to her ear, his silky hair tickling her cheek, his husky voice and warm breath setting her body to trembling. They were pressed as tightly together as two people could be, her breasts flattened against his chest and his lower region cradled intimately against her belly.

And when he pulled back, just enough to look down into her eyes, she knew that, right there on the street, beneath the gas lamp, in full view of his driver and whoever else might be around . . . he was going to kiss her.

And she was going to let him.

The contact was brief, only a light sweeping of his lips across hers, as soft as butterfly wings but no less powerful than his earlier kiss. Her reaction was just as strong, stirring a heat between her thighs and sending it fanning out to warm every place his body touched hers.

"What was that for?" Her voice was no more than a breathless whisper.

He cupped her cheek, brushing the pad of this thumb gently across her lower lip. "Just trying to get you to stop talking." His voice did not sound quite steady.

"Oh." Disappointment flooded Parris. She had thought . . .

"We'd best go."

With Dominick's hand at her elbow, she climbed into the coach emblazoned with the ducal emblem and settled back against the dark blue velvet squabs, surprised by the lavish appointments.

Dominick had always disdained the trappings of wealth, which was one of the reasons the two of them had gotten on so famously as youngsters. He didn't care that she was poor, and he cared even less that he was rich. In his eyes, they were equals.

The coach tipped slightly as he climbed in and sat directly opposite her, his long legs trapping hers and brushing the outsides of her thighs, making the roomy compartment now feel as small as a thimble.

"Comfy?" he asked, his voice a seductive cadence in the dark.

Parris nodded, not trusting herself to speak.

It was hard to think of Dominick as a high-ranking peer of the realm, his title second only below a prince.

Though, as a girl, she had elevated him to that exalted status: Prince Dominick, come to save her from an unloving father and a hateful sister.

In some ways he seemed like that old Dominick, unaffected, carefree, still teasing her. But in other ways, he had changed, matured, developed a steely edge that had not been there before—a facet that made him at times seem dangerous, and all the more thrilling.

All the more desirable.

And here she was, still the same old Parris, provincial, graceless, and finding herself two steps ahead of disaster at all times.

How ironic to have Dominick coming to her rescue again, even though he didn't know whom he had saved. It made her wonder what other females he had assisted over the years, and what forms of gratitude they might have bestowed upon him.

The thought of Dominick with other women, kissing them, touching them, loving them with his body, was almost too painful to bear. But not nearly as destructive as the image of him and Annabelle together.

Why had he hurt her like that? Of all the women he could have loved, why did it have to be her sister? And why, in that secret place in her heart, did she want to forgive him for what he had done, when he didn't deserve her forgiveness? He had deserted her, destroyed her with his silence, and yet she could not hate him as she should.

When she had seen him at the Beechams' gala, she

had wanted to run to him, hold him close, tell him how much she had missed him; how he had never been far from her thoughts, that she had prayed for his safe return every day—and then rail at him, hit him, swear that she would never again give him the opportunity to hurt her. All the while futilely wishing that they could go back to the days when life was simpler and her feelings for him were not so complex.

"What's so fascinating?"

His deep voice pulled her from her troubled thoughts. He regarded her from the shadows, his honey-colored eyes cutting through the darkness, peering at her as though he could see into her very soul.

She blinked and her dream world disappeared. "What?"

"I asked what was so fascinating? You're staring at me as though I've grown horns."

Heat rose to Parris's cheeks. What must he be thinking? That perhaps she was contemplating the weight of his purse, intending to rob him blind? Or was it quite the opposite, and he was thinking she was so enamored with him that she must stare?

She averted her gaze, wondering why he hadn't turned up the lamps that would illuminate the interior. The darkness felt too . . . intimate.

"My apologies, y'r lorship." she said, hoping to sound offhanded instead of guilty. " 'Tis just that I'm tired. Been on my feet all day. Fair to wore m'self out."

"Yes, I imagine lugging those mugs of ale around for hours and dodging all those men with grasping hands must be very hard work."

"Oh, it is, sir. Very hard, as you say. Which is why I must be off to my home as soon as y' have fixed my lip. Straight away," she emphasized.

"I understand." There was an odd note to his voice. Was he laughing at her? "And where is your home, may I ask?"

"M-my home?" Oh, drat him for being a probing beast! Why would he care one way or the other where a barmaid lived?

"Don't worry. I won't show up on your doorstep and start all sorts of rampant speculation, if that's what concerns you."

As if a man of his rank would visit the house of a serving girl. But . . . could he possibly want to see her again? Did he wish to take things beyond a mere kiss?

And what if he did?

He dashed her speculation to pieces, saying, "I just want to tell my driver where to drop you off, after my housekeeper has tended your lip."

Just when she thought she had him figured out, he went in the other direction. "Oh, well I . . . I live in Southwark." She would be long gone, slipped out a side door or even a window if need be, before going anywhere with his driver.

"Southwark, hmm? Dangerous area."

It was the only place she could think of that was sufficiently poor, which was where she suspected a barmaid would live. But the possibility of finding herself back in Dominick's coach and deposited in the East End made her shiver.

"Are you cold?" he asked.

"Cold?" No. In fact, she was far too warm. The air felt close and a fine layer of perspiration caused her blouse to cling to her.

"You're trembling."

"I'm fine."

Nevertheless, he shrugged out of his jacket, revealing the full width of his chest and how muscular his arms were, both shown off to perfection in his tailored linen shirt.

Then he leaned toward her, filling up the little bit of space between them to drape his jacket around her shoulders, its heat enveloping her as though he had wrapped his arms around her, a hint of the bay rum cologne he wore suffusing the air.

She expected him to sit back, though why she thought she could predict his moves when he had so amply proven she couldn't, Parris didn't know. Instead, he stayed where he was, regarding her with eyes that seemed almost black.

Parris pressed back against the seat cushions when he lifted his hand, a soft gasp escaping her lips as he feathered his knuckles across her cheek.

"Bruise," he murmured, reminding her of the blow Jake had given her. "Does it hurt?"

"No," she breathed, her heart hammering against her ribs.

He studied her jaw as if something there fascinated him. "I don't believe I got your name?"

Her name? Flustered, Parris said the first one that came to mind. "Meg."

Should she not escape him soon, the weight of her fabrications might very well suffocate her.

"Meg." The word rolled off his tongue in a way that swept heat across Parris's skin. "I had a cousin named Meg. She was a sweet little girl, with a face like an angel. God, I miss her," he said in a tone that had grown poignant.

He continued to absently stroke his knuckles over her cheek, not realizing that her heart ached in remembrance of the cousin he spoke of with such love. How could she have forgotten little Meg?

"She loved life," he went on. "But it dealt her a cruel blow by giving her a weak heart and lungs." A bittersweet smile touched the corners of his mouth. "She used to call me Cousin Dom because she couldn't pronounce Dominick. 'Higher, Cousin Dom!' she would squeal when I would toss her into the air. Always higher." He shook his head. "The day she died, I had just finished making a kite for her."

Parris felt tears prick her eyes, seeing that day so vividly in her mind. Dominick had been devastated by Meg's death.

Meg had been only four years old, far too young for such tragedy to have touched her life. And the fact that the little girl had known she was going to die had taught them all a lesson in bravery.

Dominick had called her Angel, and that was what Meg had promised she would be when she met her mama up in heaven. Dominick's angel.

He had been by her side when she took her last breath, and when Meg was gone, he had torn out of the house. Parris had been waiting for him as he ran full out across the field that separated his home from Archer's Pond, where she always waited for him. It was their special place.

And for the first and only time that Parris could recall, Dominick had cried, dropped to his knees before her and held her tight, allowing her to comfort him when it had always been the other way around.

She wanted to comfort him now, to banish those sad memories and renew his hope. To touch him, and infuse him with whatever strength she possessed.

She laid her hand against his jaw, a fine layer of stubble abrading her fingertips as she skimmed the rugged contours of a face that had matured and defined during his long absence.

He leaned into her palm as her fingers slid into his hair, his name whispering from her lips like a benediction as she gravitated toward him, wanting to press a kiss to his forehead, to brush her lips over his closed eyelids, feather lightly across his cheek, taste the small indentation in his chin with her tongue before slowly, tenderly claiming his mouth.

Reality intruded upon them when the coach hit a rut, forcing Dominick back against the opposite seat . . . and Parris into his arms.

"Sorry, Your Grace," Benson called from the box, but neither of them were paying attention.

Parris tried to scoot away, but Dominick coiled his arm around her waist, pulling her onto his lap. Her temperature spiked as she felt the hardness pressing against her bottom.

The knowledge that she had aroused him was heady—and frightening. This was wrong. Impossible. The stable life she had known only a week earlier had been turned upside down. But she didn't know how to put things back the way they were.

"We'll be home any moment now," the driver called down.

Home. Dominick's home.

Parris tried to ease off his lap, but he held firm. "Take this off," he murmured, his forefinger sweeping along the lace edge of her mask, which she had forgotten she still wore.

Her fingers itched with the need to tear away the flimsy barrier and let the truth be known, to face whatever came next, no matter what recriminations he may heap on her.

But as she sat there, safe in his embrace, Parris wondered how her life would ever be the same now that she had new memories of his touch to sustain her, images that would keep her tossing restlessly in her bed at night.

What would she give to hold on to him? The answer seemed so clear: whatever it took, and for however long the good Lord allowed her.

She slowly pushed his hand away. "The mask stays." She prayed he would not protest, though for a breathless moment, it looked as if he might. Perhaps, deep down, she hoped he would.

He dropped his hand. "Your choice, sweet Meg." His voice was a rumbling purr that fanned out over Parris's skin. "I happen to enjoy a little mystery. So keep the mask if it pleases you."

Relief made her sag against him. She thought he chuckled, but the driver's voice covered the sound.

"We're here, sir."

Feeling languid, Parris almost didn't register the words. When she did, she tried to scramble off Dominick's lap before Benson discovered them in that position.

Dominick held her tight, reluctant to release her. Parris's gaze leapt to his. Their faces were so close . . . their mouths even closer . . .

With a muttered oath, he placed her back on the seat across from him, righting her jumbled skirts before his driver opened the coach door and put down the stairs for them to alight.

Dominick stepped down first and held his hand out to help her. Parris's legs were not quite steady as she rose, placing her hand in his outstretched palm, warm fingers wrapping around hers, giving a gentle squeeze as though to bolster her flagging nerves.

Once she stood on solid ground, she glanced up at the elegant town house occupying an entire block of Grosvenor Square, her gaze traveling up the wide brick steps leading to a dark-paneled, double-door entrance-way.

Two blazing gold-and-glass gas lamps flanked the portal and a pair of tall mullioned windows graced both the upper and lower levels; gentle light spilled from one of the rooms out onto the cobblestone walkway, bathing her and Dominick in its hazy illumination.

She was here. Truly here. Alone with Dominick, except for the servants he employed.

Still holding her hand, he led her up the steps. Reaching the landing, he leaned down and murmured in her ear, "Be brave, my girl. You've come this far."

And as the front door opened, Parris could only wonder why it sounded as though his words held a double meaning.

Nine

I that loved and you that liked,
shall we begin to wrangle?

—Anonymous

"Ah, Hastings, good evening." Dominick sidestepped his butler, who gaped at him as though he were a headless stranger awaiting entrée into a palace of gold rather than his employer entering his own home. "Still standing sentinel, are we?"

"Of course, Your Grace," Hastings replied, his equilibrium clearly revived, and his disapproval showing in full measure. "A butler cannot see to his own comfort until he has seen to that of his master."

Dominick ushered a suddenly leaden-footed Parris into the foyer. Or should he think of her as Meg, the deceptive, beautiful barmaid, instead? Neither way brought any relief to his aching loins.

Where had his fearless Parris gone? The woman who had been brave enough to traipse among cutthroats and thieves, to fulfill some insane scheme to bring the men of London to heel?

Lady Scruples was an apt moniker, though he'd been completely wrong about her being some bitter female who had been shunned by every male who had made her acquaintance. Parris wouldn't be shunned by any man in his right mind.

But what about her ex-fiancé? Dominick had an almost obsessive need to find out more about the man, and discover what had prompted such a devastating, public fallout.

He looked down at Parris, garbed in a low-cut blouse that his hands itched to peel from her body, appearing sexy and tempting and anything but innocent, and wondered if Lady Scruples had been part of the problem.

Parris was headstrong, stubborn, maddening, and completely senseless at times. She had enough frustrating traits to lead even a sober man to the bottle.

And yet any thought of shaking sense into her fled from Dominick's mind the moment she laid her hand against his cheek in the coach, and breathed his name with the voice of a nightingale.

He had thought she was going to kiss him, which would only have saved him from himself, because he had intended to kiss her, by God. And that would have been disastrous to the plan he'd formulated shortly after discovering her ruse, a plan that seemed even more appealing now that his mind, and his body had cooled.

"May I take your coat, sir?" Hastings inquired.

Dominick would have to have been deaf not to note the censure fringing his butler's usual monotone. He suspected he could recite with a fair degree of accuracy what the man would say should he be given the chance to uncork his tongue.

A proper duke would never arouse speculation by bringing a woman of the lower classes to his home—and after dark, no less.

The fact that Dominick could read Hastings so well was ill-making, to say the least.

"You may indeed, Hastings." Dominick divested himself of his light frock coat, followed by his evening jacket and cravat. He sighed in bliss and then undid the top two buttons of his shirt, noticing that Parris's gaze lingered on the skin now exposed.

He heard someone's intake of breath and realized, to his disgust, that it was Hastings, who looked on the verge of a swoon, his bulging eyes communicating that a duke would never undress any of his person in front of a lady to whom he is not married, especially outside of the boudoir—if one must be so base as to immure themselves in premarital relations.

Dominick would agree with part of that sentiment, but Parris wasn't playing a lady tonight. And he had to put his plan into action at some point. If he did things correctly and remained in control, she would have no idea what he was up to until it was too late.

After she had been thoroughly and completely seduced.

A master plan, if ever he'd had one. Nothing overt, of course, for that might scare her off. Subtle seduction, coming-in-the-back-door seduction.

Let her find her own way to the realization that she still felt something for him. And once she did, they could put all this pretense behind them.

If a small voice nagged at him that he was manipulating her, purposely nudging her into something that she might not want, he quelled that voice.

Parris cared for him; Dominick knew it. Understanding his target was a skill he had learned well, for being ignorant to the signs of impending doom could have gotten him and his men killed.

His resolve bolstered, he turned to Hastings and said, "If you'll be so kind as to scuttle off and find Mrs. Bradshaw, Hastings. I need her to see to our guest. Tell her to bring salve, a cloth, and some warm water."

Hastings fixed quixotic eyes on Parris. "You are injured, madam?" Clearly he had not seen the cut on Parris's lip in the throes of his high dudgeon, though, in truth, the injury was barely noticeable.

Dominick noted the exact moment Hastings spotted said injury, a dubious expression sinking into his creased face as he settled his gaze on Dominick once more. Wisely, the man kept his mouth shut on whatever opinions where bouncing around in his brain.

"If you will allow me, sir, I will attend to the, er, young lady as Mrs. Bradshaw is already abed."

Dominick extracted his pocket watch, checking it as though he did not already know the lateness of the hour, or that he was not patently aware that the widowed Mrs. Bradshaw retired every evening at ten P.M., like clockwork.

God bless her.

He had anticipated this answer, and was readily forthcoming with his response. "How remiss of me, Hastings. It is quite late, isn't it? Well, it would distress me greatly should I disturb anyone from their slumber. Yours included, old boy. So why don't you bring me some ointment and then find your bed for the night?"

A rather comical look of alarm rifled across Hastings's face. "Oh, no, no, my lord. It is no trouble at all. And I am not the least bit sleepy. I shall retrieve the salve and be back in a trice. I shall also summon Benson and have him bring the coach back around so that he may return the, er, young lady to her own abode."

Dominick nearly laughed at his butler's obvious attempts to salvage his good name and debatable virtue, and the way Hastings's lips pursed as though he had bitten into an unripe persimmon when speaking of said "young lady."

"Don't be ridiculous, Hastings. No need to go to all that trouble. Just bring me the supplies and I shall see to the young lady myself. Now, hurry along. Our guest is in dire need of medical attention."

Hastings inclined his head with stiff reluctance. "As you wish, Your Grace." He cast one more woeful glance Parris's way before turning and scuffling down the long corridor as though heading to his execution.

*   *   *

Parris watched the regal old gentleman depart, feeling rather uncomfortable being alone with Dominick. Hastings's disapproval did not make this any easier. In her current garb, he likely thought her a dockside tart, the corset pushing what little bosom she had heavenward, making her breasts look as though they were being served on a silver platter.

Dominick came toward her then, moving with the sinuous grace of a predatory cat, a gleam in his eyes she had not noticed before.

"I won't bite, my girl," he said, and nothing about his demeanor as he escorted her into the library should have caused her to doubt that his intentions were honorable.

But she did.

There was a tension about him, a heat that radiated from his body and twined about her, escalating her own temperature until she was sure she had a low-grade fever and would be abed come the morning with some mysterious illness.

Dominick sat her down on the enormous couch near the fireplace. A hint of leather and brandy and cigars lingered in the air, telling her that Dominick spent a good deal of time in here.

She could almost picture him slouched in the black leather wing chair in front of the fireplace, his booted feet on the footrest, a snifter of brandy in one hand and a cigar in the other as he stared thoughtfully into the leaping flames.

"Are you feeling ill?" he inquired, drawing her gaze

back to his concerned face, and those probing eyes.

"Ill?"

"You're a bit green around the gills. Perhaps you should lie down."

Before Parris could proclaim that lying down any-where but in her own bedroom could be detrimental to her well-being, he had her flat on her back.

Then he sat next to her, his hip pressing against hers, the contact intimate and jarring. But more jar-ring was the fact that he had effectively trapped her.

"Better?" he murmured, his eyes appearing to have darkened, though it could just as easily have been the shadows behind him making it seem that way.

"I'm fine. And I'd much prefer to be sitting up, if y' don't mind." She attempted to rise, but a hand at her shoulder held her down, confirming her suspicion that she would not be allowed to leave until he had suc-ceeded in getting what he wanted.

But what, exactly, did he want?

"Why all the hurry, dear girl? Have I done anything to make you feel uncomfortable?"

"No." *Yes.*

"Well, then, are you angry with me over the kiss we shared back at the tavern? I agree, it was not well done of me, but I hope you can find it in your heart to for-give a man who had overindulged in spirits. It brought out my more impulsive side. I hope you'll be so kind as to forget all about it."

"Forget?"

Her pride stung. And in that moment, she would

have given anything to eradicate the incident completely from her mind. But eradicating it from her heart was a different matter entirely.

"Since we now have a bond of sorts, I will confide in you as to why I was at that ramshackle tavern." Lowering his voice as if they were coconspirators, he said, "I was on a mission."

His remark pulled Parris from the chiding she was giving herself for believing the kiss—kisses?—they had shared had been more than just a mistake.

"What kind of mission?" And why was she whispering as though they were speaking about top-secret information?

"Of mercy," he replied. "You see, my friend—the one who went to rescue your friend—is being terrible maligned by some harridan named Lady Scruples."

Harridan! How typical of a man to think such a thing of a independent female, to believe in a double standard of "do as I say and not as I do," to consider it acceptable to treat a woman as though she were chattel, to be bartered and bandied about to every chum within his exalted atmosphere.

Not realizing how her eyes blazed or how much the jut of her chin gave her away, Parris stated tersely, "I think she's a right old saint, I do. A veritable gem to womankind."

"Gem?" he laughed. "Not hardly. So you think she's old, too? I suspected as much. Certainly she would have to be old—and ugly, of course—to wish men such ill."

"She doesn't wish anybody ill. And she isn't old, either!" Oh, damn and blast her rash tongue! Her temper always did get her into fixes. It was as if he knew just what to say to prod her into losing control. But Dominick could provoke a saint, if doing so suited him.

"She isn't?" He regarded her intently. "And how would you know?"

Parris frowned at him and crossed her arms over her chest. "I just do, is all. And why are y' looking at me like that?"

"Perhaps because I'm starting to believe that you may be part of this ring of women avengers wreaking havoc on the innocent male population of this town."

"Innocent, my bloomin' behind!" she scoffed.

He sprang to his feet, a huge grin spreading across his handsome face. "Aha! So you are in partnership with the lady."

"I didn't—"

"I thought as much." He paced away from her, and then pivoted splendidly on his heel to face her again. "I feel a moral obligation to inform the authorities about your dealings with this nefarious sisterhood with whom you have become embroiled. You've done a grievous thing in bargaining with such a she-devil."

Parris sat bolt upright. "The authorities? I . . . we— *they* didn't do anything wrong!"

"Nothing wrong? You poor, misguided girl." Dominick shook his head, crowing on the inside. He had Parris exactly where he wanted her.

He knew her too well to think she would dissolve into histrionics—or worse, tears, which, had she ever incorporated into her repertoire of female wiles, would have brought him instantly to his knees.

No, Parris was too sensible, too wise not to see she was trapped. She settled back against the couch, eyeing him as though they haggled across a bargaining table. Little did she know that he held all the chips.

"So what is it that y' want?"

You. "Cooperation," he said.

"What kind of cooperation?"

"Information, to be precise. I want you to keep an eye on Lady Scruples and report back to me on her movements."

She regarded him with a poker face. "And if I should do this—which I'm not saying I will, mind y'—what do I get in return?"

"Freedom from facing the magistrate."

She didn't appear greatly concerned—probably because she didn't think he had seen through her disguise, and therefore felt safe from harm. Of course, she hadn't taken into account the single most important factor.

Him. He could be ruthless when he wanted something.

And what he wanted was her.

He had tried to outrun his need for her all those years ago, and where had it gotten him? Right back in the same blasted quagmire. He was damn well finished with fighting it.

"And who's to say that once I leave here I won't up and disappear so that y' can never find me?" she asked saucily, posing the question he had already anticipated.

"Did I tell you that I was in the military, sweet Meg? Covert operations are my specialty. With or without your help, I will find Lady Scruples—and I'll find you, too. Mark my words: should you force me to such desperate measures, it will be all the worse for you."

Dominick watched her internal struggle, barely refraining from laughing at the look in her eyes that told him she would love to see him hacked into tiny bits. The darling girl had never taken well to anyone's demands. But he had her trapped between the devil and the deep blue sea, and he would see this thing through to its conclusion.

"All right," she relented with complete ill grace, scowling at him.

"Good girl." He turned from her so she wouldn't see his smile of victory. "Now, where the bloody hell did Hastings go for those supplies? Waterloo?"

As though on cue, Hastings scratched on the door, entering a moment later with a tray bearing the requested items.

But it was the person who followed Hastings, bleary-eyed at having been roused from her slumber, that made Dominick's sulfurous gaze track his butler as the man marched across the room to place the tray down on the table in front of the couch, studiously avoiding looking in Dominick's direction.

"I hear we have an emergency, Your Grace." Mrs. Bradshaw's kindly gaze slid from Dominick to Parris, who unbent a little at finding herself under the housekeeper's concerned regard.

If Mrs. Bradshaw thought there was anything strange about his late night company, or that said company was a bawdily dressed female, nothing showed on her face.

His housekeeper hustled over to Parris and sat down next to her on the couch. The two women were a study in contrasts, with Mrs. Bradshaw's matronly figure and Parris's petite one.

Dominick's gaze dipped to Parris's small, pert breasts, nicely outlined in the flimsy blouse she wore, much to the detriment of his already unstable composure.

He knew the sight of those sweet mounds would bring him to his knees. He could picture them standing proud, her nipples taut, nestled in a cloud of puff pink aureoles. He groaned at the image, which brought three sets of eyes swerving in his direction.

"Are you feeling well, Your Grace?" Mrs. Bradshaw inquired, momentarily stopping her ministrations on Parris's lip, which only succeeded in drawing Dominick's gaze to his guest's full mouth.

"I'm fine, Mrs. Bradshaw. Just a bit of muscle strain." Which muscle, exactly, he need not confide. "Nothing to concern yourself with."

Mrs. Bradshaw nodded and returned her attention to her patient. Parris's gaze remained focused on him, those hot blue eyes staring at him through that damned mask that she would not remove.

He frowned as reality and fantasy momentarily juxtaposed, and he saw himself back in that moonlit garden, Annabelle writhing beneath him. But this time, as he entered her, he found himself looking down into Parris's face.

He knew the image was merely a result of his growing desire for her, yet the picture was evocative, intense. Lust and longing collided in his gut, and for a moment he wanted to forget his plan of slow seduction, forget that he was a gentleman, forget that Parris was a lady and deserved to be treated as such.

He wanted to tear the blouse off her, yank away the skirt, lay her down on the floor in front of the fireplace and pump into her until she moaned his name, begged him to end her torment, her climax sweeping through her, the sweet convulsions tightening around him.

A bead of sweat trickled down his temple and Dominick knew he had to get a grip on himself. His chances of being alone with Parris tonight were shot to hell, thanks to bloody Hastings. But it was probably for the best. In his current state, he couldn't be sure he would not act upon his raging impulses.

A disturbing thought struck him then. Was Parris still a virgin? Just because she was unmarried did not mean she had never given herself to another man. She was twenty-six, after all.

The idea that Parris, his vibrant, beautiful Parris could have been with another man rattled Dominick, chipped away at him, like a knife blade whittling down into the deepest part of his soul.

But if she had been with another man, he had only himself to blame for walking away from her eight years ago instead of telling her what she meant to him.

The only time he had been completely forthcoming about how he felt for her was in his letters—the ones he sealed and addressed, but never sent out.

Instead he had locked them away in a box in his desk, along with the mementos Parris had given him over the years: a rose she had plucked from his mother's prized blooms and presented to him on his eighteenth birthday, a feather from a baby bird she had saved, and a long lock of her hair that she had salvaged when her father had forced her to cut the thick tresses, claiming she looked like a wild heathen as he hacked it in uneven layers.

Dominick vividly remembered that day. Parris hadn't shed a single tear. Not one. Instead, she had vowed she would grow her hair down to her knees when she was old enough.

Though he had yet to see her hair down, he suspected she had kept her promise, which made him wonder how she managed to contain it all under her wig. The bloody thing had to be hot and uncomfortable, and she was probably wishing him to Hades at that moment, dying to pull the blasted thing off.

"There you go, my dear." Mrs. Bradshaw patted Parris's hand in a motherly fashion, then rose and turned to Dominick. "Will that be all, Your Grace?"

This time when she looked at him there was a hint of censure in her eyes.

Christ! Five minutes in Parris's company and a lifetime in Dominick's—a life that had been exemplary, for the most part—and he had been branded a lecher.

"No. Thank you, Mrs. Bradshaw. That will be all."

Mrs. Bradshaw inclined her head curtly and then bestowed a reassuring smile on her charge before sailing from the room without another glance in Dominick's direction, as if to drive home her disapproval.

Skulking in the corner, as though endeavoring to blend into the furnishings as he whisked dust away from the same book for the fourth time, was Hastings. The traitor.

"That will be all, Hastings. You may go."

Like a martyred soul, Hastings heaved a bereaved sigh, his chest collapsing as if he had expelled every molecule of oxygen his spare frame possessed.

Dragging his heels, he made his way to the door, pausing once to open his mouth and then quickly shutting it when Dominick raised a brow.

Once the man had reached the doorway, knob in hand, Dominick said, "Oh, by the way, Hastings?"

Hastings's stooped shoulders straightened, his eyes aglow with hope. "Yes, Your Grace? May I help you with something?"

"Yes. Pack your bags and get out. You're fired."

Hastings's shoulders sagged again and he inclined his head in humble defeat. "As you wish, Your Grace." Executing a perfect bow, he exited the room.

The door had no more than click shut when Parris's rebuke rose into the air. "That was terrible! How could you fire that nice old man?"

Nice old man, my behind.

Dominick stared at the door, figuring Hastings was hovering on the other side, his ear pressed to the wood, grinning like a wizened Satan at being defended by the, er, young lady, whose beautiful, barely covered breasts heaved in indignation, leaving Dominick momentarily transfixed by the sight.

A bolt of undiluted lust sizzled through his body, enough to incinerate him and everything within a five-meter radius, leaving only a pile of ashes to mark his remains.

He raised his put-upon gaze to her angry one and wondered if she had any idea how she looked at that moment, which was not at all like a meek, uneducated barmaid from Southwark.

Dominick decided to end this matter quickly. "Hastings!" he bellowed.

The door immediately opened, proving his suspicions about Hastings's whereabouts.

"Yes, sir?" The man's attempt at meekness and servility was comical, but clearly the only reward Dominick would receive from his hard night's work.

"Do I fire you almost every day, Hastings?"

"Yes, Your Grace."

"And do you ever leave?"

"No, Your Grace."

"And why is that?"

"Because I know you don't mean it, Your Grace. Deep down, you treasure me and wouldn't know what to do without me were I to go. You are a kind soul, generous to a fault, and merely act gruff as a—"

"You're pushing it, old boy."

Hastings grinned sheepishly, which was a sight no one should be forced to witness on an empty stomach.

Returning his gaze to Parris, Dominick demanded, "Satisfied?"

She merely gave a delicate snort. She was an item, and he must be mad to want to pursue her. But sweet mother in heaven . . . he did.

"Should I fetch Benson now, Your Grace, so that he may take the, er, young lady home?"

Dominick threw a glare at Hastings. "Are you still here? Bugger off already. And don't—"

Parris cut him off. "Yes, Hastings, get Benson. I'd like t' go home now."

Dominick knew when he was beaten. There would be other opportunities, and should things go as planned, he would have Parris where he wanted her soon enough.

With legs that had suddenly turned spry, Hastings jaunted off. Dominick wasted no time in shortening the distance between himself and Parris until he stood over her, staring down into her eyes, the mask no cover for the beauty that lay beneath.

"You've won this round, my girl. But I promise you, I will win all the rest. As part of our bargain, I expect to see you back here at the stroke of midnight, three days

from now. And should I need to track you down . . ."
He'd let her fertile mind conjure up what he might do.

He could see she was already plotting some way to best him, simply because he had told her what to do. Perhaps she was wondering how she would face him again, the very night after a day spent together at Saint Bartholomew's Fair.

His timing had been intentional. He would work his charm on her from all angles, using whatever means necessary to accomplish his goal.

Finally she nodded, and Dominick wondered if it was a good sign that she had capitulated so easily. Could she want to come back? Was her own curiosity about how the two of them would be together as strong as his?

The thought stayed with Dominick as he saw her out, watching until the coach was swallowed by the darkness, before returning to his study to plan his next move.

Ten

❧

Cupid abroad was lated in the night,
His wings were wet with ranging in the
rain.

—Robert Greene

Parris wasn't sure how it happened, but somehow she
ended up traveling in Dominick's coach with him as
they headed to Saint Bartholomew's Fair with a jab-
bering Mary and Philip in tow.

Following in another coach was her mother, Gwen,
the children's nursemaid, and Annabelle, who had not
been pleased to have been relegated to a different conveyance than the one in which Dominick rode.

Parris, on the other hand, had intended to take
whichever coach Dominick was *not* in. But when she
situated herself inside the second carriage, expecting
to see her mother entering behind her, she found
Dominick instead.

"W-where's my mother?" Parris knew she sounded
panicked, but she couldn't help it, especially considering what had transpired between her and Dominick

three days ago. Just the thought of the kisses they had shared made her burn.

Since then he had appeared at her home every day, and she had been subjected to the full extent of his abundant charm, rarely finding a moment's peace even when she went out, as he seemed to be everywhere.

He had said he wanted to renew their friendship, and his vow had not been an idle one—which only made Parris feel much more guilty about her deception, as well as cursing her with a mounting desire for him. She was unable to stop thinking about his mouth upon hers, and yearning for more.

"Your mother's taking the other coach," he told her, treating her to an utterly endearing smile, making Parris grow warm and causing her to think of things she shouldn't, wanton, wicked things that could only be set free in her dreams. "Surely you're not worried about impropriety, are you? You're no longer a schoolgirl, Parris, and we did grow up together. Remember, if you will, that I've seen you in your undergarments."

Heat rose fast and furious to Parris's cheeks. "You have not!"

"I have. You were six years old at the time, and I was a worldly man of twelve. Your mother had rigged you out in a dress of daisy yellow, and not five minutes after your arrival, you flung the dress down the foyer staircase and proceeded to tear through the house like a chubby banshee."

A snippet of the event he spoke of flashed through

Parris's mind, but one comment he made stuck in her craw. "I was not chubby."

The glint in his eyes told her he had purposely baited her. "No. You were all stick legs and arms. It's a wonder you ever filled out." His eyes took on an appreciative gleam as he boldly admired the places he spoke of. "But if you feel uncomfortable," he went on with a light shrug, "I could leave."

This comment immediately had Philip and Mary bouncing in their seats, ganging up on Parris in their pleas to keep Dominick with them.

If she asked him to leave, she would have two pouting children on her hands for the remainder of the trip. If he stayed, she would be a wreck the entire time. But did she really have a choice?

"No," she replied with a defeated sigh. "There's no need for you to leave."

He nodded, and when he briefly looked away, she could have sworn he was smiling. But when he turned back, he was serious as a monk. "Odd, but I can't help feeling your mother threw us together on purpose. You don't think she has any designs on the two of us as a couple, do you?"

Parris nearly died of mortification, certain he had summed up the situation correctly. And worrying he would think she'd had a hand in her mother's manuevering.

"I'm sorry. My mother can be a little . . . overzealous."

"You forget, I know your mother. And I suspect her

actions stem from wanting the best for you, hoping to see you wed and giving her grandchildren to adore. Not necessarily wed to me, of course. Just wed to a good man who will take care of you."

"As if I need a man to take care of me," she scoffed, her sense of independence pricked by his remark. "I am perfectly capable of fending for myself."

Parris refused to consider her mishap three nights ago in a dark alley. She could have extricated herself from that problem, she assured herself. A solution would have come to her eventually. She just hadn't been given the opportunity to formulate it.

"All women need a man to take care of them, Parris. That's simply a fact of life."

Parris's temper spiked. "If that isn't the most pig-headed, idiotic—"

His laughter silenced her. "Some things never change, do they? You're still predictably easy to rile."

Parris scowled at him, which only made him smile wider. "If you did not make such asinine comments, I would not feel inclined to comment."

"What's as-i-nine mean?" Mary inquired, her big green eyes going between Parris and Dominick.

Parris couldn't believe she had allowed Dominick to fluster her into forgetting the children's presence. She shot him another glare before addressing her niece. "It's when someone is being blockheaded, sweetie— like His Grace."

Dominick quirked an offended brow, though his lopsided grin ruined the effect.

"Oh." Mary nodded, looking rather sage for her young years. "Do you think all boys are asinine, Auntie Parris? Because Philip's a blockhead, too."

This remark earned Mary a shove from her brother, which tumbled the little girl to the floor of the coach and caused her to let out a shrill wail of protest.

Parris reached down and gathered up her niece, settling Mary in her lap to soothe her. The imp stuck her tongue out at her brother, who rolled his eyes and jammed himself into the corner, muttering something about girls being big babies.

When Parris glanced up, she saw that Dominick had settled into the opposite corner, his legs still planted firmly in her path, though not touching her.

But whenever they hit a rut, his thigh would bump into hers, which never failed to send a jolt through her. A few times when the rut had been a minor one, Parris thought he had grazed her on purpose. But she could never catch him doing it.

Either way, every touch unsettled her, made her more aware of him, how he looked, smelled, how very virile he was. While he, on the other hand, appeared completely undaunted by her nearness, so composed, in fact, he often seemed on the verge of sleep.

"You do that very well." He nodded at Mary, who nestled against Parris's bosom while she absently stroked her fingers through her niece's mass of silky curls. "Have you ever thought of having any of your own?"

Too often to count. She would have loved to have

children. Four seemed a nice number, two boys and two girls, so each would have a playmate and never have to be alone. But a husband would be required for that, and Parris was no longer willing to settle for anything less than love. She had once, foolishly, thought friendship alone was enough.

Her gaze slid from Dominick's face to the view beyond the window, not wanting him to see the truth in her eyes. "Maybe someday I'll have children, but I have a great many worthwhile pursuits in my life now."

"Such as?"

"Well . . ." Her most important calling at that moment was one she could not confide to him. Not only would he disapprove, but—he was a man. "I contribute my time to several charities, and I'm a member of the Women Horticulturists' League."

"A horticulturist's league, hmm? And do they advocate denuding rosebushes?"

Parris flushed, remembering the poor roses she had unintentionally mauled the morning he had come to visit. "I . . . that was an accident."

"An accident. I see." Then he switched subjects. "So have you heard of this Lady Scruples?"

Dominick didn't miss the way her eyes widened or how she nervously nibbled her lower lip—her very lush lower lip.

When the tip of her tongue eased out to soothe the small, reddened section, he nearly leaned forward to soothe it himself. He managed to hold himself in check only because Mary's inquisitive eyes settled on him, reminding him that he and Parris were not alone.

"Why do you ask?"

Dominick wondered if Parris realized how much she gave herself away. "Perhaps I'm wondering if I should be concerned, considering I'm a man, and my gender seems to be the target of this woman's discontent."

"They aren't targets. She's simply teaching them a lesson."

"Teaching them a lesson? In what?"

"In treating women with respect," she returned without missing a beat. "We have not been put on this earth simply for a man's pleasure."

This was a topic Dominick found entirely too interesting. "And do you have a problem with finding pleasure?" he asked, leaning forward, finding a certain perverse delight in invading her space and making her uncomfortable—for the last thing he wanted was for her to get too comfortable, to think a renewal of their friendship was all he wanted from her.

"N-no . . . I . . ." She shook her head. "This isn't about what I want."

"Isn't it?"

"No!"

He nodded and leaned back, smiling inwardly. "I can't say I'm surprised you would look at the situation in such a manner."

"And what manner is that?"

Dominick couldn't seem to help himself; he was like a man possessed. "Well, you're a woman."

"What an astute observation, Your Grace."

Her mild set-down brought a half grin to his lips. "As a man, I am inclined to notice such things." And notice he did. She looked like she wanted to fidget under his scrutiny, but managed to hold herself rigidly erect. "If memory serves, you embrace such causes. You always were one to try to right a wrong."

"And what causes do you embrace?" she inquired, deftly turning the tables on him.

"I embrace peace, Miss Sutherland. Peace at all costs. No matter how difficult the struggle."

Her features suddenly softened, and he could see the gamine-faced confidante she had once been.

"Was it very difficult for you?" she asked. "The war, I mean."

Though Dominick had consciously avoided the topic before, he found that he wanted to talk to her about his life during the years he'd been away. Perhaps he just hadn't been sure she would want to hear about it.

"It was difficult for everyone," he answered. "Good men lost their lives. Some days it all seemed so senseless. Such a bloody damn waste."

Dominick thought about the two men he had become good friends with during his army days: Lucien Kendall, colonel of the twenty-eighth Hussar division, and George FitzHugh, Dominick's second-in-command.

Both men had been instrumental in helping him stay sane during the worst of times, when so little made sense and the world seemed to have gone mad.

Fitz was the jokester of the group, keeping them laughing, an expert at diffusing tension. Many a night the three of them had sat around, whiskey in hand, reminiscing about the glory days of their youth and the lives they had known before the military.

Fitz had talked a lot about his family, how close they had all been. Dominick could hear the love in his friend's voice, especially when he spoke of his younger sister, Francine, or Fancy, as everyone called her.

Fitz's parents had died when Fancy was only twelve. He had just received his colors and had been forced to leave her in the care of a spinster aunt who he worried was not treating her right, though Fancy had never once complained in her letters.

But that was just the way she was, Fitz had told them, never wanted to upset anyone. She was an angel, sweet and malleable, never gave him a day's trouble, and would make some lucky man a wonderful wife— when she was grown up, of course, which, with the way Fitz had talked, would not be for a long while.

Dominick, like Lucien, had become a long-distance uncle of sorts, and they had all made a pact that should something happen to the other, they would see to their families.

When Fitz took a bullet that was meant for Lucien, a bullet that had caused Fitz to slowly bleed to death over the course of three days, leaving his friends to watch him die, Lucien had vowed he would take care of Fancy.

Hours before Fitz died, the chaplain had executed and witnessed the papers turning over guardianship of Francine Marguerite FitzHugh to Lucien.

That was a year ago. Lucien had recently returned to his estate, Blackthorne Manor in Sussex, having taken in Fitz's sister.

Dominick decided it was past time to write his friend and find out how things were faring with his new charge. The pain of Fitz's death had kept Dominick from doing so earlier.

But he didn't want to think about those tragedies right now. He wanted to resume his strategic assault on the beautiful woman sitting across from him, whose image had kept him sane during the worst of times.

"So, do you have anyone in mind?"

She stared at him, perplexed. "In mind? For what?"

"The position of husband. Has some young fop caught your attention?"

Parris had never known a man who had such an ability to keep her off balance, though she suspected that was exactly what Dominick wanted. Better to keep her teetering than to allow her to divine where he was going at any given moment.

Had she ever heeded the rules of what was considered appropriate conversation between a man and a woman, she might have informed him that the topic of her marital status, or lack thereof, was none of his business.

But *she* knew that *he* knew he was being brash and

meddlesome, and she would not stoop to his level by falling into the trap he had so cleverly laid.

"No, Your Grace. No one."

"Well, I wouldn't wait too long if I were you. From one friend to the other, you aren't getting any younger." His smile was baiting.

"If you wish to start a conversation about which of us is getting old, I'd be happy to oblige." To her satisfaction, the smile dropped from his face.

"Are you implying I'm beyond my prime, Miss Sutherland?"

"If the shoe fits, Your Grace."

He leaned forward. "I could run rings around you, brat."

Parris leaned forward. "I could beat you any day, Methuselah."

"*Race! Race! Race!*" the children began to chant, reminding Parris once more that she and Dominick were not alone—and that they were acting no better than Mary and Philip.

Wondering how the man always managed to rattle her, Parris sat back against the squabs, wishing Gwen were with her. Her cousin was always a great buffer.

Parris suspected Gwen was finding her predicament all very amusing, considering Parris had made the mistake of confessing more than she should have the night of their escapade at the Wrack and Ruin.

She had met up with Gwen shortly after the coach had rolled away from Dominick's town house. She spotted Travers hanging back in a shadowed corner across the street. At her first opportunity, she had hopped out of the Wakefield coach and dashed to her own.

Inside she found Gwen, looking none the worse for wear. Parris had expected her cousin to relay the details of her ordeal, but all she had said was that as soon as the foul gutterworm had released her, she had treated him to a very unladylike knee to his private area—and had enjoyed herself immensely in the process.

What she had gone on about for nearly the entire ride was the earl of Stratford and what a highhanded, arrogant, womanizing pain in the rump he was, letting it slip in her high dudgeon that he had kissed her— again, which Gwen claimed had been despicable. And yet, Parris had caught her cousin's fingers straying to her lips.

That night Parris could barely sleep, her mind replaying the kisses she and Dominick had shared, a fire burning in his eyes when he had looked at her, making her heart ache, knowing he was bestowing that heated gaze upon the serving girl he believed her to be.

And now he was sitting across from her, big and broad and so handsome it hurt to look at him, and she wished the coach would move faster so that they could get to the fair. Being confined with him was even more difficult than she'd thought it would be.

Unconsciously, Parris began to nibble her lower lip, wondering what would happen when Meg the barmaid returned to Dominick's town house that evening at midnight.

She had thought to simply not show up, but Dominick had warned her there would be consequences if she didn't appear, and the determined look in his eyes confirmed that he would follow through on his threat.

But it wasn't his threat that truly worried her. It was that she wanted to go back, wanted to be alone with him. He had told her that he had no interest in anything intimate. But did he really mean that? Or had he simply said that to get her to agree to his plan?

Mary roused from her doze on Parris's lap then, diverting her thoughts. Revived and antsy, her niece resumed her interrogation of Dominick.

Was a duke allowed to eat chocolate cake every morning? Could he ban Brussels sprouts from ever being served? When Dominick laughingly said yes, Mary promptly proclaimed that she was going to be a duke when she grew up so that she could eat chocolate cake every day.

"You can't be a duke, you dunderhead," her brother scoffed. "You're a girl."

"I can too be a duke!" She tipped her head back and glanced up at Parris. "Can't I, Auntie Parris?"

"You don't need to be a duke, Mary. You're already a princess." That answer seemed to mollify her niece.

"Nicely done, Miss Sutherland." An amused gleam swirled in Dominick's honey-brown eyes, his purposeful use of formality meant to prod her, as they both knew he didn't have a formal bone in his body.

Growing up, he hated the rigors placed on him because of his birth, the overblown pomp and circumstance, the inanities of polite society, the wearisome pecking order.

Most especially, he hated getting dressed up. He would grouse that his shirt points poked him in the neck, or that his cravat was choking him, or his jacket was too confining. Which was why Parris hadn't been all that surprised when he tossed off his jacket and cravat after they had arrived at his home the night of the tavern debacle, revealing what she had already known: that he was superbly built.

Suddenly feeling uncommonly warm, Parris glanced out the coach window, attempting to divert her thoughts by taking in the beautiful setting—the trees in lush foliage, the sun painting the leaves in shades of gold, the meadow dappled with tiny flowers in hues of lilac and rose, the air scented with a hint of lavender. The countryside was truly magnificent. It would be a glorious day for the fair.

Then Parris realized something. She frowned and turned to look at Dominick. "This is not the way to the fair."

Appearing unconcerned, Dominick replied, "But it is, I assure you. We're simply taking a more scenic route. We should be there shortly."

A scenic route? Was he was purposely holding them captive? Or was it just that he wished to torment her?

Mary, now a bundle of pent-up energy, began talk-

ing a mile a minute, and Dominick was under siege
again. She crawled into his lap and rubbed her hands
over his jaw, having developed a newfound fascination
for whiskers, or the lack thereof, in Dominick's case.

If only *she* could climb onto Dominick's lap without worry, Parris thought, and touch him without him
thinking she had gone completely mad.

In her role as barmaid, she had felt the smooth tex-
ture of his face, the underlying steel of his jaw. And
now it was hard not to dwell on touching him again.

Unexpectedly, those startling amber eyes slid her
way and caught her staring. Parris quickly glanced
away. She thought she heard him chuckle, but her
heart was pounding too loudly for her to be sure.

She should have been more persistent about traveling with her mother, especially after Annabelle had
appeared at the coach door, preparing to ride with
them, but complaining that there was not enough
room inside the coach for her to properly spread out
her skirts, staring at Parris with eyes that told her to
get out.

For once, Parris had been willing to oblige her sister. After all, perhaps Dominick wished to rekindle his
romance with Annabelle, even though he had yet to
show any signs of doing so.

But when Parris rose, Dominick wouldn't move his
leg to allow her to exit. Instead, he took her by the
wrist and uttered one word, "Sit." The fact that she
actually sat was more surprising than anything else.

Annabelle had glared at her as if Dominick's decision was all her fault. When her sister tried to wrench the children away, both of whom had grown quiet with their mother's arrival, he once again spoke up.

"I would like Mary and Philip's company, if you don't mind." As if he hadn't already endeared himself to the children, they gazed up at him as though he were the Heavenly Father.

And that had been that. Annabelle had left, furious, of course.

Now the coach rolled on at a steady clip, as did Philip and Mary's tongues, which, to Parris's chagrin a moment later, meant anything and everything was an acceptable topic of discussion.

"Auntie Parris said you were a very brave man," her niece blithely remarked, playing with the buttons on Dominick's jacket.

Looking entirely too full of himself, with that dratted raised eyebrow proclaiming his intrigue, he regarded Parris. "She did, did she? Well, this is certainly interesting. What else did she say?"

"Really, is any of this—" When his brow lifted another notch, clearly asking Parris why she was protesting, she clamped her lips shut. Fine. Let him float away on his own bloated sense of self-importance.

"She said that you got a . . ." Mary's brow furrowed as she searched for the word. Then her eyes lit up. "She said you got a carnation!"

"That's a commendation, knucklehead," Philip chided, nudging his sister in the side with his elbow.

"I'm not a knucklehead!"

"Yes, you are."

"Am not!"

"Are, too!"

"Children," Parris interjected, having learned to speak at a louder pitch than her wards so that she could be heard without actually shouting. "You're going to give His Grace a headache." Which was just what he deserved.

"Go on, Mary," Dominick urged the child, bestowing his most winning smile on the poor, unsuspecting little girl, who had not yet grown immune to it or learned how to block out its blinding effects. "What else did Aunt Parris tell you?"

"She said that you had saved her from a whole lotta scrapes when she was little, and that you were her friend once."

"We're still friends—or so I hope." His words warmed Parris against her will.

"Auntie Parris?"

Parris was forced to look at her niece, now cradled in Dominick's arms, her head nestled against his chest. "Yes, sweet?" she murmured, her voice not quite steady.

"Are you still Uncle Dominick's friend?" Uncle Dominick. The children had taken to calling him that, and Annabelle had allowed them to do so.

But to Parris the honorary title sounded too familiar, and she didn't want the children to be crushed should Dominick leave, disappearing again and breaking their hearts. And hers, should she allow herself to wish for things that should have been long forgotten by now.

"Parris?" Dominick's deep voice brought Parris's gaze to him.

"Yes?" The word was barely a whisper.

"Are you still my friend?"

The question left her at odds for an answer, though it shouldn't have. As little as a two weeks ago she would have said she would never feel anything for Dominick Carlisle again.

But just being around him reminded her of hot summer days and cold winter nights. Laughter. And companionship. Days before vows of love and broken dreams and Annabelle had interfered.

She was saved from having to answer when the children spotted the fair outside the window, their noses pressed to the glass as the coach rattled to a stop.

As soon as the door opened, Philip and Mary sprinted down the steps and dashed toward a puppet show, where a group of children already crowded, leaving Parris alone with Dominick.

She moved to exit, thinking that if she could just make it down the steps first she wouldn't be subjected to his helping her down.

But he rose before she did, his arm brushing against her breasts as he exited the coach. Parris was shocked to feel her nipples tighten from the innocent contact.

He waited for her, hand outstretched, and there was

nothing she could do but take it. His skin was warm and her palm tingled.

He didn't immediately release her when she was safely on the ground, but brought her around to face him, that errant lock of hair spilling across his brow.

"You didn't answer the question, Parris."

She should have known he would not let the matter drop. It wasn't in his nature, which only brought home more fully that he would honor his vow to hunt down Meg the barmaid, should she not comply with his wishes.

Still, Parris pretended she didn't understand what he was asking, hoping to be saved again as she saw the other coach arrive.

"Parris?" he prompted.

"Yes?"

"I'm waiting for an answer."

"What was the question?"

He said nothing. Just stood there, staring down at her from that rugged, handsome face, the sun a halo behind him, streaking his dark, shoulder-length hair with fire and glinting off the small diamond stud in his ear.

The gem never failed to remind Parris that underneath Dominick's perfectly tailored clothes was the pirate she remembered from her youth.

She wanted to reject him, knew it was the only thing to do in order to protect her heart—and yet that very same heart wouldn't allow her to deny him. Or herself.

"Yes . . . you are still my friend."

The smile started slowly, like the sun dawning over the horizon, and Parris's breath caught at the sight of it.

As her family came up behind her, Dominick leaned down and whispered in her ear, "And you are still mine, Parris."

Eleven

⁂

Now slides the silent meteor on, and leaves
A shining furrow, as thy thoughts in me.

—Alfred, Lord Tennyson

A shiver chased over Parris's skin at Dominick's words, even as she told herself not to read too much into them. Just because she had made this one concession did not mean anything was going to change between them.

The fact would always remain that he had chosen Annabelle, not her, and that was something Parris could not forget.

It wasn't about physical love, even though the image of Dominick lying naked with Annabelle, doing to her what he had once done to Parris, was almost too much to bear.

No, it was about the love that had to have resided in his heart to ask Annabelle to be his wife.

Perhaps he had gotten over Annabelle. He claimed he had never loved her. But would Parris ever know for sure? And what about her sister? It was clear that Annabelle still harbored some kind of affection for Dominick, the way she flirted with him.

As though her thoughts had conjured her sister up, Annabelle suddenly knocked into her. "How clumsy of me," she said. "My shoe must have gotten stuck. It is so very . . . grassy here, isn't it?"

"It's a fair," Dominick commented in a dry voice.

Parris wondered what he thought of Annabelle's display, since her sister made a point of leaning over to brush some invisible speck from her skirt, giving him the opportunity to peer down her bodice should he feel so inclined, as she had on numerous occasions so far.

But Dominick was looking at Parris, treating her to a heart-melting smile and a quick wink before Annabelle looped her arm possessively through his and began leading him away, chattering like a magpie about the wonderful new gowns her modiste was making for her.

Parris hung back, trying to fend off the sting of jealousy. She noticed a number of women turning their gazes his way as he walked by. She couldn't blame them; Dominick was hard to overlook.

"You should fight a little harder for him, you know."

Parris turned to find Gwen standing beside her, her cousin's gaze following Dominick and Annabelle as they stopped behind Philip and Mary, who were laughing at the wild antics of the puppets. Her mother had spotted a friend and was engrossed in conversation.

Gwen focused on Parris with intent. "Why do you let her do that?"

"Do what?"

Gwen batted her eyelashes, her expression simpering. "Oh, Your Grace," she purred in a singsong voice, mimicking Annabelle's inflections perfectly. "You are so big and strong. Can you carry me across this terrible grass-filled meadow? I fear I might scuff my shoes." The finale of her performance was a girlish giggle.

Parris laughed at Gwen's imitation, feeling cheered.

"So?" Gwen said, tapping Parris on the forearm with her fan. "Why do you let Annabelle take over like that?"

"She isn't taking over."

"She practically bowled you out of the way to get at Dominick. There's something going on here. The tension is thick enough to cut."

"It's a long story." And Gwen didn't know any of it because she had been only ten years old at the time and not privy to such information.

"I've got all day." By the look in Gwen's eyes, Parris could tell her cousin would not relent.

She sighed, and looked away. "Dominick and Annabelle . . ." Had she never said the words out loud? Parris hadn't realized until that moment how difficult they actually were. "They were to be married."

"Married?" Gwen's voice rang with shock. "I don't believe it. Dominick could not possibly be so blind as to want someone like Annabelle for the rest of his life. He strikes me as the kind of man who would look for substance in a wife, and the last time I checked, that was a commodity Annabelle had in very short supply."

Parris had no reply. She had never understood Dominick's love for Annabelle; he had always seemed barely tolerant of her. But then, hadn't her instincts been wrong before? She had once believed that he cared for her.

That he would wait for her to grow up.

"When was this marriage to have taken place?" Gwen asked.

"Eight years ago."

"Good heavens! What happened?"

"Annabelle cried off."

"Why?"

"She said . . . she found Dominick in bed with another woman." Parris had never asked who the woman was. She wasn't sure she wanted to know.

Gwen stared at her, incredulous. "That Dominick over there? The one who hasn't even looked at a woman, besides you, since he came home?"

Parris nodded.

Gwen shook her head. "Something is not right here."

"Maybe Annabelle is the type of woman Dominick wants."

"You mean selfish, self-centered, and spiteful?"

"She's beautiful."

Gwen stopped walking and turned Parris to face her. "*You're* beautiful. Both on the inside and the outside. If for some unknown reason, Dominick wants

Annabelle, then he can have her, and good riddance to both of them. But I don't think he does. I think he wants you. Good heavens, I thought he was going to kiss you right here in front of everyone."

Parris had thought and hoped the same thing. Scandalous or not. In front of everyone.

In front of Annabelle.

It felt possessive, that need, a mark of territory. She had wanted Dominick's kiss to brand her, to show that she was his, and he was hers. Perhaps she had needed that kiss to break the hold of old, painful memories. To finally be free of the past.

"Whether you both held back your feelings because of Annabelle," Gwen continued, "or there was something else going on that caused you and Dominick to miss each other the first time around, I wouldn't let it happen again, Parris. Love is too precious to throw away."

Parris reflected on the sage words as Gwen walked over to the apple-dunking barrel.

Could Dominick really have feelings for her? Could he want something more from her than her body? Or was Gwen mistaking the way he smiled at her and teased her as something else?

Desire could masquerade as love, and Dominick desired her. That much Parris knew. And as much as she wanted to tell herself that there would never be anything physical between them, it felt inevitable.

But would her heart be involved? Would his? Or would he walk away like he did eight years ago, leaving her to mend her broken heart? Did she want to give him the chance to hurt her that way again?

Parris watched him as he leaned down to say something to Philip, tousling the little boy's hair and patting him on the back while Annabelle looked on impatiently.

When he straightened, Parris saw him glance around, his roaming gaze stopping when he found her, the look in his eyes almost a caress.

She felt exposed and vulnerable standing there alone amid the rows of vendors and games, with the cries of merchants hawking various treats and children's laughter ringing in her ears.

A man came up behind Dominick then and clapped him on the shoulder, diverting his attention. A man Parris immediately recognized.

Jason Fielding.

Clinging to the earl's arm was a stunning brunette, petite, amply endowed, and gazing up at him adoringly while he patted her hand as though she were a troublesome child in need of reassurance.

Parris's gaze darted to her cousin, who was cheering on a pair of twin boys dunking their heads in the water barrel to grab an apple.

The earl spotted Gwen just as her cousin's gaze lifted and locked with his, a long, tension-charged moment passing between them.

Parris knew the exact moment Gwen noticed the woman beside Lord Stratford, as in the space of a second, her cousin's expression turned sulfurous.

With military crispness, Gwen spun on her heel, pushing her way through the crowd. The earl murmured something to the young woman that made her frown as he endeavored to extract himself from her tenacious grip, which he then transferred to Dominick's free arm before heading through the crowd after Gwen. And while the whole scene was very telling from Parris's perspective, there was only one thing she really noticed.

Dominick was now ushering around two beautiful women.

Parris was so lost in unpleasant thoughts that she didn't hear the person calling her name until he was almost upon her, and she found herself staring up into a familiar face that she had not seen in nearly five months.

"James."

"Hello, Parris." He smiled gently at her, and the look in his eyes told her he was happy to see her, even though she suspected it had taken a lot for him to come speak to her, considering the way they had parted and the things she had revealed. "How are you?"

"I'm fine." Never had she expected to feel so stilted in James's presence. There was a time when they could talk about anything. And though it was for the best that they had never married, she still missed their conversations.

"You're looking well," he murmured.

"And you."

His expression was endearing as he said, "This is awkward, isn't it?"

"Yes."

"I wish it didn't have to be like this."

"I know." She took his hand and gave a gentle squeeze. "I can only hope you're happy. Are you, James?"

"Happy enough, I suppose." He gestured over his shoulder at the small group of women standing around the fortune teller's table. "My sisters bullied me into coming. They claimed I was working too hard. And I claimed they were put on this planet for the sole purpose of driving me insane. Well, you can see who won that argument."

Virginia, the oldest of his four sisters, was watching them closely, wearing the same disapproving expression Parris had been treated to the last time she saw her: the day Virginia had come to her house and let Parris know what a wretched person she was for hurting James, and that she would never find a man as good and kind, and that she should be ashamed of herself.

Parris had been ashamed. Not for being honest with James, but for ever having allowed things to get so far that she had ended up hurting him. That, he had not deserved.

"I see Virginia hasn't forgiven me."

He laid his hand on her arm, and Parris glanced up at him. "She doesn't mean any harm. She just worries about me."

"I know. And I'm glad she's so protective of you."
Parris hesitated. "James . . . ?"

"Yes?"

"It isn't Virginia's forgiveness that I want. It's yours.
Perhaps it's too soon. So much has happened, so many
things have changed . . ."

He moved closer to her, the press of his finger
beneath her chin tipping her head up. "I should be
asking for your forgiveness, Parris."

"But—"

"You were honest with me. I was the blind one,
refusing to believe that you didn't care for me, thinking that someday you would come to love me, that
somehow I could make you do so. I realize now how
foolish that was."

"I did care for you, James."

"Yes, you did, though not in the way I had hoped.
But that wasn't your fault. You suffered a lot because of
me, Parris, and for that, I'm sorry. I never meant for all
this to happen."

She looked into his eyes and saw sincerity. Yet, what
she also saw broke her heart. James still cared for her. A
thread of hope lingered in him, and that knowledge
ached inside her.

She didn't want him to hold out hope that she
might change her mind, that there could ever be more
between them. They wanted different things, and the
disintegration of their engagement would always hang
between them.

Parris's eyes widened as James's head lowered

toward her, a protest forming on her lips, knowing he was going to kiss her. Suddenly a large, dark hand clamped down on his shoulder, yanking him back.

Her gaze flew to Dominick's furious face. His eyes slashed in her direction before focusing on James. "Touch her, my friend, and I may just have to break every bloody bone in your body."

The threat would have held more weight had her niece not been settled on his shoulders, her fingers clutching fistfuls of his black hair as she looked on with rapt fascination—as did several other people who had heard Dominick's warning.

"Who the hell are you?" James demanded as the two men faced each other, nearly identical in height and weight.

"Don't worry about who I am. Just—"

"Uncle James!" Mary squealed, wiggling in excitement and smiling at her other honorary uncle, a title inherited by any male Mary liked.

Relaxing slightly, James glanced up at Mary, giving her a wink. "Hello, angel. I've missed you."

"I've missed you, too!" Mary canted her head, her smooth brow drawing together in a frown. "Why don't you come to the house anymore? You promised me a ride on your back the last time, and then you didn't come back."

Mary had never fully comprehended that James would not be coming around anymore. Once someone was a part of Mary's life, she expected them to always be a part of it.

"I know, moppet, and I'm sorry for that. I've been very busy. But perhaps I can make it up to you. We can take a carriage ride through the park, if your Aunt Parris accompanies us. I'll even let you handle the ribbons for a few minutes. Would you like that?"

Mary bounced with delight, her fingers yanking Dominick's hair in her excitement. "Can we, Auntie Parris? Please!"

Parris couldn't believe another man had resorted to using her weakness for her sister's children against her. "We'll see, precious."

Surprisingly, Mary didn't put up a fuss. Instead she said, "See how tall I am, Uncle James? Uncle Dominick lets me ride on his shoulders—and he didn't even yell at me when I dropped ice cream on his shirt."

Parris had been studiously avoiding looking at Dominick, hating the fact that she had known even a moment's thrill about his having sounded so very possessive.

When she finally met his gaze, she nearly flinched under that forceful regard. And yet, everything inside her melted. Never had a man looked more endearing than Dominick did at the moment, with a squirming Mary on his shoulders and his once pristine white shirt sporting a stain from her niece's ice cream. Parris felt the strongest urge to reach out and hug him, but his forbidding expression held her at bay.

James turned to her. "Uncle Dominick?"

Parris knew what he was thinking: that he had already been replaced in her affections. She only prayed he would not make other connections, as well. Her prayer came a moment too late.

"This is him, isn't it?" His words were not loud or abrasive, but spoken low and with a hint of hurt in his voice.

"Yes." She nodded. "It is."

As though realizing they had come to their final turning point, James gave her a sad smile. Leaning forward, he said close to her ear, "I hope you get all your heart desires, Parris." Then he straightened and told Mary he would see her soon, which Parris knew was a lie, before blending into the crowd.

Parris's gaze followed him, an odd sense of wistfulness filling her, knowing she would most likely never see James again.

A strong hand grabbed hold of her arm then, bringing her attention back to Dominick. She didn't know what was reflected in her eyes or on her face, but whatever it was made him release her.

Annabelle sidled up next to him, sparing Parris a cutting look before saying with an exaggerated sigh, "Poor James. He did so love you, sister. In truth, I think he still does."

Parris had never known such a desire to slap her sister as she did in that moment, but Mary had spotted a merchant selling candied apples and begged for one.

Casting a calculated glance at Dominick, Annabelle opened her reticule. "Oh dear, it appears I haven't brought enough money with me. I'm sorry, Mary darling."

Everything tightened inside Parris. She knew her sister had come with plenty of money, having seen her helping herself to the supply maintained for the housekeeper to buy household items, which Parris would have to replace or else tell Mrs. Keaton that Annabelle was a petty thief.

Without hesitation, Dominick handed the money over to Annabelle, who treated him to her most flirtatious smile before sailing off to get Mary her treat.

Mary, so wonderfully precious and innocent, leaned over the top of his head and kissed his brow. In return, Dominick bussed Mary's cheek. It was the most heartwarming sight Parris had ever seen.

But if she had expected her niece's sweetness to soften Dominick, she had been greatly mistaken, for the gaze that came to rest on her once more was turbulent.

"So that was him," he said tersely.

Parris nodded, not wanting to talk about James. "I think you have permanently won Mary's heart."

"And what about you, Parris? What would it take to win your heart?"

For a moment, the world seemed to stand still as Parris asked herself if he really wanted to know the answer. But Mary began to bounce again, having spotted her mother returning with her treat, effectively silencing whatever Parris had thought to say.

"Here you go, darling," Annabelle chirped. "Oh!" Her foot seemed to catch on something, her hand reaching out to steady herself on Parris's shoulder . . .

Entangling the candy apple in Parris's hair.

"How clumsy I am today!" Annabelle blinked wide, unrepentant eyes at Parris. "Oh, dear . . . your hair."

Parris could feel the sticky heaviness of the thickly coated apple clinging to her hair and felt a sudden rush of emotion well up inside her.

"Damn," Dominick swore fiercely, his angry gaze cutting to Annabelle, who flinched.

Gingerly, he lifted Mary from his shoulders. Reaching into his pocket, he peeled off another bill, but this time he handed it to Mary rather than her mother and instructed her to get herself another apple.

Then Dominick came to stand beside Parris, and with a gentleness she had not expected, he carefully peeled the sticky treat away.

Parris reached behind her to feel her hair and nearly sobbed as her hand ran over a large clump. Dominick thrust the apple into Annabelle's hand, leaving her to gape unbecomingly as he took Parris by the hand and led her away.

"Where are we going?" she asked in a quavering voice, hating the fat tear that rolled down her cheek, knowing it was silly to cry over such a thing. It was only hair. Hadn't her father told her that often enough, when she would beg him not to cut it? When he would chop it unevenly, while she sat there numbly, refusing to show any emotion.

He had wanted to break her will, change her into someone she wasn't, but she would not give him the satisfaction. Her stubborn refusal to bend would earn her a whipping, but she would take it without so much as a whimper, for to do otherwise would be a victory for her father.

Dominick maneuvered them between two booths, stopping in front of a barrel of water. He looked down at her, his expression grim as he wiped his thumb across the wet path left by her tear.

A salty drop lingered at the corner of her mouth and Parris licked it away, watching Dominick's gaze dip to her lips and wishing she was brave enough to press her mouth to his. She wanted to feel the heat that had coursed through her when he had kissed her before, thinking her someone else.

Her body burned with images of what she could do to him in her role of Meg, a need that grew stronger the more she was with him.

But at that moment, all she could manage was a prayer that she did not blink, for fear the remaining unshed tears would tumble down her cheeks and have him thinking her foolish and weak.

"Turn around," he murmured, and Parris obeyed without question.

He took her hair in one hand and she heard the ripple of water, knowing he was bathing the snarled tresses carefully. Her heart expanded with feelings almost too strong to contain.

"Dominick . . ." His name caught on a sob.

"Let me do this for you." His request was closer to a plea and Parris could not bring herself to make him stop. The way he touched her was almost reverent, as if she was something cherished and rare.

She wanted to lean back into his hands, to feel his fingers on her skin. Instead she closed her eyes and enjoyed the sensations he evoked.

"Will I have to cut it?" Her voice was not quite her own as Dominick moved closer to her, the whole heated length of him only inches behind her, his nearness making her shiver.

"No," he said softly, his voice sounding hoarse. "I won't let anyone cut your hair."

It was as if he was speaking to the girl she had once been, when he used to enfold her in his arms and promise her that someday she would be free of her father's cruelty, that he would take care of her, as he always promised to—before the currents of life had swept him away from her.

"Do you still love him, Parris?"

It took a moment for Parris to understand his question, as all her senses were wrapped up in the sensual haze his hands created.

"No." The word was no more substantial than a breath of air.

"Did you love him once?"

"I cared for him, but not the way he wanted me to. Not in a way that would have ever made him happy."

"Then why were you going to marry him?"

"He was good to me. He treated me like an equal and not some girl to be coddled and tolerated and draped over his arm as though I was an ornament. He was a friend. Sometimes . . . I miss that friendship."

Dominick's fingers momentarily stilled. "He would take you back. He still loves you."

Parris wished she could deny that James still cared. "I know, and I hurt him when I never meant to."

"Hurt him?" Dominick's voice took on an edge of anger. "What about how he hurt you? He left you on your wedding day, for Christ's sake."

"I gave him little choice."

"Jesus, what are you saying?"

"I don't want to talk about it. Please." She prayed he would not press her.

He let out a low expletive, and then asked, "Would you have gone through with it?"

"Yes," she answered in a barely audible voice. "I'd pledged myself to him, and if he had not cried off, I would have married him."

The hands on her hair tightened, becoming almost rough. Perhaps she deserved it for what she had done.

"Why didn't you write me, Parris? Why didn't you tell me what was going on in your life? I would have been there for you."

"Would you?"

"Of course, damn it! Why do you question me? Wasn't I always there for you as a child?"

"Yes. But then . . . things changed. You left."

"I had to go."

"Yes. Because of Annabelle."

"Because of you."

"Me?" Parris shook her head, her chest constricting with painful memories.

"Yes, you. I never loved Annabelle. I told you that."

"Then why did you ask her to marry you? Why did you hurt me so? God, Dominick . . ." Emotion clogged her last words, threatening to close off her throat.

She had never expected to have this conversation with him, never expected to see him again. And now, here he was, back again, and something was building inside her that wouldn't release her from its grip, that continued moving forward whether she wanted it to or not.

"I made a mistake, Parris. A stupid, foolish mistake. I didn't realize it until it was too late, and there was no turning back."

What mistake did he mean? Was he referring to the woman his sister had found him in bed with? Or . . . an indiscretion with Annabelle?

She closed her eyes. "Did you and Annabelle . . ."

He hesitated, then said in a raw voice, "Yes."

Oh, God. Even though she had thought he and Annabelle had made love, to hear him admit it was almost too difficult to bear.

"Won't you ever forgive me?"

Forgive him. He had asked her once for absolution. She had not had it in her to give it to him then. Did she have it now?

His fingers brushed the base of her neck, caressing her skin. Her stomach jumped as though he had harnessed lightning in his hands, sending sizzling currents along her arms and down her spine.

Her traitorous body responded to his touch, her

nipples straining against the material of her dress, and heaven help her, she wanted him to smooth his hands over her shoulders and cup her, to ease his hands beneath the suddenly taut material of her bodice and soothe her, then replace his fingers with his mouth.

If only she had not once tasted this fruit, hadn't understood what the yearnings of her body pushed her toward, hadn't the memories to torment her now, with his hands skimming softly down her sides.

"*Parris . . .*" Her whispered name wrapped around her like sweet seduction. She opened her eyes to find him standing in front of her.

She wanted him to kiss her, and she didn't want him to be gentle, to treat her as though she were breakable. She wanted his passion, every rough ounce of it, his body telling her how he felt.

Her eyelids felt heavy, weighed down by desire as she looked up into his handsome face, an emotion there that she wanted to believe mirrored her own.

"Please," she murmured, asking for something she could not bring herself to say.

His head descended; her every sense was alive and yearning for this moment, knowing that only in his kiss could she find what she sought: the answer that would break the chains that had bound her for so long.

"Auntie Parris!"

The voice jolted Parris like a bucket of ice water. How could she have forgotten the children were close by? Or her family?

Oh, God. It was happening all over again. All the things she had been running from since she was sixteen years old, before she realized how deeply the knife of unrequited love could cut, how devastating the wound. To love and not be loved in return was one of life's worst tragedies.

She pushed passed him, trying not to run, praying she would not cry . . . and never seeing the despair etched on his face as he watched her go.

Twelve

When the sun sets, shadows, that showed at noon
But small, appear most long and terrible.

—Nathaniel Lee

Parris ignored the soft knock on her bedroom door, and her maid informing her that dinner was being served. She was too absorbed in the melancholy that had gripped her since her return from the fair that afternoon.

She could not face anyone and pretend that all was well, as she tried to shut out the memory of Dominick's hands in her hair, his warm breath on her neck, the expression in his eyes as he stared down at her.

The ride back to London had seemed endless, even though she had been spared having to travel with Dominick.

Spared, yet utterly miserable. More so when he had entered the other coach with Annabelle and the children. The very thought of the two of them together had been a torment. She could not give Dominick the absolution he sought. Not at the expense of her heart.

She stared out her bedroom window, watching the sun die beyond the horizon, the shadows drifting into her room to steal over her until nothing remained of the light, and darkness all but enshrouded her.

Tomorrow . . . tomorrow she would act as though nothing had happened, remind herself that she was strong, that no man was worth such heartache.

But for tonight, she wanted to give in to those softer emotions and pray they would be a balm to her tattered pride and wounded spirit.

A light scratching at the door barely moved Parris as she called out once more, "I don't want supper. Now please go away."

"Tain't about supper, miss," her maid replied. "A letter come for ya."

Parris sighed. "Come in, then."

A shaft of light beamed into the room as Millie opened the door. "Where is ya, miss? Have all y'r lamps gone out?"

"No, I . . . fell asleep. Light the one near the door."

Parris could hear Millie's low expletive as she knocked into the bureau before finding the oil lamp and lighting the wick, bringing a soft glow to the room.

Rubbing her side, Millie trudged over to Parris's chair and handed her the letter. Parris studied the envelope for a moment, wondering who would be writing her.

The seal on the back was a simple, unremarkable dollop of red wax without an imprint to give her any idea of the sender's identity.

She began to open the letter, but realized Millie still hung over her shoulder, looking all too eager to see the message contained in the missive, which she would certainly spread among the gossiping servants.

"Thank you, Millie. That will be all for now."

Appearing dejected, Millie sighed and muttered, "Aye, miss," and shuffled to the door, casting one last longing glance at the vellum in Parris's hand before closing the door after her.

Feeling nervous, and not quite understanding why, Parris broke the seal, pulled out the single sheet of paper, and began to read:

My love,

I am in hell, my heart tortured as I struggle with irresolution, endeavoring to deny the feelings I have for you, for which I will confess to have failed.

It was impossible not to be drawn to your winsome smile, your indomitable spirit, your passion for life . . . and to want to bring out that passion in other forms. Yes, that, too, has haunted my mind.

It haunts me now, as I write this.

Parris stopped reading, her hands trembling. To think that someone had been watching her, desiring her.

She glanced at the last page, looking for a signature

to identify the author, but there was nothing. She felt a stinging disappointment, realizing that she had been hoping the letter was from Dominick.

Though why would he write to her now? He hadn't thought her worth the time or effort during the years of his absence.

Could the letter have come from James? The timing, along with his appearance at the fair, seemed questionable. She knew he still harbored feelings for her, but she had believed he'd finally understood there could never be anything between them.

But the thought was far less disturbing than the possibility of a stranger watching her, perhaps following her without her knowing.

Almost against her will, Parris was drawn back to the letter.

> At first, I involuntarily allowed the visions of your charms into my mind until, finally, they became incessant, gnawing at me with an unfulfilled hunger.
>
> I entertained no one fantasy beyond that of the immediate pleasure brought about by thinking of you. Though it should not surprise you to discover how quickly this became a habit, an obsession, if you will.
>
> It was as if I awoke from a long delirium and found that I harbored a dark passion for you, and I had neither the will nor the strength to resist.

It seems as though I was forever trying to suppress the need you brought out in me, and then some inexplicable thought would crush my attempts.

But I have discovered that when passion takes thorough possession of a man's soul, it leaves him unfit for anything else. And so, I have concluded only this . . .

We cannot outdistance our fate.

But for the present, this second, if you do nothing else, dream of me when you close your eyes . . .

As I dream of you.

The words lingered in Parris's mind, and her traitorous body responded to the heat that seemed to rise from the paper to envelop her, caress her.

Dream of me when you close your eyes . . . as I dream of you.

She wanted to ascribe those words to Dominick, but his eyes, his touch, his kiss did not speak of love. And she could not be another one of his conquests, another Sutherland girl who had fallen prey to his charms. If Dominick cared for her, he would not hide behind a letter.

So who, then, had written her?

Parris resolved to question her maid, to discover whatever she could about the bearer. Rising from her chair, she rang the bell.

Barely a minute later, Millie knocked and stuck her head in the room. "Yes, miss? Do y' need me?" Millie's gaze went immediately to the letter, perhaps hoping Parris would divulge its contents.

"Who brought this letter, Millie?"

"A scruffy young lad appeared at the door, miss. Said I was ta give it ta y'."

"Did this young lad tell you who entrusted him with it?"

Millie shook her head. "No, miss. He was right mysterious, he was. Dropped him a tuppence, I did. He grabbed it up quick like and took off without even a by your leave." She sniffed disdainfully at that rudeness.

Parris sighed, no closer to the truth than she had been a moment ago. "Thank you, Millie. That will be all."

Parris returned once more to the window, searching for something in the darkness, though she knew not what.

Her gaze shifted to the east, in the direction of Grosvenor Square, though nothing could be seen at this distance but the high dome of Saint Joseph's Cathedral. Only a few hours remained before her midnight meeting with Dominick . . .

A few hours in which to steel herself for whatever was to come.

Dominick stared into the fire in the hearth, listening to each tick of the clock, his restlessness increasing as the evening progressed. Waiting . . .

It seemed as if he was always waiting. First for Parris to grow up, then for himself to forget her, to expunge the passion she evoked in him and find a common ground in friendship. But he could no longer delude himself. He desired far more than friendship from her.

He wanted it all.

He took a sip of his wine and glanced one more time at the clock on the mantel.

Ten minutes past midnight.

She wasn't coming.

Damn! He should have known better than to try and coerce Parris into doing something she didn't want to do. She did not take well to orders, and since his army days, giving orders was what he did best.

The cards were stacked in her favor. Unless he intended to confess that he knew "Meg" was a fraud, he could not hunt her down and demand answers.

Christ, after his display that afternoon at the fair, he couldn't blame her for not showing up. He had very nearly kissed her; would have done so right there in broad daylight, had little Mary not squealed Parris's name because Philip was tugging on her braid. Mischief their mother should have handled, but as usual, Annabelle was oblivious.

Annabelle—what had he ever seen in her? She was shallow, self-absorbed, clingy. She had bonded herself to his hip most of the day, pressing her bosom into his arm and purposely finding reasons to lean over, affording him every possible opportunity to ogle her breasts. Her behavior disgusted him, even more than usual because Mary was there to witness it.

Dominick could only pray that the bright, vivacious

child took after her aunt rather than her mother. It would be a shame if all that sunshine was squelched and packaged into another simpering debutante.

In truth, Dominick was more than three-fourths in love with the little imp. Mary made him think about what his life would be like if he had children of his own.

With a winsome smile, she had wrapped him around her finger and he found himself indulging her more than he should. He suspected she had tasted every treat at the fair—and dropped more than half of them on him.

Annabelle had screamed like a fishwife at Mary when she innocently dirtied his shirt with her ice cream. When he had knelt down to soothe Mary, her eyes held huge tears, and Dominick had wanted to wring Annabelle's neck.

He had told Mary the shirt could be cleaned as he wiped away a fat tear coursing down her cheek, thinking how stoic the little girl was. In many ways, Mary reminded him of Parris.

Sniffling, she had peeked up at him with those big, luminous green eyes and bestowed a hesitant smile upon him. Shyly, she inched closer, running her hands over his face, having discovered some sort of fascination with his jaw.

Then she tugged the handkerchief from his pocket, and acting quite grown up for her young years, she wet it in the cup of water her harried nursemaid had produced and began to clean the stain. Annabelle had hovered over them with a sour expression on her face.

"Oh, Uncle Dominick!" Mary had gasped a minute later. "Look at your bruise!"

Dominick had glanced down and then laughed. "That's not a bruise, Mary. It's a tattoo."

"A tattoo!" Annabelle had exclaimed, bending down to stare at the dark shape of the snake's head, revealed by the wet spot on his shirt. "Why, that's positively heathen!"

Mary darted a glance over her shoulder at her mother, then leaned close to Dominick and whispered, "Can I see it?"

Dominick knew he should say no. She was only a child and a snake was a snake. He didn't want to give her nightmares. But the expectancy wreathing her cherubic face played havoc with his heart, and he didn't have the strength to deny her.

"Yes," he replied in a conspiratorial voice. "But not right now."

"Promise?"

"Promise."

"Will you show it to Auntie Parris, too?"

Dominick would give his eyeteeth to show it to Parris, knowing she would be fascinated rather than repulsed. He very nearly groaned thinking about her fingers tracing the design, winding her way down his chest until she came to the snake's tail coiling around his nipple.

The image was so vivid he could almost feel the pad of her forefinger sweeping across the hard pebble, see her leaning down to taste him, her tongue gently rasping over his heated skin.

He cursed fluidly beneath his breath and realized he was hard as a bloody stone. Jesus, even innocent thoughts of Parris eventually digressed into fantasies, need burning in his gut and growing more insistent with each passing day.

He forced his thoughts back to the matter at hand, his gaze cutting to the clock once more and noticing that another ten minutes had passed with no sign of her.

Disappointment sluiced through him, and he felt very much like getting drunk. Otherwise, he'd spend another restless night plagued with images of her, of things he wanted to say to her.

Things he wanted to do with her.

Good Christ, he felt like a steam kettle ready to blow. He had hoped he'd instilled enough curiosity in her from the kisses they had shared to bring her back. Either he had not affected her enough . . . or she was sensible enough to stay away.

At least she was showing some common sense, unlike him. Maybe it was time to reconsider his backdoor method of seduction—the only person he was tormenting was himself. Parris was probably at home fast asleep.

Perhaps dreaming about the mystery man who had written to her?

Dominick shook his head. Another lackwit idea. But when he had returned her and her family home after the fair, he had been nearly mindless with jealousy over that moronic ex-fiancé, and boiling over with long-suppressed desire for her.

At the time, the idea had seemed a perfect vent, a way to tell her how he felt without pushing her further away. How ironic to find himself using the same clandestine method Lady Scruples employed. Perhaps it was fitting.

He finished off the Madeira in his glass, intending to find something stronger to dull the ache in his loins, when a light tapping sounded against the window across the room. He wanted to howl in triumph when she saw the masked faced peering in through the glass.

Parris—or rather Meg—had arrived.

His mood vastly improved, Dominick strode across the room and shoved open the window, smiling down at her, not realizing that his grin was almost wolfish and his eyes inscrutable as the moon slid behind a cloud, his shirt partially unbuttoned and begging for fingers to caress the hard flesh.

Parris reveled in every glorious inch revealed to her hungry gaze, her heart thumping even harder than it already had been.

Ever since she had crept from the house, not even confiding in Gwen about her midnight rendezvous, she had felt as though she couldn't get enough air.

Several times she had stopped and nearly turned back, telling herself that no good could come from this escapade. But the need to see Dominick, to be alone with him, had been too strong to resist.

"I thought perhaps you weren't coming," he murmured, his sultry voice washing over her like a breeze on a warm summer night.

"Y' told me I must," Parris countered just as quietly. "So here I am."

"Yes . . . here you are." Something about his words sent a shiver down her spine. "Why didn't you come to the front door?"

"I didn't want anyone to see me."

"Ah, yes . . . best to keep things a secret. Although," he drew out the word, "some secrets are a great deal of pleasure to unravel."

Parris didn't want to be drawn into the trap of wondering what he was referring to, and chose to assume he was speaking of Lady Scruples—whose identity would remain a mystery if Parris had anything to say about it. If nothing else came from this excursion, she could at least steer Dominick in a different direction.

"Come around to the French doors," he told her.

Her feet once more feeling leaden, Parris walked around the corner of the house to a quaint brick-paved terrace, with a wrought-iron bench sitting under a tree and the smell of honeysuckle scenting the air, as well as a slight autumn nip, even though it was still summer.

The smoky scent of wood burning in the fireplace only increased the allure of the setting as a faint warm breeze ruffled the leaves and teased the exposed flesh of her shoulders and arms.

She turned toward the house then and found Dominick lounging on the threshold to his study, his shoulder propped against the jamb, those beautiful ginger-colored eyes gauging her every move.

With his shirtsleeves rolled up and a few of the buttons undone at his neck, his silky black hair tousled as though raked by impatient fingers, he had never been more glorious. He epitomized virility, temptation— and every aching, lonely place inside Parris responded to him.

He pushed away from the doorjamb and started toward her. Parris was rooted to the spot, a voice clamoring inside her to flee, to get out of there as quickly as she could.

But she doubted she could have taken a single step, even had she wanted to. His every movement hypnotized her, and when he stopped before her, she wanted to wrap her arms around his neck and press her body close.

He said nothing. Instead he lifted a length of her hair—no, not her hair, that of the wig. She held her breath, wondering what he would say, if he would recognize that she was a fraud and demand that she unveil herself.

His eyes glinted a silvery gold in the light of the moon, the rays etching hollows and contours on his face, as though he had been created by whatever gods roamed the darkness in the hours between midnight and dawn.

"Do you have any information for me?" he asked,

his gaze slowly drifting over her face before fastening on her eyes.

Parris blinked, rousing herself from the sensual haze he had so easily woven around her. "Information?"

"About Lady Scruples."

"Oh . . ." How could she have forgotten the reason she was there? "I . . . I heard she's left town for a while."

"Left town. I see." He studied her and Parris chided herself to stand firm, though it was difficult. "Are you sure you're being completely honest with me, sweet Meg?"

"Yes." The word issued from her mouth without any conviction.

"You know I would be very angry were I to think you were holding back. You wouldn't hold back on me, now, would you?"

Parris could do no more than shake her head.

"Good. Sherry?"

"Excuse me?"

"Would you like a glass of sherry?"

At that moment, Parris felt inclined to drink whiskey straight from the bottle. "Yes. Very much so . . . Y'r Grace." She had to be more careful to remember she was a barmaid.

He nodded and returned to his study while Parris followed him with reluctant fascination. She spotted something against the far wall that brought a small sound of delight to her lips.

Her old fishing rod.

Without thinking, she picked up the rod, surprised at how well it had held up over all these years. She had lost it to Dominick on a bet. The next day, he had presented her with a brand-new one.

She had thought he had simply thrown the old rod away, and couldn't believe he actually still had it. Her finger lightly traced the tiny notches she had cut at the base, which had kept track of how many times she caught more fish than he.

"Do you fish?"

Startled, Parris's head jerked up. She reluctantly returned the pole to its place and took hold of the glass he held out to her, trying to quell her nerves as well as the longing to talk about the days when they had sat on the banks of the pond, not needing to speak to feel content.

"No," she murmured. "I don't fish."

He lifted the rod, his thumb running over the supple wood. "This belonged to a friend of mine. I won it in a bet." He turned to look at her. "Between you and me, she couldn't catch a fish even if it jumped out of the water and into her hands."

Indignation rose inside Parris at his blatant lie. She wanted to call him on it, but in her role as Meg, she couldn't. "What was the bet?"

"Well, there were these large flat stones that ran across the pond we used to fish in. They were spaced pretty far apart, and she bet me I couldn't make it all the way across to a small isle in the middle of the pond. She went first and almost made it. I'll give her that. But she missed one of the rocks and dropped into the water like ninety pounds of deadweight."

Deadweight, her behind!

"Then I went across," he continued. "I made it all the way to the other side. As the winner, I received her beloved rod. Poor girl didn't realize she was beaten before we even started."

What an exaggeration, especially since he had nearly missed the same stone as she!

Parris folded her arms across her chest and glared. "I bet she could have beaten you had she wanted to."

"Nope. I had something she didn't."

"And what was that?"

He leaned forward, almost indecently close, and replied, "Longer legs."

His smile was so infectious, Parris had to bite the inside of her lip to keep from returning it. Never had a man been more adept at prodding her into a temper and then immediately disarming her as Dominick did.

A pained expression suddenly crossed his face, alarming her. "What's the matter?"

He gripped his thigh. "An old wound from my army days. It aches every now and again, especially when the weather changes or it's about to rain."

Parris glanced out the open French doors and noted no change in the weather, other than a slight increase in the wind. She turned back to Dominick, unsure of what to do. He looked in agony.

"Shall I fetch someone for you?"

"No, I don't want to disturb anyone from their slumber." He hesitated and then said, "Perhaps . . ." He shook his head. "Forget it."

"What?"

"Nothing." He took a swig of his drink, as if hoping the liquor would dull the pain, and yet he gritted his teeth, which told her it would take more than mellowing effects of the alcohol to help him at that moment.

Her concern grew. "Let me help. Please," she added when he appeared ready to protest.

Finally, he relented. "If you insist. Perhaps you might . . ."

"Yes?"

"Well, if it isn't too much bother, perhaps you could massage my thigh? Sometimes that helps."

Massage his thigh? She would have to lay her hands on him to do that, touch that hot, hard flesh. Just being near him was difficult.

"Forget I asked." He walked away with a slight limp, making Parris feel guilty. He was in pain and all she could do was think about herself.

She hastened over to him, lifting his arm and draping it over her shoulder. "Here, let me help you."

He regarded her for a moment, his eyes delving into hers. "Thank you."

Parris nodded, not trusting her voice.

She gingerly assisted him onto the couch, not realizing that the front of her peasant blouse sagged rather alarmingly when she leaned over, which gave Dominick an unfettered glimpse of her breasts. Only her taut nipples seemed to be keeping the material in place.

"Better?" she asked.

When his gaze lifted to hers, Parris's breath locked in her throat at the heat reflected back at her. She realized how close she was to him—and that she stood directly between his legs.

"Much better." His voice sounded thick.

Parris wasn't sure what to do next. There seemed to be no way to access his thigh without coming in direct contact with him, either by sitting next to him, which would put her far too close to his mouth, or kneeling between his legs. Either way seemed untenable.

"Meg?"

Parris barely recognized that he was speaking to her. Her gaze had been riveted to his heavily muscled thighs and the buff-colored breeches that gloved every taut inch of him, cupping his . . .

She shook her head, a blush rising rapidly to her cheeks. She was thankful for the mask that covered most of her face and hopefully hid the yearning pulsing through her at that moment.

"Are you all right?" he asked.

Parris blinked, realizing she was staring at him. "Fine."

"You don't have to do this, you know. The throbbing will stop in an hour or two. I've dealt with much worse. I'm sure—"

Parris silenced him by slowly dropping to her knees

in front of him, every nerve ending tingling as she rubbed her sweaty palms over the front of her shirt, which pulled it tight across her chest. The material felt like the coarsest of linen as it rasped over her sensitive nipples.

Then, taking a deep breath, Parris laid her hands on his thigh.

Thirteen

*He will hold thee, when his passion
shall have spent its novel force.*

—Alfred, Lord Tennyson

Heat seared Parris's palms as they made contact with hard muscle. She heard Dominick's soft groan as she began to massage his old wound, which was precariously close to his groin.

"Harder," he said in a pained voice that made Parris glance up, a slight breath breaking from her lips as she saw the glazed look in his eyes, an expression swirling in their depths that bordered on hunger. "Harder . . . please."

Parris willingly obliged. The heat rising from his body was heady and intoxicating, a languorous warmth spreading up her arms and over her chest before coursing lower, his heat becoming part of her as a heaviness built at the juncture of her thighs.

Parris couldn't tear her eyes away from his. He wouldn't let her. She nearly jumped when he took hold of her hand and moved it up his thigh, her fingers almost brushing the hardness centered there.

But she wanted to touch him, knew this moment was inevitable the second she had taken the first step from her house and traveled down this road. She wanted every masculine inch of him wrapped around her, inside her, to know if the real thing was as sweet as the memory.

To seduce him as she had eight years ago.

The knowledge burned inside her.

Her body thrummed as she inched her hands up, close enough so two of her fingers swept against his rigid length. She heard his sharp intake of breath and felt satisfaction in the purposeful taunt.

What would he do if her hands slid from his thigh and cupped him? If she massaged the hardness pressing against his buttons?

She knew he hadn't meant her innocent ministrations to turn into something else, and she couldn't blame him for his body's reaction.

He was a man, a virile, heavenly-made male in the prime of his life. What gnawed at her was the fact that "Meg" had brought about this response in him.

The desire for honesty, coupled with her need for Dominick, raged inside Parris. She wanted him to know the truth, to know who touched him. Yet what she wanted even more was what they shared long ago on a sultry summer night in a garden.

And if the girl forever hiding behind a mask could not have him, then Meg, the lustful serving wench, would. Parris could no longer deny what her heart and her body yearned for.

Her gaze still locked with Dominick's, she skimmed her hand over his erection. Air hissed through his teeth as his jaw clenched and his body jerked.

She massaged him through his trousers and could feel him swell. He let her go on with her sensual ministrations for a few moments, and then his hand clamped down over hers.

Parris's heart slammed against her ribs. A small part of her was relieved, thinking he was pushing away Meg. But another, larger part wanted him so desperately, she would do whatever it took to have him.

But instead of finding rejection on his face, she saw passion raging almost out of control. He did not push her away, but dragged her up from her kneeling position on the floor and across his lap, straddling him.

Wet heat dampened her pantalets, and she wanted Dominick to touch her there. He pressed up against her, as if discerning her thoughts, rocking his erection against her barely shielded cleft.

Parris threw her head back, forgetting why she shouldn't let this go any further and how her own actions might break her heart again.

She didn't care.

He cupped her breasts and she let out a long, low moan as his thumbs swept across the turgid peaks, making her mindless with desire as he increased the tempo. When he began to roll her nipples between his fingers, her inner lips clenched, a throbbing starting deep inside her.

She pushed against him, feeling another rush of warmth between her thighs as he began to weave his erotic web around her with his mouth and hands and body.

His fingers slipped beneath her skimpy blouse and slowly eased the material down, getting caught up on her erect peaks, his single tug freeing her, baring her breasts to his hungry gaze.

Parris saw herself through his eyes, how she gyrated against him, moaned so that the room captured the sound and amplified it, pleasure flushing her skin, her scent rising hot and musky between them.

"Please," she whispered as he stared at her breasts, wanting his mouth on her.

He did not disappoint her. His large hands gripped her buttocks, pulling her forward. While she watched through passion-hazed eyes, his tongue slid out and flicked one nipple. She jolted as he teased the peak, moistening it, circling, lapping, her body quickening with each passing second.

Then he moved to her other nipple to lavish it with the same attention he had shown the first, before cupping her breasts and pushing them together, drawing one sensitive nub deep into his mouth and then moving to the other to offer it the same attention.

Parris thought she moaned his name, but she was so wild with desire that coherent thought had totally deserted her. All she could do was hold on to his shoulders and revel in the friction her own movement created between their bodies.

"Yes," she breathed, as he continued to tug on her nipple while his free hand skimmed up her calf, pausing to stroke the tender flesh behind her knee before resuming its journey along her outer thigh, bunching up the material of her skirt as he went.

His fingers brushed the base of her spine, leaving a path of prickling skin in its wake before slowly, methodically drifting around to the front of her . . . and delving into the opening of her flimsy pantalets.

The first touch of his finger against her clitoris made Parris cry out with pleasure; the erect nub was hot and exquisitely sensitive, pouring bliss through her veins. His mouth created wet paths between her breasts as he massaged her.

Her nails dug into his shoulders. "Oh, yes . . . yes . . ."

"That's it. Let me feel it. Let me know I'm making you as crazy as you're making me."

"Please," she moaned, as his finger slowed to torturous circles. She wanted him to stroke her, faster. But he wanted to torment her, to tease.

Each time she felt on the brink of heaven, it was as if he knew and would purposely ease back, kiss around her nipple, lick beneath her breast, making one taunting sweep with his tongue across the aching tip. Then he would start again, building the tension, the need, until Parris thought she would disintegrate.

Her fingers were wild as she tore at the buttons of his shirt, needing to lay her hands against his hard flesh, pressing against the muscles that bunched and flexed with every move he made.

"Dominick . . . please, *please!*"

"Whatever you want, love," he murmured in a passion-roughened voice, as his mouth latched onto her nipple and his fingers resumed their torture on her throbbing core, flicking back and forth so that she was bucking and writhing, dying inside for that sweet release she knew he could give her, until her back arched, her entire body tensing, lightning gathering deep inside her and spiraling downward as her first convulsion tore through her, followed by a second and a third and a fourth as Dominick made light circles before his finger slid down to her opening to feel her pulse.

Without warning, he eased his finger inside her. Parris moaned at the sensation, her sheath clutching him with each contraction.

He began to pump inside her and she closed her eyes, the intoxication stirring once more. She wriggled, yearning for him to go deeper, and heard his harsh groan.

"Damn it, you're killing me. If you don't stop, I'll take you right here."

Parris ground her hips against him, hoping he would lose control.

He grabbed hold of her wrists, pinioning them at her sides as he stared into her eyes, looking fierce and tender, as though he wanted to kiss her as much as he wanted to push her away. It was maddening. He was maddening.

With a growl, he leaned forward and kissed her nipple, the tip so incredibly sensitive from all the attention he had given it that her inner lips contracted one more time.

With a deep, almost desperate breath, he leaned back against the cushions and gently righted the blouse that had puddled around her waist.

Parris didn't want him to stop. She didn't want to be reasonable or sensible or drift back to that place of pretense. She wanted to feel his hands on her, flesh against flesh, with no more barriers. She had missed him so much, and she longed for him to ease the ache in her heart as well as her body.

She reached out to run a finger down the deep V of his half-open shirt, smiling as she heard his sharp intake of breath.

Something caught her eye then and she eased back the left side of his shirt, gasping as a magnificently depicted serpent peered out at her, its body coiled as though ready to spring, its scales reflecting blue-black, its forked tongue flicking out.

Parris traced its shape with her finger, feeling the smooth, solid flesh beneath, the muscles that delineated Dominick's rock-hard upper chest and rippled down his stomach, her gaze fixed on the silky brown disk neatly wrapped inside the snake's tail.

She leaned forward and kissed his nipple, lapping gently at it until it hardened. Then she drew the pebble into her mouth as he had with her, reveling in the way his body tensed. Raising her head, she pressed her mouth to his, her tongue slipping across the taut line of hard-won control.

With a groan, he reluctantly parted his lips, and she stroked inside, wrapping her arms around his neck and pressing closer, wanting to get closer still ... wanting him inside, to be one with him in a way she had only dreamed about for a very long time.

Boldly, Parris put her hand between them and discovered he was still erect. She unbuttoned his trousers, praying he wouldn't stop her.

He didn't.

Her mouth still fused to his, she reached inside his drawers and found him, silky and hot, flame hot. He moaned into her mouth as she began to stroke him.

He tore his mouth from hers and tipped his head back, his expression one of rapt ecstasy as her hands glided over him. He had taught her so much eight years ago, things she had not forgotten, desires long suppressed and waiting for this moment.

Parris hated her skirt, the clothing hampered her. She shoved the material out of the way and pressed his erection against her moist cleft, and began sliding back and forth over his heat.

His eyes snapped open, passion glazing them as he looked at her. With a growl, he coiled an arm around her waist and used his free hand to drag her blouse back down, latching onto a nipple and sending a rush of sensation straight to the center of her.

She rode him faster, wanting him inside, yet she was too frantic, too wild, a thundering climax looming over the next horizon as he took possession of her mouth and toyed with her nipples.

Parris cried into his mouth as her release tore through her, her entire body tensing with that sweet saturation, the pulses coming hard and fast, and then a moment later, Dominick reached his own release.

"Jesus God!" He dropped his head back against the top of the couch and Parris rested her head against his shoulder, feeling utterly ravished. And utterly happy.

She lightly kissed his neck, every part of her body thrumming, the blood singing through her veins, her entire world encompassed in a blissful euphoria that she did not want to end. She felt insatiable.

"No more, sweetheart," he rasped, the words more a plea than a statement.

As Parris eased back, reality began to invade her dream world, reminding her of who Dominick thought she was. A lowly barmaid.

And he had let "Meg" touch him.

Parris couldn't believe it. She was jealous of herself! Worse, insidious thoughts crept in, making her wonder about the other women who might have touched him like this . . . and whom he might have touched.

Bedded.

Her anger was irrational, but it wouldn't let go of her. Why did he never see *her*? And why did her heart break each time she thought about how he would react if he knew the truth?

Abruptly, she moved off him, furiously tugging up her shirt and fixing her skirt before pushing herself away from the couch, away from arms that reached for her.

"What's the matter?"

"Nothing." Parris wanted to throw something at him, to scream and rail like a ten-year-old.

She whirled away and moved to the fireplace, staring at the flickering flames and hugging herself as a cool breeze blew in through the French doors.

She heard him get up. Heard him walk toward her. She couldn't face him until she had her emotions under better control.

He came up behind her. Parris tensed in anticipation of his touch. Perhaps he would wrap his arms around her waist and pull her back against his chest, and if he should, she would be lost. But he did not touch her, and she knew both relief and disappointment.

"You're angry."

"I'm not."

"Is it because—"

"No." Then, because she wanted to lash out, she said, "That meant nothing to me. Less than nothing."

He clasped her shoulders roughly and swung her around to face him. He looked furious, a muscle working in his jaw. "Don't lie to me. You loved it, moaned for it, so don't tell me it meant nothing to you!"

She tried to jerk away from him. "Leave me alone!"

"Look at my chest, damn you! Those are your marks, your claws raking into my flesh as you writhed in my lap, begging me for more."

"Stop it!" Parris wanted to clap her hands over her ears to keep from hearing the truth. Once more, she had lost herself in him. Would she lose him again, now? Would he walk away and leave her with more haunting memories?

Parris closed her eyes as a lone tear rolled down her cheek. "I can't go on like this," she whispered.

He cupped her chin and lifted her face to his. "Jesus, don't cry."

"I can't . . ." She shook her head. "I just can't do it anymore." Her voice choked with emotion.

He tried to pull her into his arms, wanting to comfort her, but she resisted. She wasn't sorry for the tears. They seemed inevitable, like this moment.

Her true sorrow was for all the time she had lost living in the past, all the years she had spent loving this man, mired in a fantasy that existed only in her mind.

She took a step back, a sob welling up in her throat, and then shoved past him, racing out through the French doors.

She could hear Dominick's booming voice calling after her, but she kept going, the black night swallowing her. She didn't know where she was running to. She only knew that she had to get away.

For a moment, Dominick thought about letting her go, knowing he had pushed her too far, gone way beyond what he had intended.

But Christ, all his good intentions had flown out the window the second she laid her hands on him and he stared into those riveting blue eyes. He had seen desire smoldering there and knew it was for him, all for him.

Parris had never looked at him like that before, and he could no longer wait to kiss her, to hold her, and do all the things he had dreamed of during their years apart.

He had waited so long, denied his feelings, pushed them down until he had thought he had conquered them. But as soon as he had seen her at the ball, he knew he was still hopelessly ensnared. He couldn't let her go. This madness had to end—no matter the outcome.

He took off after her, cursing himself for waiting even a moment, as the night nearly eclipsed her small, fleeing form. Were it not for the whiteness of her blouse, he would have never spotted her.

In her wild flight she had lost the blonde wig; it and the mask lay like cast off memories on the ground beside his front gate, leaving her long banner of blue-black hair to fly out behind her.

Like a frightened animal, she darted a glance over her shoulder and saw him gaining on her, her legs beginning to tire.

Then, suddenly, in her haste to be free of his pursuit, she veered left . . . out into the middle of the street. The square was still as death, except for the thunderous clatter of a single hackney barreling down the road.

Dominick blasted out a warning; saw Parris glance up as the hackney bore down on her. The scream she let out pierced him to his very soul as he threw every ounce of strength he possessed into lunging across the distance that separated them, grabbing her around the waist and sending them both tumbling toward the curb. He tried to cushion her blow with his body, rolling so that she ended up on top of him.

They were both breathing hard, her hair in wild disarray, wrapping them in an isolated world, separated from the people who now slept, content and blissfully unaware of the turmoil existing outside their doors.

Dominick gazed up into Parris's turbulent eyes, saw the sheen of her tears, and felt all his anger at her reckless behavior boil to the surface.

"You little idiot!" He grabbed her upper arms tightly. She winced and he recognized a certain savage satisfaction, wanting her to feel the same pain he was feeling. "You could have been killed. God damn it, Parris!"

Dominick felt her entire body grow still, knowing she had realized he'd called her by her real name. Now it was out in the open, and they would have to deal with what had just transpired between them—and what he still wanted from her now, and every day to come.

Her eyes widened and her face blanched. Her gaze darted to her hair, now fully revealed and pooling on his chest. Dominick knew she was thinking that the loss of her wig had been what had given her away.

He wanted to tell her the truth, that he had known her identity all along, but she had too much to deal with just then. And perhaps he didn't want to face her reaction to his revelation yet.

"Dominick . . ." His name came out a low, desperate plea, for what, he didn't know. Perhaps as penance for her deception? Who was he to cast stones? He, too, had been dishonest, using her disguise to his advantage to get closer to her, threatening the exposure of Lady Scruples should she not comply. What choice had he given her, really?

"We need to talk," he told her sternly.

She bowed her head, refusing to look at him. "What is there to say?" Her voice was flat, emotionless.

"Damn it, Parris. You know damn well what we have to talk about—what just happened between us. You don't think I can simply forget it, do you?"

"I wish you would." She spoke barely above a whisper. "I wish it had never happened."

Each word was like a knife blade sinking into his chest. He wanted to hold her close, to wipe away the tears brimming in her eyes, tears that threatened to make him leave off questioning her, to let it go for another hour, another day.

But he had been skirting what lay between them for years. Now it was time to get everything out in the open, to steel himself against those tears and that look of despair etched on her face.

"Get up, Parris." His abrupt command made her flinch.

Obediently, she eased off him, and Dominick hated the fact that simply having her on top of him, her breasts crushed against his chest, her silky hair skimming his still-heated flesh, had aroused him, had him gnashing his teeth with the desire to ruck up her skirts and take her against the tree she now stood in front of.

Wordlessly, he took her by the hand and led her across the street. He felt incapable of speech, and knew it was best not to look at her. He would only lose his resolve.

"Dominick," she pleaded, trying to draw him to a stop.

He didn't respond, didn't loosen his hold, even when she begged him to let her go.

He would not allow her to escape that easily.

Fourteen

*It is well to observe the force and
virtue and consequence of discoveries.*

—Francis Bacon

Dominick hauled Parris through the French doors and blocked her path when she attempted to get around him. His gaze locked with hers as he turned the key in the bolt, bringing home his determination to finish what they had begun, to know her feelings for him, come what may.

"Sit down," he said in a tone that brooked no argument, his blood running hot with equal parts anger and desire.

A single smudge of dirt marred one of her smooth cheeks, and it was all he could do not to brush it away, and then follow his thumb with his mouth.

His gaze trailed down her body, and his simmering sexual hunger slammed into him like an iron fist. Her nipples strained against the light fabric of her blouse, the right shoulder sustaining a rip that left the material dangling, nearly exposing her breast to his lustful gaze.

She lifted a shaky hand to the spot and clutched the torn material between her fingers, so tightly that her knuckles shone white.

He met her eyes again. "Sit, Parris. Don't make me tell you again."

Her eyes sparked defiantly. Good—she was showing some fight. That was what he wanted, not the Parris who stared at him with anguish. She could make him lose focus, and he couldn't let that happen.

Stiffly, she moved to the couch, taking up the position he had so recently vacated, bringing back visions of her straddling his lap, those pert, pink-tipped nipples thrust forward, begging for his mouth, sweet little moans issuing from her lips as he suckled the tight buds.

Dominick balled his hands into fists and abruptly turned away from her, striding to the liquor cabinet, needing a stiff belt of whiskey to help him through whatever revelations the next few minutes might bring.

He poured a draught, drained the contents, and then refilled his glass before he felt able to face Parris rationally.

She hadn't moved from her spot, and she wouldn't look at him. He didn't know where to begin. There was so much he wanted to say to her, eight years' worth of her life he had missed, and things about his own life he wanted to share.

And yet, only one word issued from his mouth. "Why?"

Slowly, she turned to look at him, her eyes pools of despair, and Dominick wanted to beat himself. He had pushed her too fast, and now he had pushed her away.

She opened her mouth, and then glanced down at her hands, responding softly, "I didn't mean for you to ever find out."

God, just the thought that she had no intention of telling him the truth restored his anger. What had he ever done to earn such distrust?

You left her.

The possibility that he could have truly lost her cauterized his soul. He had meant to hold his ground, remain at a safe distance, and yet he came to stand in front of her, forcing her to meet his eyes or risk discovering the simmering volatility inside him.

She trembled before him, and Dominick put the drink to his lips, needing to refortify himself. But instead of tossing back the remaining liquor, he paused, and then dropped his arm and pressed the glass into her hand. "Drink that. It'll take away the chill."

She looked at him another moment, then wrapped both her hands around the tumbler and hesitantly put the drink to her lips. She sipped slowly but steadily.

When she had finished, he took the glass from her. She flinched when his fingers brushed hers, making him want to shake her and ask her what he had done to cause her to be so wary of him, when only a short while ago she had moaned his name in ecstasy, holding his hand while he stroked the fevered peak between her downy curls.

He hunkered down in front of her, unaware that his shirt was still undone, or that the serpent on his chest fascinated and frightened her, as if beckoning her closer and simultaneously warning her away.

"Parris, talk to me."

She shook her head and whispered, "I can't."

"Why? You could always talk to me when you were a little girl. Nothing's changed. I'm still here for you."

"No." Tears clogged throat. "Everything's changed. Don't you see? It changed a long time ago. I'm not a little girl anymore."

"I know that, Parris. Don't you think I see it? You're a beautiful, desirable woman, and what happened here—"

She touched a finger to his lips. "What happened here was my fault. I deceived you. I thought I wasn't hurting anybody, but everything got away from me. When you kissed me at the tavern, I . . . I couldn't bring myself to tell you the truth. I've wanted you to kiss me for so long."

Her simple honesty made him ache, made him want to howl like some lovesick schoolboy. She had longed for his touch as much as he had craved hers.

"Parris, I've always cared about you, don't you know that?"

"As a pesky child who lived next door."

"No, it was more than that. Much more."

She lifted her wounded gaze to his. "Really?"

He smiled gently at her and cupped her cheek. "Really. But, Jesus, there were days when I had wished I could still see you as the young girl who used to chase after me and drive me mad with questions. I didn't want to see that you had grown up, that men would be looking at you. Even Frederick started to pay attention to you, and Christ, I was jealous as hell."

Tentatively, she returned his smile. "You were?"

"Seething with it. You were my girl, and I wasn't letting Frederick have you, even if he would have lowered his standards and married a baron's daughter."

Too late Dominick realized how his words had sounded. Her face clouded over with hurt, to be replaced a moment later by bitterness and pain.

"Is that why you made love to Annabelle and then left her? Because you were too good for her? And me?"

"God, no. That isn't—"

She shoved at his shoulders, trying to push him away. When he wouldn't budge, she began to punch at him until he had to shackle her wrists to her side.

"Stop it, Parris."

"Leave me alone!"

"My words came out wrong."

"You never thought any of us were good enough for the precious Carlisles! You're just like your father."

"That's not true, damn it! You know me better than that!" Dominick saw her wince as his grip tightened on her wrists, her comment slicing him to the very marrow of his bones.

Scalding tears rolled down her cheeks. "I don't know you anymore! You left me when I needed you so desperately." A choked sob broke from her lips. "You left me . . . and I loved you so much I wanted to die."

Her confession burned a hole in Dominick's heart. He released her wrists and gathered her into his arms. She struggled, but it was brief, her fight spent as she wept against his shoulder, each sob of anguish slicing into his gut like a razor.

He stroked her hair until she quieted, then he murmured, "I'm sorry I hurt you. I was confused."

She eased back and stared up at him, her eyes luminous from her tears. "Because of your feelings for Annabelle?"

"Because of what I let happen." He had allowed desire to take control of his better judgement, much as he had tonight, and the outcome had been disastrous. "I tried to do right by Annabelle, but I was just another trophy to her. She never wanted me. She wanted Frederick."

"What?"

"I don't know that I can completely blame her. Frederick would inherit the dukedom. I was just a second son."

"No." Parris shook her head. "She was devastated when you left."

"That had nothing to do with me. Frederick didn't want her." He paused and then added, "I found them in bed together the night of our engagement."

Her eyes widened with shock. "I . . . I never knew. She said that she found you . . ."

"With another woman?"

"Yes," Parris whispered.

"Damn her," he bit out. "I should have known she would say something like that."

"Did you . . ." She stopped abruptly, her gaze dropping from his, and Dominick braced himself, waiting to hear her ask him again about Annabelle, what it had been like making love to her sister, if he had enjoyed it, if he wanted to be with her again.

He couldn't deny her if she wanted answers. That onetime mistake would dog him the rest of his life. A single night of passion with the wrong woman had cost him a lifetime of passion with the right one.

"Did I what?"

She hesitated, and then quietly asked, "Did you ever care for me?"

Not until he had left, had he realized just how much Parris meant to him. She had been an integral part of his life and he had felt incomplete without her.

"Yes. I cared for you. A great deal, in fact."

"And now?"

"Nothing has changed."

Again, she could not meet his eyes. "What just happened . . ."

"Was beautiful." And just the thought of it made desire flare to life again, a need only this vibrant, headstrong woman could assuage.

The devil on his shoulder prodded him, an internal

battle waged that he could not hope to win, forcing him to say, "I want you again."

"You do?"

"I burn with it." He captured her gaze. "Tell me no, Parris. Push me away."

"I can't. I want you, too."

"You have to be the one to stop this. I'm not strong enough to walk away. Jesus, I wish I was."

"Don't leave me alone again."

Seeming shy, and heartbreakingly vulnerable, she slid forward on the couch, spreading her thighs around his hips, her skirt bunching up in her lap, her sweet innocence seducing him, setting his body on fire.

She was a temptress, a siren luring him to the rocks where he would shatter into a million pieces the moment she laid her hands on him.

"I've waited for you for so long," she whispered. "Touch me."

"Parris . . ." Dominick's throat went dry, his body rigid with the control he was trying to exert over himself.

When she took his hands from where they were fisted in the material of her skirt and placed them over her breasts, her taut nipples pressing against his palms, Dominick knew he was lost, utterly and completely lost.

His self-preservation in ashes around him, he growled and massaged the rigid peaks until she moaned. Then he cupped her buttocks, pulling her tight against the erection straining the buttons of his trousers.

She tossed back her head as his mouth slid along the sleek column of her throat, his thumbs teasing her nipples and then gently plucking at them, feeling them grow even harder and fuller.

When he could take no more, he yanked down her blouse and laved one swollen tip, then the other, before drawing the tight point into his mouth.

She panted and ground her hips against his. In the next instant, she was on her back on the couch, one leg hooked over the top.

He wanted to take things slowly, but he had waited too long for her. He pushed her skirts up to her waist and tore her pantalets off, feeling like a man possessed when he saw the ripe beauty of her sex, pink and moist and waiting for his mouth.

Sinking down between her thighs, he flicked her clitoris with the tip of his tongue and she arched up, crying out his name, her hands gripping his head as he pushed tighter against her, taking the heated pearl into his mouth and sucking as his hands cupped her breasts and teased her nipples.

Then he stroked the tip of his forefinger over her tender peaks, matching the rhythm with his tongue on her throbbing pulse point until he felt her entire body tighten and then convulse.

His hunger for her raged through his blood, searing his very skin. He gave her only a moment to recover before settling himself between her thighs, needing to tell her with his body what he felt in his heart. To possess her, to make her his own, as he had fantasized about doing since the moment he had laid eyes on her in the Beechams' ballroom.

Some small part of his brain told him that he was going too fast, that he should simply pleasure her and leave it at that, that taking her innocence was wrong.

But he knew that he was ready to go to the next step, to settle down and finally become the man his father had always wanted him to be.

He wanted Parris to bear his children, to bless him with at least one gamine-faced little girl who would love to fish and drive him to the brink of distraction with her maddening behavior, just as her mother had.

Dominick looked down into Parris's passion-glazed eyes as he spread her thighs wider and unbuttoned his breeches. "If you don't want this, Parris . . ."

She combed her fingers through his hair and breathed, "I will always want this . . . and you."

Her words filled every aching place inside him as the last vestige of rationality blew away, leaving only a solitary shred of sense that warned him to take things slowly, not to frighten her.

She tugged her bottom lip between her teeth to keep from moaning as he slid his rock-hard shaft along her cleft, rubbing over her moist, hot peak, wanting to bring her to a fevered pitch again, to feel her climax around him when he entered her.

She closed her eyes and released her bottom lip, allowing an erotic sigh to whisper forth. Dominick caught the sound with his mouth, lips slanting across lips, sweat beginning to break out on his body as she squirmed beneath him, the tight points of her nipples teasing his chest as he held his weight on his arms.

She moved her hips in opposing friction to his, groaning when he would purposely slow down to prolong the building fever, wanting her release to be long and deep, as deep as he ached to go inside her.

The thought made him half crazy with desire as he increased his pace and dipped his chest lower, so her nipples would make better contact to increase her pleasure.

He heard her whimpers, felt her writhe beneath him, and his last ounce of control snapped. At her first convulsion, he thrust into her waiting warmth.

Her muscles tightened around him like a glove, yet all he could think, for the first few moments that he was deep inside her, was that she was not a virgin.

The realization was a blow to him. He had no right to expect her to still be pure, no right to expect anything from her, yet he did—making the truth all the worse, because he was the man who loved her.

Who had she been with? That bloody bastard James? Had he compromised her and then left her at the altar? Dominick had never felt such a need to kill a man.

"Dominick?"

He shook the haze of anger from his eyes and found Parris staring up at him, concern mixed with pleasure in that deep blue gaze.

Christ, he shouldn't be angry with her, and yet he was. Damn it! Why couldn't it have been him? Why couldn't she have waited? Why did he believe, even for a moment, that she should have?

He said nothing to her. Instead he took her hands and raised them above her head, any intention of going slow burned from his brain after his discovery.

He clamped his mouth to hers and thrust into her. He wanted to prove she belonged to him now, but he forced himself to slow down and bring her to climax once more before finding his own release.

But even then, his anger at himself, at her, did not abate. Something had torn inside him, and as he eased out of her, he knew he had to have her again.

He wanted to imprint the memory of this moment, of his full and total possession of her body, on her brain, to obliterate whatever man—or men—had come before him.

He snaked his arm behind her back and sat her up. Then he turned her over so that she was on her hands and knees. Heedless of her questioning voice, he grabbed hold of her hips and slid into her again, felt her instantly clench his shaft, any words or protests dying on her lips as he stroked in and out of her.

He reached around, separated her moist folds, and massaged her. She cried out, panting his name, and he wanted to keep hearing her say it as he rocked inside her until her sweet warmth poured over him again and he found his own release, thinking about the consequences of his madness only after it was too late.

He eased out of her, noted her slight flinch, and felt disgusted with himself. He stood, needing to put some distance between them in the hopes of finding a measure of sanity.

He fixed his trousers and watched as Parris turned around, her body flushed with her pleasure, her hair a silken jumble around her face, the long length cascading over her shoulders and partially covering her breasts, giving him a tantalizing glimpse of her nipples through the dark veil.

She looked at him and he knew she was waiting for him to speak, but he felt too volatile. He caught the pain in her eyes before she forced her gaze away, her hands trembling as she righted her blouse and skirts, her torn undergarments, lying on the ground, a testament to his frenzy. She stared at them, her hands clutching the edge of the couch.

Say something, damn you! his conscience shouted. *Talk to her. Tell her how you feel.*

But he couldn't. Not then. He needed time to think, to sort out the emotions running rampant through him.

"I'll have Benson take you home."

Mutely, she nodded, and less than ten minutes later, Dominick watched the coach rumble away from the curb, Parris's pale face haunting him long after she was gone.

Fifteen

❧

The desire of the moth for the star,
Of the night for the morrow,
The devotion to something afar,
From the sphere of our sorrow.

—Percy Bysshe Shelley

Parris was glad for the cover of darkness that cloaked her, that hid her shame and despair as she quietly let herself into the town house on Park Lane through the servants' entrance.

She leaned back against the door and closed her eyes, absorbing the sounds of the house, seeking a balm for her wounded heart and damaged pride, but her thoughts would not release her. The too-recent memories of Dominick's lovemaking thwarted her attempts to find her balance and attain some semblance of peace.

She could smell him on her skin, feel his mouth on her breasts, his hands probing between her thighs, the thick ridge of his shaft entering her, filling her, bringing her fantasies to life.

How could she ever face him again, knowing what

they had done together? How intimately he had touched her, how she writhed and panted beneath his expert touch, begging for more?

She pressed a fisted hand to her midsection, seeking to hold back the sob welling inside her at all that she had gained and then lost.

Why had she allowed things to go so far? She should have listened to herself and stayed away. Now he knew what she had done, how she had deceived him.

She had seen the look in his eyes after he had made love to her. He had regretted his actions. His need for completion had eclipsed common sense and he had done the unthinkable with her, and he could not forgive himself.

Parris knew too well about acting rashly. Her life had been fraught with impulsive behavior, always teetering on the very edge of trouble. She had hoped that she had grown out of such antics, but after tonight, it was clear she had not changed.

She dug her fists deeper into her stomach, remembering how she told Dominick that she had loved him—and how he had not said the words back to her. Not tonight, and not when she was sixteen. She had given him the chance, had allowed him past her defenses, only to find her feelings rejected once more.

She had become the kind of woman Lady Scruples could not tolerate, allowing that side of herself to drift to the background since Dominick's return.

He had laughingly implied that Lady Scruples was a

bitter woman out to crucify men because she had no one in her life to love, or who loved her.

Parris had not allowed his comments to penetrate, but now they seemed insidious, prodding her, making her look deep inside herself to seek the truth.

Could she have become bitter? Resentful? Could that really be the reason Lady Scruples had come to life, and why she had faded away once Dominick returned?

She didn't want to believe it, because to do so nullified everything she had come to know as real and worthwhile, making her a fraud.

A sob broke from her lips as her entire world splintered into pieces around her, and there was nothing she could do to stop it; no way to go back and erect the barriers, or save the walls of the life she had known from crumbling.

She pushed away from the door, her feet leaden as she made her way through the kitchen and out into the hall, moving by rote toward her bedroom.

As she headed up the main staircase, something caught her eye. Her breath locked in her throat as a shadowy figure dashed across the top of the landing and disappeared around the banister.

Someone was sneaking through the house!

Parris pressed back against the wall, trying to catch her breath, her heart hammering away as a hundred thoughts tumbled one on top of the next through her mind.

Had she come upon a burglar in the act of robbery?

Had he seen her? Was he up there in the dark, waiting to accost her? Or did he have something far more sinister in mind than mere thievery?

She glanced toward the front door, but knew she could never leave her family in jeopardy. The children were up there, as well as Gwen, Annabelle, and her mother.

Swallowing her fear, Parris kept her gaze riveted to the landing as she grabbed the nearest object to her, a chunky silver candleholder, and proceeded cautiously up the stairs. Her heart was beating so loudly, she thought the entire household must hear it.

Cresting the top of the stairs, her eyes scanned the pitch-black corridor. All the sconces had burnt themselves down and only the faint smell of candle wax lingered in the air.

A creaking floorboard sounded behind her. She whirled around and raised the candleholder above her head, an aborted scream bursting from her lips as the figure moved out of the shadows toward her.

"Parris, it's me!"

Her heart in her throat, Parris rasped, "Gwen?" The darkness peeled away, revealing her cousin's pale countenance. "My God, what are you doing? You scared me half to death."

"Imagine how I felt," Gwen replied in a hushed voice. "I thought I was all alone, and then I saw a person at the bottom of the stairs when I knew everyone was in bed—or should be, at least."

Almost simultaneously, they noticed that neither of them was wearing nightclothes.

"Where have you been?" Parris asked, surprised to see that Gwen was also dressed in her barmaid outfit.

"I could ask you the same question." Gwen raised an eyebrow as her gaze skimmed over Parris's garb.

Parris sighed. "I guess we are both caught."

"I believe so."

A faint noise sounded at the end of the hallway, bringing their gazes in that direction. Gwen said, "I think we should get out of this hallway before someone discovers our nocturnal activities."

Parris nodded and they headed down the corridor, slipping soundlessly into Parris's room, where they breathed sighs of relief.

Parris lit the oil lamp on the table next to her door while Gwen sank down onto the edge of the bed. Warm, golden light banished the darkness.

"Good Lord, Parris!" her cousin gasped. "What has happened to you?"

Parris caught sight of her reflection in the mirror and saw that her blouse was partially ripped, her skirt sporting a tear at the hem, and her hair a riotous mess around her face.

Gwen pushed away from the bed, concern stamped on her features as she came to stand in front of Parris. "Who did this to you?"

"No one did it to me. I . . ." How to explain that she had nearly gotten herself killed dashing in front of a hackney in her wild flight from Dominick? "I was clumsy, that's all."

"Why don't I believe you?"

"It's the truth." But Parris could not quite meet her cousin's eyes.

Gwen took Parris's hands in hers. "Why won't you confide in me? What have I ever done to make you distrust me so?"

"It's not that I distrust you. It's me. I . . . I have done things I'm not proud of, and I don't want you hating me, too."

"Too? Who could possibly hate you?"

Parris hesitated, and then replied in a trembling voice, "Dominick."

"Dominick?" Gwen stared at her in confusion. "I don't understand. Why would he possibly hate you?"

Parris realized there was no longer any reason to keep her secrets. What good had they done her? "I've been dishonest with him."

"He discovered you were not a barmaid, I presume?"

Parris nodded, unable to confess the rest of her deception, though it was there on her tongue.

"That doesn't surprise me," Gwen remarked. "The man is too clever to be fooled for long. So is that where you were tonight? With Dominick?"

"Yes."

"Did you make love to him?"

Parris opened her mouth and just as quickly shut it, wondering why she was startled by the question. Her cousin had always been astute and never hesistated to say what was on her mind.

With a sigh, Parris confessed, "Yes." Then to further her shame, she added, "Twice."

Instead of being shocked, Gwen actually smiled. "Oh, Parris, that's wonderful! I knew you loved him, and that he loved you."

Her cousin's words pierced her, and Parris eased her hands from Gwen's grip. "Dominick doesn't love me."

"Oh, but you're wrong! I've seen the way he watches you. His gaze devours you whenever you're not looking. And I heard from Mary that 'Uncle Dominick looked madder than a stirred-up hornet's nest' when he saw you and James together. That, my dear, foolish cousin, does not sound like the actions of a man who isn't madly in love with you."

Parris had never in her life been prone to weeping, but tonight she could not seem to stop. She covered her face with her hands.

"Oh, Parris." Her cousin sounded anguished. "Come with me." Gwen led her over to the bed and they sat side by side. "Please tell me what's happened."

The tears flowed in earnest now and Parris could no longer hold back the floodtide of emotions. "He hates me, Gwen. He thought . . . that I . . . was the barmaid, and he . . . he . . ."

"Kissed you?"

Parris nodded weakly. "Then he found out the truth and things went too far."

"If he didn't want you, he could have stopped, Parris."

"No, it was all my fault. I . . . excited him."

"And that's a bad thing?"

"Yes. Because everything was based on a lie. I could

have told him who I was so many times and yet I said nothing—just as I did that night eight years ago." The words were out of Parris's mouth before she could stop them.

Now Gwen looked stunned. "Are you saying that you and Dominick . . . ?"

Parris looked down at her hands. "Yes. I loved him so much, but he didn't love me back. I should have let him go, but I couldn't. He was gone for so long that last time, after he left for Cambridge, that I thought he was never coming home. Then he did, and I just wanted to have something of him before he was gone again—perhaps not to return this time.

"His parents were holding their yearly costume gala. So I dressed up like a courtier, with a mask and powdered wig and I . . . I seduced him in his parents' garden. Just like I seduced him tonight.

"All these years I've been angry with him, but he never deceived me the way I did him. He never led me to believe there would ever be more between us than friendship. He wanted Annabelle, not me. Then the engagement was called off . . . and he left."

"And you never told him it was you that night in the garden, did you?

Parris shook her head. "I intended to, but then . . . there was really no point anymore. I never thought I would repeat the same mistake. But I did tonight."

"Are you sure you're not imagining how bad things are? Dominick had just made love to you. Perhaps he was suffering from the same confusion you're feeling."

"You should have seen the look in his eyes. They were cold."

Gwen wrapped her arms around Parris's shoulders. "Men are fickle creatures, cousin. Sometimes it takes them a bit longer to see what's right in front of their noses."

"I'm living a lie, Gwen. All this time that I've played the role of Lady Scruples—and here I seduced Dominick! Not once, but twice. Had a man used these tactics, we would have been outraged."

"The gentlemen—and I use that term loosely—that we set out to teach a lesson deserve exactly what they get."

"Even Lord Stratford?"

Gwen stiffened at the mention of the earl. "Most especially him. The lout." Parris could see she had brought up a sore subject. "How dare he turn out to be a contradiction! The man should be flogged, leading a female to believe he's a complete rake, and then when she wants him to show her just how wicked he is, he turns saintly and talks about being married first! Even when she has come to his home for the express purpose of being seduced!"

For a full ten seconds, Parris could only stare at her cousin. When words finally came, she said incredulously, "You went to Jason Fielding's home to . . ."

"Make love to him, yes. But the horrible man refused me!" Gwen's indignant expression crumbled. "I thought he cared for me. But he wouldn't . . . you know."

Parris wanted to shake her cousin. "Of course he cares for you, Gwen. He asked you to marry him! Now who's being ridiculous?"

"I would not marry him if he was the last man on the face of the earth," her cousin stated vehemently, looking utterly miserable. "I bet he never hesitated to take any of his other women to bed! Well, if he doesn't desire me enough to make love to me, then I . . . I don't want him." The lie was emblazoned on Gwen's face; clearly her cousin did not intend to be rational about the subject.

Parris sighed. "It seems neither of us have fared well this evening."

Gwen nodded and dabbed at her eyes. "True, but I suspect that sap-headed duke of yours will come to his senses by the morning. He's probably just in shock. God forbid a woman should go after what she wants. Men just fall all to pieces."

Sixteen

‿‿‿✆✆‿‿‿

The unfathomable deep
Forest where all must lose
Their way, however straight,
Or winding, soon or late.

—Edward Thomas

Dominick didn't go to see Parris the next day, or even the day after that.

Instead he drank steadily, alternately hissing at bloody Hastings for intruding on his binge, or cursing his own stupidity for ever leaving Parris in the first place and allowing her to fall victim to some unscrupulous bastard who took her virginity and then walked away from her.

Was it that benighted ex-fiancé? Dominick wondered for the seven hundredth time. Had he been the one to get the gift that should have been Dominick's? To stroke inside that tight valley, hear Parris's sweet moans, and know he had been the first?

Christ, why did it even matter? He loved her to the point of obsession, and he was trapped inside that hazy realm where the rest of the world ceased to exist.

Hence, his bender to the jagged edge of no return.

It was his fault. Had he not left her, not run away from his feelings, she would have been his. All his life, he had stupidly allowed himself to believe that Parris would always belong to him. Perhaps he had truly thought she would wait for him to come around, to pull his head out of the sand and stop fighting.

Did she love him still?

After what they had shared, the way she had been in his arms, he would have said yes. She had given herself so freely, so passionately.

Insane.

All of it. Him. Her. The endless whirlwind of love. It was enough to make a man want to plunge headfirst into a vat of whiskey and let the liquor be absorbed through every pore until he was insensate.

"Christ, you look how I feel."

Dominick's head wasn't quite steady as he elevated his gaze from the scotch bottle in his hands to the person framed in the threshold. Bloody Stratford. Behind him stood an antsy-looking Hastings.

"I told him you were not receiving, Your Grace," the butler droned.

"And I told him to bugger off," Jason retorted, shooting Hastings a warning look before stalking into the room and heading straight for Dominick's favorite spot: the liquor cabinet.

"That will be all, Hastings," Dominick managed to utter. Getting rid of his butler would be easier than getting rid of Stratford.

"You heard the man," Jason shot over his shoulder. "Scuttle off."

With a disdainful sniff, Hastings reluctantly decamped.

His glass filled to the rim, Jason threw himself into the chair across from Dominick, slouching down, his legs tossed out in front of him, ankles crossed.

He lifted his tumbler and stared at it, muttering, "Women. The bane of a man's calm, orderly existence." He downed half the glass, grimaced, and then eyeballed Dominick. "So what's the matter with you, old man? Someone kill your dog?"

"I don't have a dog."

"I was speaking metaphorically, or figuratively— one of those, and don't be difficult. It's too early in the day for a brawl, and in my present state, I'm feeling greatly inclined to punch someone. Wouldn't mind planting you a facer on principle alone, seeing how my woes are all your fault anyway, thank you very bloody much."

"What the hell are you talking about? And why are you talking in the first place? Or even here, for that matter? Can't you see I'm wallowing in a bout of self-pity and working on what may very well turn out to be my best hangover yet? Why must you ruin everything?"

Jason straightened in his chair. "What am I talking about? Had it not been for you and your 'Go after her, Stratford' when we were at the Wrack and Ruin, I would not have met the woman who is to be my future marchioness—whether she bloody well likes it or not—and who will henceforth lead me around by the nose, bear me a passel of screaming brats who will call me Papa—which I shall, no doubt, find most endearing, in the gruffest sort of way imaginable—and who will leave me not a single servant who will heed any of my demands, but rather defer to her ladyship instead.

"In short, I will be shackling myself to a female who will have me crawling around on my hands and knees for the rest of my days for the most minor of infractions, and turf me out of my own bedroom when I have displeased her—and I ain't too fond of the couch or sleeping alone, and will therefore drift about most pathetically until I have restored myself to my wife's good graces. And that, old man, I lay entirely on your doorstep. I hope you're happy. Sod."

Dominick stared at the man he had, for some unearthly reason, called a friend for seventeen years. "I think you've cracked. I haven't the first bloody idea what you're going on about."

"The sweet little barmaid at the tavern—the blonde, or shall I say the fake blonde? I see you're deducing my meaning at last."

Now it was Dominick's turn to straighten in his chair. "What are you saying?"

"I'm saying that I love the girl, and now I'll have to be bloody respectable. Give up all my mistresses. Lost my taste for them, anyway. Girl's tainted me for anyone else. Have to put a ring on her finger, even if she fights me all the way to the altar, which she will, I tell you. Never met a more stubborn bit of female pulchritude in my entire illustrious life." He shook his head, clearly disgusted with himself.

Slowly, Dominick rose from the chair, his insides churning with the thought of Stratford and Parris. Could Jason be the man Parris lost her virginity to? Dominick distinctly remembered Stratford telling him that he had his eye on the blonde that night in the tavern. Certainly Parris wouldn't . . . not with Jason . . . not his best friend.

"I'll kill you," Dominick ground out, a red haze of anger descending over him.

"Excuse me, old boy?" Jason rose from his chair, the two men facing each other. "What did you say?"

"Stay the hell away from her," Dominick growled. "Or I swear by all that's holy, I'll be meeting you at Guilford Crossing at dawn."

"You're challenging me to a duel?"

"If you don't leave off seeing the woman I'm going to marry."

"That *you're* going to— Over my dead body!"

"That can be arranged."

"Good Christ, I can't bloody well believe it would come to this. Wanting to murder my best friend—and over a woman, no less."

"Never thought you were that noble, Stratford. Women have always been a sport to you. My advice is to keep it that way. Healthier for you."

"And you, old man. The girl wants me. Granted, she's being difficult about the whole thing. Wouldn't be a female if she didn't make some poor, hapless man insane. Nevertheless, I want her."

"Well, you can't have her."

"I *can* have her and I will, if I have to break both your legs to get her. Hell, and here I was acting like a gentleman when she tried to seduce me two nights ago—which was deuced hard to do, mind you."

"Seduce you?"

"Bloody amazing, I admit, and quite the most erotic thing that has ever happened to me. But I couldn't take her like that. Damn me, but I want her for more than just one night."

Dominick felt the veins in his neck throb and his hand clench with the distinct desire to put his fist through Stratford's face.

"*I* made love to her two nights ago." He pointed to a spot behind him. "On that very couch."

"The hell you say!" Jason took a threatening step forward, bringing them nose to nose. "She was with me until my coachman brought her home."

"You lie, old man. She was with me." Dominick thundered, "Hastings!"

Less than a heartbeat passed before Hastings, looking pale, poked his head in the door. "You bellowed, Your Grace?"

"Did Benson take a young woman home for me the other night?"

"He did, Your Grace."

"Straight home?" Stratford barked.

"I'm not sure."

"Get him here," Dominick commanded.

In short order, a confused-looking Benson, cap in hand, gingerly stepped into the room, assessing the two combatants, his Adam's apple bobbing convulsively. "Y' called for me, sir?"

"Yes, Benson. I want you to tell this buffoon here that you took my guest straight home the other night."

"That I did, Your Grace. Straight away. And if I may say so, sir, she didn't look none too well. Her face was all pale and it looked as if she had been cryin'."

That bit of information concerned Dominick. Why had Parris been crying? He had thought she'd appeared tired, more than anything else. It *was* rather late when she left and they had shared an evening of passion, along with some rather startling revelations.

"Did she say anything to you, Benson?"

"Only 'thank you,' sir. All quiet like, as if speakin' were too difficult. Watched her until she made it into her house safe and sound."

"Thank you, Benson. That will be all."

The man bobbed his head and departed, leaving Dominick to wonder why Parris was upset. True, he had not said much to her when she left.

He suspected he had looked rather forbidding, but he'd been tangled up in jealousy, a jealousy he hadn't known he possessed until he fell in love with Parris.

"Well, this makes absolutely no bloody sense," Stratford muttered sourly. "No bloody sense at all."

Suddenly it all made a great deal of sense to Dominick, and he nearly wanted to laugh with relief.

"What an ass you are, Stratford. You were with Lady Gwen."

"Don't you think I know who I was with?" Jason groused. "Even though the girl did try to keep her identity a secret with that horrible wig, covering up the most lush mahogany hair I've ever had the good fortune to see. Must say I'm delighted that the rest of her is completely real." His smile was wolfish, and all Dominick's anger deflated. "Who did you think I was with?"

"Parris."

"Miss Sutherland? Lord, man, why would you think I was with her?"

"Because she, too, was disguised. Though I recognized her from the start."

"Holy Christ, this is priceless." Jason shook his head and picked up his drink. "She was the other barmaid, was she?"

Dominick nodded.

"Unbelievable. What are the odds that we would end up with the two most willful females in all of England?"

"I've had more time to get used to the idea than you. I grew up with Parris." And whether she had succumbed to temptation no longer seemed important. She must have cared for the man; she wouldn't have given herself to him otherwise. That much Dominick was sure of.

But at the moment, all he cared about was that she no longer had any feelings for the man. Dominick would wipe whoever he was from her heart.

He had let her go once. He would not do so again.

But that didn't mean he had no intention of confronting the ex-fiancé. The man had some explaining to do. And when he was finished, Dominick would belt him in the jaw for hurting Parris, then thank him for getting the hell out of her life.

And now seemed as good a time as any.

Parris stared absently out one of windows lining the dining salon, watching a family of swallows settle into their nest in the old elm tree at the edge of the terrace, as the sky above faded from blue to black, signaling the end of another day with no word from Dominick.

On the table behind her arose the smells of her solitary supper, duck in apricot sauce, braised leeks, artichoke hearts, an endive salad, and fresh fruit. All uneaten. She had no appetite.

It had deserted her since that night with Dominick.

For two days she'd remained in her bedroom, unable to sleep, to eat, refusing all visitors. Wanting simply to be alone. She pretended illness to keep everyone at bay.

Her maid had turned away Annabelle more than once. Parris suspected her sister was not coming to inquire about her well-being, but rather to taunt her about something, most likely Dominick, whose disinterest her sister had been seething about since the fair.

As though Parris's thoughts had conjured her up, Annabelle's mocking contralto voice sounded from the doorway. "Well, well, my darling sibling has overcome her illness and decided to join the rest of the world once more."

Reluctantly, Parris swiveled to face Annabelle. She was not up to a confrontation. "I was just leaving. I find I am without an appetite today, so I will bid you good night." Parris headed for the nearest exit, but her sister's next words stopped her cold.

"I imagine you wouldn't be hungry, after acting like a whore with Wakefield."

Had Annabelle hit her with a blunt object, Parris could not have reeled any more. Slowly, she turned. "What did you just say?"

"You heard me."

"Certainly I couldn't have heard you correctly, then."

"You did." Her sister's smile was no more than a baring of teeth. "I know all about your tryst with Dominick, going over to his home in the middle of the night and spreading your legs for him like a little tart."

Parris's hands balled into fists at her sides. "You'd best retract your words, Annabelle."

"Or what? Lay a finger on me and this entire household will know what a slut you are." Her sister closed the double doors leading to the hallway. "What will Mother think of her precious darling then? You have amply fulfilled Father's every prophesy about your outcome."

For some reason, that comment was more of a blow than Annabelle's others. "You know nothing about my relationship with Dominick."

"I know more than you think," her sister countered with a smirk. "The doors around here are not very thick."

Parris gaped at her sister. "You listened at my door?"

Without an ounce of remorse, Annabelle nodded. "Mary was ill, if you recall, and her whining kept me up half the night. For once, something worthwhile came out of having those mewling brats."

"What did you hear?"

"Everything. I know how you stole Dominick from me."

"I didn't steal him from you."

"You did! You hated the fact that he loved me. That he looked at me in a way he would never look at you. We used to laugh about how you would follow him around, gazing at him like some moonstruck calf when we were alone together."

"What are you implying?"

"God, are you that blind? Dominick and I were lovers long before he asked me to marry him. You don't really think he didn't have me first, did you? Oh, Lord—you did! How gullible can you be? Even now, you're just a replacement for me. It was always me he adored."

Parris's hands trembled. "I'm not a replacement!"

"You would like to think that, I'm sure. You always wanted to believe that Dominick belonged only to you. Well, I hate to disabuse you, sister dear, but he didn't. I enjoyed his hands on my body, his mouth on my most intimate places, before you even understood how a man could pleasure a woman."

Annabelle laughed, a hideous sound of loathing directed at Parris. "You know that little island in the center of Archer's Pond? I would make him take me out there just because I knew you loved it so much. There were times I saw you on the banks waiting for him, while he was making love to me."

"I don't believe you."

Annabelle's jaw tightened. "Well, believe it. And now I'm going to do to you what you did to me: steal Dominick."

"He doesn't want you, Annabelle! Whatever happened between the two of you is in the past. It's over."

"It isn't over!" Annabelle stormed across the salon, her face suffused with fury. "I will have him back."

"You won't!"

The slap was unexpected, sending Parris staggering back into the wall, holding her hand to her face and staring in shock at her sister.

"You're a fool," Annabelle hissed. "If he loved you, then where has he been for the past three days? Your grasping for a man who never wanted you has pushed him away."

"No." Parris shook her head, her cheek on fire.

"Yes. And in case you still hold out any false hope that what I'm saying isn't true, then know this: I was with him the very night he came to visit Mother. I licked every inch of the writhing serpent on his chest as he made love to me."

Seventeen

*This is the monstrosity of love,
that the will is infinite, and the
execution confined; that the desire is
boundless, and the act a slave to limit.*

—Shakespeare

The home of James Montgomery, Earl of Kerrick, was in Mayfair, on the very cusp of the fashionable district of London. Should the line of demarcation shift a scant block, the residence would be considered gravely unfashionable, which would quickly make Kerrick a social pariah should he not uproot posthaste to a more acceptable address.

As it was, the house was a nondescript redbrick, standing a mere two stories tall, with a short climb to the double-door entranceway.

As Dominick waited for someone to answer the summons of his pounding fist upon the door, he thought about Parris, of the feelings he had for her, and what Stratford, of all people, had forced him to see: that regardless of the howling of his stupid male pride and his wanting to be Parris's first lover, none of it made a damn bit of difference to his heart.

He had treated her poorly and he intended to make it up to her—as soon as he was finished wringing the truth from bloody Kerrick about why he had humiliated her.

Dominick raised his fist to pound again when the portal creaked open, allowing him a glimpse of a wizened old face. "May I help you, sir?" came the phlegm-ridden voice of the ancient butler.

"I'm here to see Kerrick. Is he in?"

"He is just taking his supper. If you would care to come back—"

"No, I wouldn't care to come back." Dominick shoved past the man and headed into the foyer.

Flustered, the butler scuttled after him. "This is most unseemly. If you will just—"

"Give him this." Dominick handed over his calling card.

The butler stared down at it and then back up at Dominick with wide, rheumy eyes. "My most sincere apologies, Your Grace. I shall fetch him at once. If you would be so kind to wait in the blue salon." With a shuffling gait, the man led Dominick to the room and then excused himself.

Dominick stared into the fireplace's cold grate, figuring he would be waiting half the day for Kerrick at the speed his butler moved.

He wondered if Parris was cursing him to hell. She had a great deal of pride, and he suspected it would take a concerted effort on his part to get back in her good graces. But he would do whatever was necessary.

He jerked slightly when a voice sounded behind him a few minutes later. He swung around to face the man he had come to see, and quite possibly take a swing at.

"Kerrick."

"Wakefield," the man returned with an equal amount of distaste. "To what do I owe this unexpected visit?"

"I think you know."

"I think I do. But I doubt you hied all the way over here so that I could tell you." He strode into the room then and headed toward the sideboard to pour a drink. "Care for anything?" he called over his shoulder.

"No."

"Suit yourself."

With Kerrick's back turned, Dominick regarded the man that Parris had nearly married, trying unsuccessfully not to think about what she had seen in him—his air of confidence, the self-assured way he held himself, the muscular body that proclaimed his fitness, the sculpted features and dark eyes, and the thick, black hair just long enough to defy convention. A rebel. Just like Parris.

All the jealousy Dominick had believed sufficiently tamped down when he had left his residence threatened to choke him. Just the image of Parris lying naked with this bastard made Dominick's jaw ache from the pressure of gritting his teeth.

He didn't know his fists were clenched until Kerrick turned around and drawled, "Want to hit me, do you?" before putting his drink to his lips, appearing monumentally unconcerned that Dominick had pushed his way into his home, intruded on his meal, and now looked as if he wanted to do him bodily injury.

With effort, Dominick forced himself to relax. "I'm giving you fair warning to stay away from Parris, Kerrick. She wants nothing more to do with you."

"She told you this, did she?"

"She didn't have to."

"I see. And how long were you gone, Wakefield? Seven, eight years? Bloody amazing, how you seem to still know what Parris wants after all this time."

"I've known her a hell of a lot longer than you."

"Things change, my friend. Parris is not the same little girl who followed you around and believed you were her hero, tarnished as you may be."

"And what the hell do you know about it?"

"A lot more than you think. Parris and I used to be very close."

"How close?"

"That's none of your concern. But know this, she is a woman now, one with wants and needs, and you don't know the first—"

Without a thought, Dominick shot across the room and grabbed Kerrick by his lapels, shoving him up against the sideboard, jealousy consuming him like nothing he had ever known before, obliterating the cool rationality with which he had fought in the army. Nothing had ever made him this blindingly angry.

"Remove your hands," Kerrick said in a measured tone, "and I might feel inclined to forgive your hot-headed behavior instead of putting a bullet through your heart tomorrow at dawn, as I realize that only a man desperately in love could act without a shred of sanity."

Blood was singing through Dominick's veins, his entire body throbbing with the need to do violence. He gnashed his teeth and eased his grip on Kerrick. With an insouciant manner that grated on Dominick's nerves, the man quaffed the remainder of this drink.

Stiffly, Dominick took a step back and demanded, "Why did you leave her?"

"Leave her?"

"You know damn well what I'm talking about. You were to be married. I want to know what you did to her. And why, if you care for her, did you run off on her?"

"Because I was a fool," he answered without hesitation, tension bracketing his mouth. "If I could go back and change everything, I would. I know she would have followed through and married me. But I also knew she would never feel for me the way I feel for her. I loved her."

Dominick winced at Kerrick's words. "And now?"

He shrugged. "I still care for her. I certainly wouldn't turn her away if she came back to me. But she won't come back. She loves someone else."

Everything inside Dominick froze. "Who?" Could there have been another man Parris had fallen in love with? But why was she no longer with him, then?

Kerrick shook his head, his expression grim as he looked Dominick dead in the eye. "Don't you know?"

"No, damn you! If I knew, would I be here?"

"Why *are* you here, exactly? I sense there is more to this visit than a simple reconnaissance mission to gauge the competition."

"You're not competition."

"Then why are you worried?"

"Have you two ever . . ."

"Made love?" A hint of a smile curled the corners of Kerrick's lips. "So that's what's bothering you so much? Don't want the question hanging over your head, do you?"

"If you took Parris's innocence, then you should have done the honorable thing instead of being a god-damned coward."

Now it was Kerrick's turn to step to Dominick, bringing them face-to-face yet again. "Think twice before you bring my honor into question, Wake-field."

The earl's jaw flexed as they squared off for another moment. Then he took a steadying breath, admitting, "I never touched her. Is that what you want to hear? But at this moment, I would like nothing better than to tell you I bedded Parris, if for no other reason than to have you take a swing at me, so I could happily bloody your face. But because of the affection I feel for her, and the fact that—for some godforsaken reason—she loves you, I will refrain."

"And how the hell do you know how she feels about me?"

"She told me quite a bit. Now that I've had time to ruminate on my relationship with her, I think I was a substitute for you."

"Well, she doesn't need a substitute anymore, so keep your distance."

Kerrick shook his head. "Christ, you really are belligerent, aren't you? No need to beat a dead horse, man. I understood your meaning the first go-around. As for my staying away, that will be Parris's decision. I won't interfere, but I won't turn her away if she needs me."

"She won't," Dominick snapped before heading for the door, anxious now to see Parris and set everything to rights.

On the threshold, Kerrick's words stopped him. "One word of advice before you go, Wakefield."

Sharply, Dominick turned to face him. "And what is that?"

"Keep your eyes open this time."

"What the hell is that supposed to mean?"

"The next time a mysterious woman comes to seduce you in a garden, perhaps you should wonder about her motives."

Less than a half hour later, Dominick was being ushered into the house on Park Lane, once more finding himself sequestered in another room, this time awaiting Parris.

From the strained look he had received from the butler, Dominick figured he would have a great deal of explaining to do. He was surprised Parris had not banned him from the house, which would have forced him to either hold his ground until she came down or stand outside on the pavement and shout his feeling for all of London to hear, which might very well be what he deserved.

God, he was a jackass. A stupid, ignorant, blind jackass. How could he not have known it was Parris he had made love to in that garden—masked or not?

He had never been able to put that sensuous, forbidden woman and Annabelle together. Annabelle had never possessed such passion, the kind that leaves a man feeling as if he had been ravished.

Images flooded Dominick, memories of those pert breasts, the pink tips, the breathy moans, even the way she had clutched his shoulders during her release.

All the same.

Why had she done it? Why had she given him the gift of her virginity and never told him? Never expected him to do the honorable thing afterward?

Why had she let him walk away?

Christ, he would have stayed—and happily. Parris understood him, knew him in a way no one else did. And to think of how rough he had been when he had made love to her on the couch, taking his anger out on her ... God, it didn't bear contemplation.

Hearing the rustle of skirts, Dominick swung around, expecting Parris and finding Annabelle instead.

"Your Grace," she demurred, dropping into a curtsy that, as usual, afforded him a view of her bosom, which moved Dominick not one damn bit. When she glanced up and noticed, anger sparked in her eyes.

"I'm here to see Parris," he said tersely, uncaring that his manner was less than polite. He wanted to see her, needed to see her. The longer he waited, the more desperate he became.

"That is what I've come to speak to you about." Annabelle closed the door behind her and then glided into the room as though making an entrance at a ball. An odd sensation settled in the pit of Dominick's belly, wondering what she was up to.

"Where is Parris?" he demanded when Annabelle came to stop in front of him, standing very close and glancing up at him with sea-green eyes that he had once thought guileless. He knew better now.

"She's gone."

"Gone? What are you talking about? Where did she go?"

"I'm not at liberty to say."

Dominick's jaw tightened. "What game is this?"

Her gaze widened with practiced innocence. "Game? How hurtful of you to say such a thing. It was not I who ran away, denouncing you with every breath and hoping never to see you again."

"Where did she go?"

"As I said, I have been sworn to secrecy by my sister, and I think it's best if you heed her wishes. She is most overwrought at the moment. She really wants nothing more to do with you. Who can blame her? You really are a wretch, Your Grace. Was ruining one Sutherland not enough for you?"

"No one ruined you but yourself," Dominick retorted. "It wasn't you that night in the garden. I know the truth now. I should wring your bloody neck."

With the acting capabilities of a true professional, Annabelle put a hand to her mouth and stared at him, aghast. "That's a lie. I lost my virginity to you that night."

"I don't know when you lost your virginity, but it sure as hell wasn't to me. Frederick, probably. You two seemed to be very well acquainted with each other the last time I saw you. You do remember that, don't you? You were on your knees." She lifted her hand to slap him and Dominick grabbed hold of her wrist. "I don't advise it."

"You're a hateful bastard," she hissed.

"And you're a vindictive bitch. To think I almost fell for your ploy. Your little stunt took away eight years of my life, damn you."

"Your life!" Her eyes hardened to chips of ice. "Who cares about your life! I had to marry the first man who came along, because your swine of a brother had taken my innocence and left me with no options."

"Perhaps had you kept your thighs closed, that wouldn't have happened."

She screeched and leapt to her feet. "You've lost Parris and it's just what you deserve for what you did to me!"

Dominick towered over her. "Where is she?"

"She told me everything, you know."

"Good. Then it's out in the open."

"Good?" Annabelle uttered in a strangled voice. "You have ruined my sister and you call that good!"

"I'm going to marry her."

Annabelle gasped, and for a full moment, she stared at him unblinkingly, her face leaching of color. "Marry her? You . . . you can't."

"I can and I will, if she'll have me."

A bubble of hysterical laughter burst from Annabelle's lips. "She won't want you. Not after what I've told her. I'll rot in hell before she becomes the next Duchess of Wakefield, when it should have been me!"

Dominick grabbed Annabelle's upper arms. "What did you say to her?"

She wore a strange smile. "I told her all about us."

"There was never any 'us,' Annabelle, and you damn well know it."

"Oh, but there was. You made love to me. You took my virginity—and for that, you owe me!"

With a strength born of hysteria, she wrenched her arms from his grip and lunged at him, her fingernails just missing his face. She came at him like a wild woman, her fists flailing, shrieking about making him pay.

Dominick didn't want to hurt her, so he waited for

an opening and then got behind her, locking his hands around her waist and pinning her arms to her sides.

"What did you tell Parris?"

She laughed again. "All about how you used to fuck me."

Dominick whirled her around to face him. "I never touched you!"

"Yes, you did. We were lovers for years. Then I got pregnant and you proposed, but you couldn't keep your cock in your pants. Parris knows it all now." Her smile was full of malice as she added, "And she knows Philip is your son."

Dominick pushed her away and staggered back as though struck by a physical blow. "You're insane."

"Don't call me that!" She lunged for a vase on a side table and hurled it at him. Dominick ducked and it sailed over his head, crashing against the door.

A moment later, the door opened. "Mama?"

Dominick swung around to find Philip standing on the threshold, looking scared and bewildered, his gaze moving from the broken glass at his feet—lilies scattered everywhere—and then glancing up at Dominick with frightened eyes.

"What's the matter with Mama?" he asked in a terror-stricken voice.

"This is your father, Philip!" Annabelle ranted in a shrill, half-crazed tone. "Your father, who left you because he didn't want you!"

"Shut up, Annabelle!" Dominick growled, grabbing for her, intending to subdue her. But she fled around the side of the couch, her eyes glazed with triumph.

"Philip," Dominick said as calmly as he could manage. "Find your grandmother and tell her to summon the doctor. Your mother is unwell."

"How dare you, you bastard!" Annabelle shrieked, snatching a marble paperweight off a bookshelf and hurling it at him.

The paperweight whistled past Dominick's ear and shattered one of the panes in the window behind him.

"My God!" a new voice cried. "What is going on here?" Dominick glimpsed the horrified expression on the baroness's face.

"He took advantage of me, Mother!" Annabelle accused wildly, pointing at Dominick. "He stole my innocence and now he has taken Parris's as well!"

The baroness shifted startled eyes his way. "Dominick? Is any of this true?"

"I just told you it was!" Annabelle screeched. "Why don't you ever believe me?"

"Annabelle, stop it! Get a hold of yourself!"

"He has to marry me, Mother. He has to! Philip is his son."

Her mother gasped, and clapped her hands over her grandson's ears, looking shocked. "My God, what has gotten into you, Annabelle?"

"He has ruined me, Mother! Ruined me!"

The children's nursemaid came rushing up then, and the baroness bade in an urgent tone, "Take Philip upstairs, and have Timmons fetch Doctor Reynolds immediately."

Matilda did as she was told, hustling Philip away.

"I never touched your daughter," Dominick asserted.

"Neither of them?"

"That I cannot claim."

"I see. And how do you feel about Parris?"

"I love her."

Annabelle screamed and flung a Limoges bowl at him. The bowl clipped his shoulder and shattered behind him. "She tricked you, seduced you, and yet you love her! That conniving little bitch!"

Swiftly, the baroness strode into the room, took her daughter by the arm, and slapped her. Annabelle gaped at her mother, stunned.

"I'm sorry, but I had to do that. You're acting hysterical, Annabelle. And I won't have you talking about your sister in such a despicable way."

"You have always taken her side over mine!"

"That is untrue."

"It isn't! You love her more than me. You always have! I hate you!" Annabelle hissed venomously, and with a cry of rage, she bolted from the room.

Her mother moved to the doorway and called for the butler. "Timmons, keep an eye on my daughter— and make sure she stays away from the children until she has calmed down."

"Yes, ma'am."

"Has the doctor been summoned?"

"Yes. And I have stressed the urgency of the situation."

"Thank you, Timmons." The butler nodded and dissolved from sight. With a weary sigh, the baroness faced Dominick. "I'm sorry for that outburst. I do not wish to make excuses for Annabelle's behavior, for it is reprehensible, but her mental state has steadily deteriorated since her husband left her."

"I understood him to be deceased."

"He is. Killed in an unfortunate stagecoach robbery, but his death came after he had left my daughter." She moved across the floor and took a seat on the settee, the strain around her eyes evident. "Come, sit beside me. We must talk."

Dominick glanced toward the door, thinking about Parris, wondering where she had gone to, and knowing a strong desire to find her.

"She's not here," the baroness said as if reading his thoughts.

Dominick moved to the settee and sat down. "I need to know where she's gone. Please."

"I do not think she wishes to see you."

Dominick raked a hand through his hair. "I don't blame her. I handled everything miserably."

"It would seem so. The question is, what have you done to make Parris leave? My daughter has never been one to run away from a problem before. You know this as well as I."

"I do." Parris's ability to brave the worst situations was one of the qualities he most admired in her. He seemed to be the only one she ran from.

"I despair, thinking about the heartache she must be suffering to compel her to leave her family. I am at a loss for what to do. The entire house seems possessed of some sort of madness. Even Gwen has been moping about in her room."

Dominick didn't think Gwen's moping was due to Parris as much as Jason, whom Dominick had left at his home, slouched in a chair, looking miserable.

"I just don't understand what is happening." The baroness pinned her silvery blue eyes on Dominick. "And I expect you to enlighten me on whatever role you may have played in my daughter's decision."

Where to begin? Their story went back a long way, far more than the few weeks it had taken Dominick to make a muck of whatever life he hoped for with Parris.

"I'm not proud of my actions," he said, finding it difficult to meet her eyes. "It seems I possess a certain aptitude for letting down the one person who means the most to me."

"Were you being honest before when you said you loved Parris?"

"I couldn't live without her," he confessed, the release of that long-held burden like a weight off his shoulders.

A slight smile played on the baroness's lips as she murmured, "I suspect the feeling is mutual."

"I didn't realize how much she meant to me until it was too late and I couldn't go back. After proposing to Annabelle, how could I ever have made Parris believe that I didn't love her sister?"

"You could have written to her, told her how you felt. I think the silence was worse than the crime."

"I did write . . . I just didn't send the letters." Except one, Dominick reflected. But he had been too much of a coward to sign it. Maybe if he had, Parris wouldn't have run away from him. "I need to speak to her. I want to make things right."

"Why don't you wait awhile? Perhaps when things have settled down, you'll both see the situation more clearly. "

"I've been waiting all my life for her. I beg you, don't make me wait any longer. Tell me where she is. We need to talk this out."

The baroness cast a sideways glance at him, looking uncertain. "She would be most unhappy with me should I confide to you her whereabouts."

"Please."

She hesitated another moment, and then sighed. "She went home. To Kent. Back to face her past, she said. In order to put it behind her forever."

Eighteen

Tears, idle tears, I know not what they mean,
Tears from the depth of some divine despair

—Alfred, Lord Tennyson

The bitterns had returned to Archer's Pond.

Parris sat in the grass watching the birds, the mottled brown plumage on their small heads dancing in the breeze as the mother bird guided her babies into the water, creating the barest ripple in the glasslike surface, while the father soared into the sky in search of food for his family.

Parris smiled as the nestlings followed their mother, carefully attending to how she did things and trying to learn from her example. The mother doted on her babies, preening them, nurturing them, and the sight warmed Parris's heart.

She was glad to see that the birds had returned. This was their sanctuary, their home. Just as it had always been hers. And she hoped, with her own return, that she would find the solace and peace of mind she sought.

She reclined against the fat trunk of the ancient oak tree whose thick limbs, laden with rich green leaves, shaded her from the afternoon sun, and dappled the ground around her with patterns of gold. A light breeze shirred the grass and ruffled the tall willows.

In another lifetime, she and Dominick had carved their names into the tree. The markings were still as sharp and defined today as they had been ten years ago when they had used his bait knife to etch them deeply into the wood, and when she, in her youth, had said that their friendship would last as long as the tree remained standing.

As the oak had stood for centuries, through storms and droughts and the old duke's plans to use the fallow fields for additional crops—which would have meant cutting down the tree and filling in the pond, only Dominick's fierce intervention keeping that from happening—Parris had never doubted the bond they shared would remain equally as strong.

But the tree had outlasted whatever they had once meant to each other.

The booming cry of the male bittern startled Parris, jerking her back to the moment. Back to the reasons she had left Gwen in the middle of her cousin's first Season, left without giving her mother much of an explanation as to why she had to go.

"I see the bitterns are still coming here."

Parris tensed at the familiar deep voice, her heart drumming erratically against her breast as she slowly turned her head up to the man who had caused her flight, whose handsome face and penetrating eyes would stay with her no matter how far she ran.

Dominick stood only a few feet from her, looking devastatingly handsome—and ruthlessly determined. The sun framed his big, muscular body in bas-relief, making him look like a dark angel come to earth to torment and tempt her.

"What are you doing here, Dominick?" For all her efforts, her words rang with hurt.

"I came for you."

He advanced a step and Parris pushed to her feet, putting her hand out as if to ward him off.

He stopped, a glint of anguish touching his eyes, though it could have been a trick of the light, a reflection off the water.

"I don't want you here," she told him with as much conviction as she could muster. "Please. Just leave."

As though he hadn't heard her, he took another step forward, and she took another step back. He leaned against the trunk of the tree, his arms folded over his chest, his tawny eyes never leaving her face.

"Do you remember the day we carved our names into this tree?"

Parris stared at him mutely.

"Your father had forbidden you from seeing me again," he went on, his voice a velvet rumble that made her shiver and hug herself. "He told you that if he ever found out you were spending time with me, he would beat you.

"That day, he discovered you had disobeyed him

and he caned your bare back until he raised welts. After searching for hours, I found you sitting up in this very tree. Dark was rapidly approaching, and I was frantic that I would not find you before night fell—and as the nights are black as pine tar around here, I feared you would be out here alone, and scared. Every horrible image my brain could conjure up ran through my head during those hours."

"I saw you," she said in a low voice, her body trembling. "You were running across the field, calling my name."

"I was out of my mind with worry. But you never made a sound, never let me know you were up here."

Parris bowed her head. "I . . . I didn't want you to know what my father did. I knew . . ." She stopped.

"That I would be furious. And you were right. I was."

She glanced up and met his piercing gaze. "But you kept it to yourself."

"For the time being, yes."

"Then you coaxed me from the tree and carried me to the summer cottage and rubbed salve on my back."

"You told me nothing about what happened, but I knew."

"I didn't want you to do anything rash."

A faint, bitter smile creased his lips. "I wanted to kill your father, Parris. I wanted to wrap my hands around his throat and choke him until his eyes rolled to the back of his head. Only the thought of you hating me kept me from doing it."

The young girl who had loved him with all her heart nearly confessed that she could never hate him. The mature woman whose mind and soul were torn by visions of him and Annabelle together, her sister touching Dominick's heated flesh, writhing beneath him as he entered her, seared Parris's throat, keeping her from speaking the words.

Instead she murmured, "But you went to see my father a few days later."

"Yes," he replied soberly. "I did."

"I watched from my bedroom window as you galloped toward the house." Her savior, she had thought then. How many nights had she waited by that same window, hoping he would come back for her? "I hid in the shadows at the top of the landing as you strode into the house and headed straight for my father's office."

Never in her life had Parris been so afraid. Her father had a volatile temper, and he kept a loaded gun in the bottom drawer of his desk.

"I dashed down the stairs and pressed my ear to the door, but your voice was too low and I couldn't hear what you were saying. But my father never laid a finger on me after that. And he never again forbade me to see you. What did you say to him?"

He shoved away from the tree and Parris could not move. Her lips went dry as he approached, her chest constricting, making breathing difficult.

Then he stood before her, tall and incredibly broad, casting a shadow over her as she tilted her head back and forced herself to meet his gaze.

What she saw in his eyes made a sensual heat blossom inside her, her body responding instantly, traitorously, her nipples tightening, making even the slightest movement of her bodice rasp against her sensitive flesh.

His hand slid around the nape of her neck, his fingers entangling in her hair, releasing the pins holding up the heavy mass and sending it tumbling over her shoulders and down her back.

"I told him that you belonged to me, Parris . . . and that I would protect what was mine with deadly force, if necessary."

His possessive words resounded through Parris's head. "You really said that?"

"I did."

Parris swallowed, her gaze dropping to his lips that hovered so near she need only lift on her toes to touch him. "Dominick, I . . ."

He smothered whatever she had been about to say with his mouth, and Parris melted into him, feeling as if she truly did belong to him, knowing she always had, her body overruling her mind as her arms wrapped around his neck, her breasts flattened against his chest as he pulled her tighter to him.

He growled low in his throat and gripped her waist, hauling her hard against him, letting her feel his desire for her. He nudged her head back as his lips moved to nuzzle her throat, his hands sliding up her sides to cup her breasts, his thumbs sweeping across the swollen, aching tips through the thin material of her bodice.

Never had Parris been more grateful to be wearing one of Annabelle's old castoffs, which left a good deal of room in the bodice, making it easy for Dominick to slip his hands inside and lay his hot palms on her bare skin before tugging the material down and taking one hard peak into his mouth, drawing harder and harder with each tug, creating a pleasure-pain that was nearly unbearable.

Parris's head dropped back and she moaned as he toyed with her, laving each nipple to soothe her before suckling once more. He wedged his muscular thigh between her legs and Parris rocked against him, liquid heat gathering at the very core of her.

A small voice chided her to stop, that making love to Dominick would change nothing, that too much lay between them. But she needed him desperately, just one more time. She wanted to imprint the memory of his touch in her mind, ingrain the feel of his hands on her flesh into the deepest part of her.

He bore her to the soft grass, keeping his weight on his forearms as he feathered her face with sweet, hedonistic kisses, leaving no flesh untouched.

He kneed her thighs apart, and Parris gazed up at the canopy of leaves above her with passion-glazed eyes, a sigh of rapture breaking from her lips as his finger slid between her cleft and found her swollen nub, rubbing in circles until she was panting his name.

He flicked her nipple with the tip of his tongue as he worked his magic between her thighs, bringing Parris to the brink of ecstasy time and again, only to sense when she was on the verge of climaxing and pull back.

Then he slid down her body and his mouth replaced his fingers. The first touch of his tongue upon the engorged pulse point made her hips buck wildly.

She tossed her head back and forth. "Dominick . . ." she whimpered over and over again.

His fingers came up and circled her nipples, but he would not touch them. Parris thrust her breast into his palms, and still he tortured her, so that she finally clamped her hands over his and made her touch him. He groaned as if it was she tormenting him and not the reverse.

His forefingers flicked her nipples once, twice, three times before her entire body tensed, holding her on the brink for a heartbeat, before she began to convulse, long and deep and hard.

In the next breath, he slid into her, her swollen tissue clenching around him as he began to pump, her body sighing into him with each thrust.

He lifted her hips and wrapped her legs around his flanks, which brought him deep inside her. It was as if he had touched her soul.

"Parris . . ." Her name on his lips was the most glorious thing she had ever heard.

He rocked her, his thrusts growing frenzied, his face wracked with an expression that was near to anguish, sweat glistening on his brow as he forced himself to slow, easing out of her entirely in the next moment.

A protest sprang to her lips, but then he began to

massage the nub between her dewy folds with his hot, silky shaft as he sucked on her nipple, rapidly taking her to that bright spiraling place once more.

She cried out with her second release, her nails digging into his back as he drove into her again, his hands gripping her buttocks, pulling her tighter against his groin as he plunged into her, her last convulsion squeezing him, his body shuddering as he found his own release.

Too soon reality returned to bombard Parris, ruining everything with the vision of Dominick doing to Annabelle what he had just done to her.

Even as she told herself that he must have had many other women, the one woman she could not bear picturing him with was her own sister.

She pushed at his shoulder, his heavy, solid weight thwarting her efforts. "Get off!" she cried with all the agony that was in her heart.

His head snapped up and he grabbed her wrists as she began to hit his chest, pinning her arms to the ground. "Goddamn it, Parris. Stop it!"

"I hate you!"

"Don't say it, Parris. By God—"

"I hate you!"

A muscle worked in his jaw and his eyes were like twin flames. With a wordless sound of disgust, he released her and rolled away.

As though she were on fire, Parris bounded to her feet, turning her back on him to fix her skirt and bodice, shame washing over her for having succumbed to him so easily, so willingly—even now, her treasonous body ached for him.

Scalding tears welled in her eyes, a sob rising in her throat.

Too late, she sensed him behind her, his hands on her arms, her name a plea on his lips. She swung around to face him, the tears tumbling down her cheeks, making her want to die with a need for him that she knew would follow her all her days.

"Please . . ." he begged, reaching for her as she jumped back, eluding hands that would pull her close, comfort her as he whispered sweet words to her, making her forget once more that he had left her.

That he had made love to her sister, over and over again.

"Go away," she told him with all the coldness she could find within her. "I don't ever want to see you again."

"I'm not going away, Parris."

"I told you when you came back that I didn't want you. Nothing has changed."

His jaw worked. "Then I'll make it change, damn it."

"You can't make me love you!" she cried. "You can't make the past go away!"

"No, but we can go forward from here."

"You asked my sister to marry you. How can I ever forget that?"

"It was a mistake."

"Yes, a mistake. We've both had our share of those."

"Jesus, Parris, we've already let too much come

between us, but we've survived. Don't allow Annabelle's lies to destroy us now."

"Now?" The sound that escaped her was a tear-roughened laugh. "Eight years, Dominick. You walked away and it nearly destroyed me. I won't let that happen again. Please . . . just go away."

Then she fled from him.

Dominick took a few steps, intending to go after her, to finish what should have been put to rest all those years ago, but he stopped and watched her flight, feeling as though his very soul had been ripped from him.

Knowing this time he had lost her forever.

Nineteen

The high that proved too high,
the heroic for earth too hard,
The passion that left the ground
to lose itself in the sky

—Robert Browning

With nightfall came the howling wind, followed by the rain.

Watery knives slashed against the windowpanes and rattled a loose shutter, cursing it to bang against the house. A draft of air whispered through the mostly shadowed room, coiling around Dominick's ankles and causing the flames in the grate to leap and dance.

The weather suited his black mood. His temper had been escalating throughout the day, rising with the tempest brewing outside—and the tempest brewing within him.

The huge grandfather clock in the hallway began to toll out the hour, a heavy *bong* that reverberated along the empty corridors of the dark house, soaring into the vaulted ceiling above his head and echoing within his chest, mingling with the despair and desire that had led him to the brandy bottle he now clutched desperately in his hand.

He tossed back a hearty swallow, even though he was already numb, except in the one place he longed to discover no feeling left. His heart.

Parris. There seemed to be no escape from the vision of her tear-streaked face or the accusation in her eyes as she fled from him that afternoon. When had everything gone so terribly wrong?

When you seduced her, his mind taunted viciously.

God, she had been so passionate, so giving. He closed his eyes against the onslaught of images, her body beneath him, ripe and lush, her breast thrust against his mouth, her hands digging into his hair. She hated him, yet he hungered for her. And now that he'd had a taste, he only wanted more.

He had left himself open for this pain, but in his arrogance, he had believed she still loved him.

Now, she was in possession of his letters.

Eight years' worth that he had never sent. Eight years of pouring his heart out to her, telling her exactly how he felt, what she meant to him. All the things he had been too afraid to confess in person.

He'd had a footman deliver the box to her house shortly after his ill-fated meeting with her.

Since then he had waited, believing she would come to him, throw herself into his arms, weeping for an entirely different reason this time.

But as each hour ticked past with no sign of her,

the more desperate and furious he became and the more he drank to ease the turmoil roiling inside him.

As the clock chimed one final time, he shouted with rage and threw the brandy bottle into the fire, the flames licking hungrily at the liquor, logs crackling and spewing out wisps of ash.

He churned with the need to get out, to merge with the storm, outdistance the beast beating against his chest, drumming in his ears, growling inside his head, demanding he make Parris listen to him.

Then he was at the front door, throwing it wide, the wind blasting against him as he stepped out into the night, the rain plastering his clothes to his body as the darkness swallowed him.

Parris could not sleep.

It seemed as though she had done nothing more than toss and turn for hours, her gaze continuing to drift to the scarred wooden box perched on her bed-side table that contained a large packet of letters.

Dozens of them. All from Dominick.

She had been hesitant to open the door when she had spotted the footman garbed in the Wakefield colors of blue and gold. She was even more reluctant to accept the offering the man held out to her. But he had orders not to leave until Parris received it. Knowing Dominick might very well appear at her door next, should she refuse, Parris reluctantly took it.

For an hour, she had sat in the library, staring at the box, afraid to open it. Then she had paced before it, and finally lifted the lid, her fingers trembling as she touched the envelopes, yellowed with age.

For hours she had been immobilized, reading Dominick's letters, almost able to hear the despair in his voice when he wrote of the loss of one of his closest friends, George FitzHugh, relaying how the man had taken a bullet that had not been meant for him.

Tears welled up in her eyes when he had gone on to confess his deepest vulnerabilities, reliving the nights when he had hunkered in the darkness believing he was going to die, only the thought of her sustaining him.

He had explained why he had to leave, of the feelings he had for her that he had done his damnedest to block out, to deny, fearing he was going to lose her, as she had feared losing him.

And then there were the long letters that spoke of the fantasies he had about her, of touching her, making love to her, detailing all the things he wanted to do to her, his words suffusing her entire body with heat until she had to put the letters back in the box and walk away.

Why . . . why couldn't he have told her this before? Why did he have to come back and make her fall in love with him all over again, only to betray her by bedding her sister?

If only Parris could forget Annabelle's crude words, but they rang in her head like a mocking, unending knell until Parris had to clap her hands over her ears.

How could she ever think to make a life with

Dominick, when every time she saw Annabelle, it would bring everything back? She had so desperately wanted to discount her sister's claims, knowing Annabelle reveled in her petty cruelties . . . until her sister had mentioned the tattoo. Then all Parris's hopes and dreams had shattered under the weight of her despair.

She had sought forgetfulness in sleep, but even that eluded her. Each time she closed her eyes, images of Dominick and Annabelle together, limbs entwined, mouths fused, awaited her, taunting her, reminding her that the man she loved had slaked his lust on her sister, making Parris want to curl into herself as all her youthful insecurities washed over her and she found herself once more standing in Annabelle's shadow.

Now, helplessly, Parris stared at the ceiling, every creak and groan of the house causing her to sit up in bed, clutching the counterpane as she stared wide-eyed around her small, sparse room, fearing the dark, what might lie beyond the range of her vision, her veneer now stripped from her, causing old weaknesses to surface.

Many nights she had curled up with a blanket on her window seat, staring out across the dark expanse separating her house from the Duke of Wakefield's grand estate, moonlight glimmering off the slick surface of Archer's Pond as she strained to see the distant lights flickering at the mansion.

Her heart would warm whenever she caught sight of Dominick's signal: a candle being waved back and forth, telling her all was well and then waiting on her own response.

The winters had been the worst, when the fog rolled in and it was impossible to see any distance. And yet, she would still sit at her window seat, watching and waiting.

When Dominick had gotten older, he would sometimes appear beneath her window on his horse on his way to the local tavern, against his father's dictates, the duke railing that a son of his did not mingle with the lower classes.

So many times Parris had fallen asleep in that nook, trying to keep her eyes open to catch a glimpse of Dominick returning. But after he had left for the army, she had forced herself to put away her childish dreams and try to move on.

It seemed she was still trying.

Parris started as a loud bang suddenly reverberated through the house, her heart lodging in her throat. She knew all the doors and windows were locked, and there was no one around for miles.

Grabbing her thin cotton wrapper from the end of the bed, she tossed her arms into it, and padded swiftly to her bedroom door.

Barely breathing, she eased the door open, the creak of the hinges amplified in the utter stillness of the house.

She peered out in the corridor and saw nothing. Tuning in to the sounds around her, Parris could detect nothing out of the ordinary.

She released her breath and closed her door, chiding herself that she was allowing her imagination and the fact that she was alone to rattle her.

She longed for a breath of fresh air, to feel a cool misting of rain on her face to soothe her troubled spirit. The embrasure seemed to call to her as a sliver of moon worked its way from behind a black cloud, sending a silvery beam through the window and creating intricate patterns on the bare wood floor.

Rubbing her arms to ward off her lingering anxiety, she hastened over to the double windows, unlocked the latch and pushed them open, closing her eyes as a rush of rain moistened air swept in, molding her nightclothes to her body, making her feel as if nothing stood between her and the elements.

The whicker of a horse brought Parris's eyes snapping open, and her gaze locked on the large figure looming at the edge of the treeline, his features obscured by the night.

Parris's heart thumped wildly against her ribs as the rider nudged his mount forward, stopping directly below her window as though her memories had conjured him up.

Dominick's clothing was plastered to his muscular frame, his white shirt flush against his torso, a wide V revealing most of his powerful chest. His black pants clung to rock-hewn thighs, and his blue-black hair was slick and wet, running over his collar.

But it was his piercing, ruthless gaze that captured

Parris, leaving her breathless and rooted to the spot. The anger in those eyes singed her.

"Let me in, Parris." His tone was as dark and dangerous as the night, warning her not to disobey.

But she couldn't let him in, couldn't be near him. Too easily, he could tear down her defenses. With a mere look he could seduce her, and she could not allow that to happen.

"Come down and open the door. Now."

Parris shook her head and saw his eyes glitter and his jaw clench. The next moment, he jumped from his horse and strode determinedly toward the house.

He was coming in whether she wanted him to or not!

The realization made Parris race from her room, her robe billowing out behind her as she ran blindly along the darkened hallway and down the flight of stairs, her breath rasping through her lungs as she dove upon the front door, checking the latches, knowing only a moment's relief at finding everything secure as she heard Dominick's boots pounding up the front steps.

He did not knock, did not say a word. But she knew he was there, and he knew she was there. Certainly he could hear her erratic breathing, the pounding of her heart.

Then his footsteps receded and she turned and leaned against the door, a bead of moisture trickling between her breasts as she lifted a shaky hand to her chest.

Out of the corner of her eye, she caught a movement, a towering figure stalking past the windows in her father's old office.

Parris's gaze locked on the French doors at the other end of the room, panic rising inside her like a flood tide, knowing that was where Dominick was heading.

She propelled herself away from the front door and flew into the office, knocking over a small table and sending the oil lamp upon it crashing to the ground, splintering glass and sending jagged pieces skittering across the floor.

Then, like some mythical god, Dominick appeared before the French doors, formidable and furious, and Parris stopped dead in her tracks, her hand climbing to her throat, her head shaking wildly as he leaned back and kicked the doors open with a booted foot.

The panels slammed against the walls, shattering the glass and littering the floor with even more spiked shards. They surrounded Parris, leaving her nowhere to run, even if she could.

But she would not have been able to take more than a few steps, for Dominick's ground-eating stride closed the distance between them in less than a second. He loomed over her, virile, hard, his features completely unflinching as he glared down at her.

"Dominick . . ." His name had barely passed her lips before he scooped her up in his arms and started out of the room, the glass crunching beneath his booted feet.

Dread settled into the pit of her stomach. She had

never seen him like this, so ruthlessly determined. It frightened her.

She squirmed in his unrelenting grip. "Let me go, damn you!"

Fierce dark eyes slashed her way, the look he sent her silencing her . . . until she realized he was heading straight for her bedroom.

"What are you doing?"

"What I should have done years ago. Claiming what is mine."

"Dominick, don't!"

He carted her across the threshold and slammed the door shut with his heel, the sound ringing with finality, telling her without words that she would get no quarter.

He carried her to the bed and deposited her before him, one massive thigh trapping her nightgown against the mattress, thwarting her attempts to scramble to the other side. He was taking no chances.

With trembling fascination, she watched as he undid his cuffs and then gripped the edge of his shirt and yanked, sending buttons skittering over the floor, leaving him naked to the waist and utterly glorious, all hard planes and flexing bands of muscle.

Desire washed over her. No matter what he had done, she could not stop herself from loving him. The emotion sang through her veins, heated her blood, made her want to weep with despair and joy.

"Undress, Parris."

Parris wanted him, but not like this, not when her

thoughts beat a tattoo with Annabelle's name, remembering her sister's words about the serpent on his chest, how she had touched it, kissed it . . . while Dominick made love to her.

The image seared her, blanking her mind to any potential danger of pressing Dominick when he was in such a turbulent mood. She began to hit him, swear at him. He easily manacled her wrists, not hurting her, but not releasing his hold either.

She wanted to punish him for his betrayal, and the words "I hate you!" spewed from her mouth like acid, knowing how angry he had become that afternoon when she had said them.

Until that moment, he had merely restrained her. Now, his mouth twisted into a harsh line, as though she had finally pushed him to his limit.

In a flash, his hand was at the bodice of her nightgown, the sound of rending material filling her ears along with her howls of protest as she writhed against his hold, trying to cover her breasts and the dark nest of curls at the apex of her thighs.

"Don't!" he commanded hoarsely, yanking her hands away. "Don't hide yourself from me."

Parris lifted her only free arm and slapped him hard across the face, the sound of flesh against flesh echoing in the room, her hand stinging from the force of the blow, her stunned gaze moving to his cheek, then his eyes.

"Damn you, Parris," he growled, before his towering frame came down over her, pressing her into the mattress, his mouth bruising as it took hers, his knees opening her thighs, his hardness driving against her.

She could taste the brandy on him, the hint of smoke and rain that clung to him, feel his heat, the completely male scent that belonged entirely to him, and she responded to all of it.

When she whimpered, his lips softened, slanting over hers, forcing her to respond against her will to the mastery he held over her body, his thumb finding one turgid peak and sweeping over it, capturing her moan in his mouth.

"God, Parris . . ." he lamented in a husky voice as his warm lips trailed along her jaw. "Don't do this to me." He sounded tortured. And when he lifted his head and gazed down at her, she could see the sorrow and the regret in his eyes. "Jesus, I feel . . . crazy."

He had frightened her, hurt her, made her love him and yearn for him for eight long years, and defiled her feelings for him with her sister.

Even as her fingers itched to smooth his wild hair, to press her mouth to his, she wanted to lash out at him even more, perhaps knowing how he would respond.

Perhaps wanting it.

"I don't want you, Dominick. Not now. Not ever."

The look that came into his eyes was frightening in its intensity. "Then I'll have to make you want me." His mouth cut off any protests, plundering, delving, allowing her no place to hide from the force of his passion.

He cupped her breast, pushing up the peak before

drawing it into his mouth. Parris wanted more, arching up, urging the tip farther into his mouth as his tongue circled and flicked and his fingers worked magic on her other nipple.

"Dominick," she begged, when he removed his sweet, wet mouth from her aching nub.

"Yes, sweetheart. I know . . . I'll give you whatever you want."

Parris arched off the bed when his finger slipped into her damp, hot valley, stroking her, building the magic only he could weave.

With shaking hands, Parris freed him from his trousers, his hard, silky length jutting free. She could not resist touching him, wrapping her hands around the hot satin and stroking him, feeling his body tense. His eyes jammed shut as if he were in agony. A bead of moisture wet the hooded tip and Parris smoothed her finger over it.

"Jesus," he hissed through clenched teeth.

Parris wanted to feel all of him, every solid sinew. With his help, she divested him of his shirt, then trousers, coming to sit before him on the edge of the bed. He cupped the back of her head and kissed her with such fierce tenderness that everything inside her liquefied.

When he released her, she felt bold and wicked and on fire for him. Before he knew what she was about, she wrapped her lips around his shaft and tasted him, played with him as he had played with her, reveling in the feeling that, this time, she had mastered him.

Before she had a chance to truly enjoy herself he moved on top of her, the taste of him on her lips as he melded his mouth to hers, his hardness probing against her entrance, the thick ridge of his erection slowly filling her, building the pressure, until, sweet heaven, he was in her to the hilt.

He captured her gaze with his own, his eyes filled with passion and possession and an emotion Parris was too afraid to hope for.

His hands shackled her wrists, raising them above her head, refusing to allow her to touch him, leaving her with only the ability to feel every erotic thing he was doing to her body.

He kept her gaze locked on him as he lowered his head to lave her nipple, a storm as wild as the one raging outside building within her.

He metered his movement and she moaned, arching her hips into his, silently begging him to end the sweet torment, but he would give her no reprieve.

"Do you love me, Parris?"

How could he do this to her? Now, when her feelings were so raw, so at the surface, when the two of them were so very intimate? She couldn't tell him, couldn't give him the chance to hurt her.

She shook her head, biting her bottom lip as he brought his slow, torturous thrusts to a near stop, going deep, so very, very deep, and then nearly pulling all the way out, bringing her to the cusp of release and then refusing her.

"Tell me you love me, Parris."

Oh God, she did love him, had always loved him.

"Parris . . . please, God, put me out of my misery."

Parris closed her eyes, feeling the sting of tears, emotions threatening to overwhelm her. All her life she had been waiting to love this man. He had fulfilled her every fantasy.

For so long she had been afraid of her feelings for him, afraid of losing him, knowing that if she gave him all of her heart, the pain of his not loving her in return would destroy her. But she could no longer deny those feelings, or deny him the words.

She cupped his face. "Yes . . . I love you. I always have."

He closed his eyes, a shudder passing through his long frame as he groaned, "Thank you, God." When he opened his eyes, a new light shone in them, whipping her breath away with its intensity as he whispered in her ear, "Let me show you how I feel about you."

Parris moaned as his mouth slanted across her, his tongue mating with hers as he plunged into her, pushing her legs up and over his shoulders so he could get deeper, sweat gathering on both their bodies as he pumped into her, making her frenzied. Mewling sounds poured from her mouth with each thrust until, together, they climaxed, ascending to heaven on a burst of white light before returning, spent and satiated, back to earth.

Dominick rolled off her, but brought her with him, and even though reality was intruding on her world once more, she needed to be close to him, to lay her head on his chest and listen to the heavy beat of his heart, knowing she had made him as wild as he had made her.

He tilted her chin up, his dark, unfathomable eyes staring down at her, his silky, ebony hair mussed and beautiful. Parris couldn't resist sweeping the stray lock from his forehead.

"Why did you run away from me?" His voice was a sensual rumble in the shadowed stillness of the room.

Parris wanted to avert her gaze, but he wouldn't let her.

"Don't shut me out again, Parris. You've always been able to talk to me. I want that back. I was a fool to have ever walked away from you, but I'm here now and I'm not going anywhere. And if you'll have me, I—"

Parris pulled away from him, even as a part of her longed to stay in his arms. He reached for her, but she hastened from the bed, staring at the tatters of her nightgown and robe on the floor.

Dominick had seen every inch of her, and yet she wanted to cover herself. He made her feel too vulnerable, too susceptible to his charm.

She grabbed his shirt. No buttons remained but it was large enough to wrap around her.

"You look delectable," he murmured seductively.

And he looked far too virile and masculine with his big body encompassing most of her bed, his bronzed skin standing out against the white sheet, his chest a broad slab of muscle.

Her appreciative gaze skimmed down to where the

sheet draped his lean waist, the thin material gloving his loins, her eyes widening as she noted the evidence of his arousal.

He chuckled at her expression. "You see what you do to me. I fear I have been constantly in this state since I set eyes on you at the Beechams' party."

Heat rippled in the pit of Parris's belly and rapidly fanned out. Her reaction was shameful, wanton. How could a mere glance at him raise her body temperature to such a degree?

She forced her gaze away and padded to the window seat, the cold air just now touching her as she closed the windows, hugging herself close as she looked out across the landscape.

She tensed as she heard the rustle of the sheet, and the creak of the mattress as Dominick stood up, her body becoming more tense with each step that brought him closer to her, knowing she would shatter if he should touch her.

When he laid his hands on her shoulders, she jumped, whirling around and stepping away, the backs of her knees bumping into the seat behind her. She dropped onto the cushion, unable to look away from him.

He scowled. "What's the matter with you?"

He had donned his trousers, but the top button was undone. It didn't matter. The clothing could not disguise his raw, physical presence, his overwhelming appeal that only made the wound in Parris's heart bleed that much more. Few women would be able to resist him—sophisticated, beautiful women like Annabelle, who knew how to pleasure a man.

He sank down to his knees before her, his hands resting lightly on her thighs. "Parris, talk to me. Tell me what I've done. I know I was an ass for not coming to you after we made love at my house, but so many things were running through my mind." He shook his head. "I was rough with you, and I'm sorry."

Her words, when she finally spoke, were so soft Dominick barely caught them. "I thought you hated me."

"I could never hate you. I let stupid male pride get in my way when I realized . . . you weren't a virgin. I wanted to be the first. I couldn't bear the thought of another man making love to you. I blamed myself for not being man enough to tell you how I felt long ago." Dominick paused, waiting for her to confide her secret. He had purposely left the door open.

"You hypocrite." The words were a low, sibilant hiss as she stared at him with cold eyes. "You didn't like the idea of a man touching me, and yet you debauch any woman who steps into your path."

"Christ, Parris, that's not—"

She shoved at his chest, pushing him back, but he caught at her wrists. "How could you?" she cried. "How could you hurt me like that?" A sob broke from her lips and she jammed her eyes closed, tears seeping between her lashes. "She was my sister, Dominick . . . my sister!"

The realization of what Parris was telling him

rocked Dominick back on his heels. "Parris . . ." When she wouldn't look at him, he caught her chin between his fingers and forced her head up. "There was nothing between Annabelle and me. Not eight years ago. And not now."

"Don't try to deny it!"

Damn bloody Annabelle! She had taunted him about telling Parris they had been intimate, but he hadn't known what to believe until that moment.

"Parris, listen to me—"

"No!" Her tears fell in earnest now. "God, how I loved you. So much so that I ended up losing myself to become more a part of you. I would have done anything to make you happy. After all these years I've spent missing you, of feeling my heart disintegrate one small piece at a time, I won't give you my heart again, Dominick. I won't."

"You already have, Parris, and I'm not going to let you take it back because you have chosen to listen to your sister's lies. And that's what they are, Parris. *Lies.* I have never touched Annabelle. God, you have to know how single-minded your sister can be when she wants something. But nothing, I repeat, nothing, ever happened."

"You were always breaking my heart." Her words were spoken on a whispered sob that clawed at Dominick. He tried to gather her up into his arms but she wouldn't allow him to touch her.

"I'm sorry, Parris. The last thing I ever wanted to do was hurt you. That's part of the reason I left."

"Because you loved me," she scoffed.

"Yes, I loved you, and if you read my letters, you would know how much."

"I read them."

"I meant every word I said."

"Then why didn't you say them during the years you were gone, Dominick? You didn't care enough then to worry about the possibility of my finding someone else to love—to bed."

Dominick knew she wanted to hurt him, and she was amply succeeding. "Maybe I thought it was best if you did." Then they never would have come to this pass.

"Maybe you're right. We've quenched our curiosity now, haven't we? Was I everything you fantasized about? Was I as good as my sister, Dominick? Was I?"

Dominick's hands fisted at his side. "God damn it, Parris, it wasn't like that! I loved you when you were a little girl. I loved you when you were a young woman on the verge of adulthood. And I love you even more now. For the love of God, don't let Annabelle's lies poison us."

Rain splashed against the windowpane, a heartbreaking backdrop to the tears that spilled from Parris's eyes as she reached out and laid her hand against his chest, slowly tracing his tattoo. Dominick trembled from the force of that innocent touch.

"Is this what Annabelle did to you?"

"No. Jesus, no." He took hold of her wrist. Her struggle was minimal, her body drained of fight, allowing him to tug her down onto her knees before him.

He pulled her limp form into his lap and she turned

away from him, hiding her face against his chest, her wet cheeks burning him, making him die that much more inside.

He searched desperately for words to convince her of how he felt. But how could he convince her when she was bound and determined not to believe him?

Then the truth suddenly dawned on him about what Annabelle must have told Parris to get her to believe that he had bedded her.

The snake.

"I swear to you, Parris, I never touched Annabelle and she never touched me." He took her hand and placed it over his heart, over his tattoo. "She never touched me like this. That's what she told you, isn't it? Because she knew about the snake, you believed everything else she said."

She remained mute, only the nod of her head telling him that she had heard him.

"And now you believe her, because you think she couldn't possibly have known about the tattoo unless she had been with me in a sexual way."

"It's true."

Dominick cupped her chin and tipped her head up, forcing her to meet his gaze. "It's not true. The only reason your sister knew about the tattoo is because of Mary. She spotted it at the fair when she was trying to clean the stain off my shirt made by her ice cream. Annabelle was there. Ask Mary, if you don't believe me. But, God, I wish you would believe me. You have my heart, Parris. You've always had my heart."

Her eyes were luminous blue pools, the desire to believe him lingering there. "Dominick, I . . ."

"Tell me you love me again, Parris. You told me the first time when you were sixteen. Do you remember? Because I'll never forget. You've imprinted yourself on my soul. You were and still are my salvation. The girl who gave herself to me unselfishly and without reservation under the cover of moonlight, on a warm June night eight years ago, loved me. I want her back. And I'll do anything to win her over. I deserve a second chance, Parris. Can't you find it your heart to forgive me?"

She blinked up at him. "You know? About the garden . . ."

"Yes. I nearly came to blows with your ex-fiancé over it. That's why you couldn't marry him, isn't it, Parris? Because you had given yourself to me and I owned your heart. Please tell me I still do."

She hesitated, fighting a battle within herself, until she finally gave up the struggle.

Shyly, she reached up and wrapped her arms around his neck, pulling his head down to whisper, "You've always owned my heart."

Her words and the look in her eyes granted Dominick the most precious of gifts.

One he would never throw away again.

Epilogue

There's in you all that we believe of heaven,
Amazing brightness, purity, and truth,
Eternal joy, and everlasting love.

—Thomas Otway

TWO YEARS LATER . . .

"Women."

Dominick glanced away from his contemplation of the hunter's moon overhead to see Jason walking toward him, looking disgruntled.

"What's the matter, Stratford? I seem to have heard that lament before."

Jason stopped beside Dominick, flashing him a scowl before looking back toward Carlisle House, which was shining like a beacon, lights blazing from top to bottom, making his ancestral home glimmer like a magnificent jewel against the dark, velvet sky and endless stretch of land.

It was the night of the annual costume gala. Parris had coerced Dominick into dressing as a pirate, finding a certain perverse delight in reminding him of their childhood games.

Philip and Mary, who had come to live with them after Annabelle had run off with a destitute marquis, had seconded their aunt's suggestion.

Dominick thought he would never again take part in another Carlisle gala, least of all this one, or that he would come to find such profound joy in it.

Parris had changed all that.

"God, will you look at her?"

Dominick followed Jason's gaze back to the veranda, lit by hundreds of candles. Parris's idea. She said the candles reminded her of when she was a child, waiting in her bedroom for his signal in the window. The sight was breathtaking and the guests were thoroughly enjoying themselves.

Including Lady Gwen, whose tinkling laughter rang across the long expanse of lawn between the house and garden, digging the scowl deeper into Jason's face. Dominick managed to contain his amusement at the jealousy oozing from his friend's every pore.

"Your wife looks radiant tonight, Stratford."

"She does," he groused. "Damn it."

"That does not sound like the remark of a happily married man."

"Too happily married, blast you! Look at those buffoons fawning all over her. That's my wife!"

"She's just enjoying herself."

"A fat lot you know. And don't you dare laugh, you rotter! That woman is supposed to be looking lost without me by her side. Blessed Jesus, why will she never do what she's supposed to?"

"She's a woman, Stratford. My advice would be not to strain what little brain you possess by endeavoring to figure them out. They know from birth how to flummox us. Best to simply flow with the tide."

"I tell you, it's not right for a woman to look that beautiful when she's eight months pregnant! She's supposed to be weepy and dependent on her husband—and waddle. That woman still glides like she's floating on air. Unless you see her from the side, you can't even tell she's with child!" That seemed to really irk Stratford. "Worse, she belongs to every blasted charity and is doing far too much to settle my husbandly nerves."

Dominick chuckled. "Is that all, Stratford? Or is there more?"

"Plenty. She's makes me crazy. Why, dear God, did I set myself up for this kind of torment?"

"Because you love her, perhaps?"

"Damn, but this love business is bloody hard."

"That it is." But it was worth every minute. The rewards were beyond measure.

"I still blame you, old man," Jason grumbled.

"What did I do now?"

"You had to marry Lady Scruples, that's what you did. And then your wife has to go out crusading for woman's rights, and my wife, of course, has to be involved, too. Joined at the hip, those bloody two are. Full of all sort of opinions, I tell you."

Dominick had always known Lady Gwen would give Jason a chase before he got her to the altar, and then drive him crazy every day thereafter. Bless the girl, she was amply succeeding. It almost made being friends with the rousing pain worth the aggravation.

"This is your life now, Stratford. Better get used to it. Your first child is on the way."

Jason's expression mellowed. "Our first child. Damn if those aren't the sweetest words. I'm going to be a father, old man. A father." He smiled dumbly, as though he had invented fatherhood. But Dominick had felt the same way.

"It is wonderful."

"And when is the next little Carlisle coming along? Megan is going to be two this year."

Dominick still couldn't believe his good fortune. His daughter was a blessing. Meg was as much of an angel as her namesake, and had all the makings of being a hellion just like her mother, with her feisty personality, head of dark curls and pale blue eyes. He figured he was in for some very interesting years ahead.

"Oh, now that tears it!" Jason growled. "There's bloody Shelby flirting with Gwen. Now I'm going to have to kill him."

Dominick chuckled and watched Stratford storm across the lawn, ready to do battle but melting as soon as his wife touched his shoulder as she met him at the steps.

Dominick wondered where his own darling wife

was. Most likely she was giving their daughter her final feeding before putting Meg to sleep.

He had difficulty being present during the feedings. The sight of their child suckling Parris's breast made his body respond in a less than dignified manner. Parris would laugh at his predicament even as her eyes promised him delights he could collect in their bedroom.

Just the thought of what she could do to him made his blood run hot. He decided he'd had enough hanging around in the garden to keep from staying too close to temptation.

He caught sight of a cloaked figure departing from a side door then, and glimpsed a feminine ankle, the scene eerily reminiscent of another night.

He watched the woman as she made her way to the summer cottage. What was afoot here? Word had obviously spread about the lovers' hideaway. But damn it, this was his home! If anyone was having a tryst, it was going to be him.

The sound of a throat being cleared brought Dominick's gaze swinging around. Hastings stood behind him, a small silver tray held aloft.

"What is it, man?" Dominick said gruffly, his gaze darting back to the cottage as the woman ducked inside.

"A letter has come for you, Your Grace."

"A letter? At this hour? Who's it from?"

"I am not privy to that information, sir." Was that a smile on the old coot's face?

Dominick grunted and swiped the missive from the tray, staring daggers at his butler for the interruption as he opened the envelope . . . and grinned from ear to ear.

"Good news, I hope?" Hastings queried, his owl-eyed expression giving him away, telling Dominick his butler was in cahoots with the author of the letter. For once, Dominick didn't mind the old boy's interference.

"I'd say an increase in your wages is called for here, Hastings."

"Why, thank you, Your Grace. You are most kind, truly the most wonderful of—"

Dominick had already blended into the night before his butler had finished his sentence, missing the smile on Hastings's face as he turned back to the house.

Quietly, Dominick let himself into the cottage, grateful for the military training that had taught him the value of moving with stealth.

He came upon the beautiful woman, garbed in the sheerest of lingerie, which momentarily distracted him before he wrapped his arms tightly around her waist, startling her.

"Ssh. Don't fight me," he murmured in her ear, not allowing her to turn around. "I've captured you now, my Lady Scruples, and if you don't do as I say, I will be forced to call in the magistrate."

She wriggled in his arms, rubbing her backside invitingly over the bulge in his trousers. "I'll do whatever you say, my Lord Pirate," she purred, taking his hands and moving them up to cup her breasts, her nipples pushing against his palms. "I only have one request."

"Which is?"

She turned her head to look up at him, love and desire and everything Dominick could have ever hoped for reflected in her stunning blue eyes.

"I would like you to give me a little boy who looks just like you."